CHOSEN

BOOK 1 OF THE DJINN WARS

CHRISTINE POPE

Dark Valentine Press

CHOSEN

ISBN: 978-0692357552
Copyright © 2015 by Christine Pope
Published by Dark Valentine Press

Cover design and book layout by Indie Author Services.

To learn more about this author, go to
www.christinepope.com.

To anyone who has been left behind...

CHOSEN

CHAPTER ONE

THE DYING BEGAN ON MY TWENTY-FOURTH birthday. Even now I truly believe that was nothing more than a sad coincidence, but if nothing else, the synchronicity helps me to remember when the end began. September twenty-sixth. There was a certain crispness in the air, a bite after the sun went down that told me fall was on the way, and winter soon to follow. We didn't get as cold in Albuquerque as they did in Santa Fe, but we could feel the shift in the seasons even so.

I was out with friends doing tequila shots at Zacatecas when the first reports about a strange illness in New York showed up on the evening news. Maybe I caught a glimpse on the TV in the bar, but I don't think so. To be blunt, I was pretty wasted. Getting plowed like that wasn't in my usual repertoire, but my friend Tori kept ordering round and after round, and since I wasn't driving, I didn't try too hard to stop her. Maybe in the back of my mind I was thinking that this year I was twenty-four, and twenty-five would come sliding along soon enough, and I might as well party with abandon while I still could. Sooner or later I'd have to be a good, responsible adult, but not on my birthday.

The next day was a Saturday. No school or work for me; I was getting my master's in English, mostly because I couldn't really figure out what else to do with myself, and staying in college for as long as possible seemed pretty attractive compared to what awaited me in the real world. Since I'd been lucky enough to snag a T.A. position teaching lower-division English classes, I didn't have to worry about dragging my sorry hung-over ass into work, either. I had until Monday to recover.

Around noon I finally wandered into the kitchen, after taking a shower so long the hot water began to run out. Good thing we had a separate water heater for the little apartment over the garage where I lived, or I probably would have heard about it from my mother. All right, so I was still living at home, but the apartment gave me at least the illusion of independence, if not the real thing. It also allowed me to pay much lower rent than I would have otherwise. My parents didn't want to charge me anything—well, not my mother, anyway—but I'd insisted. It was a pittance, but it did cover the utilities and helped give them some extra wiggle room.

My mother had the little white TV on the kitchen counter turned on and was frowning as she watched some cable news talking head go on about a new illness that had begun appearing in New York and Los Angeles the day before. Reports were also coming in from up and down both coasts about this unnamed disease, which left its victims hospitalized with extremely high fevers.

"More Ebola?" I asked, blinking against the too-bright light in the kitchen and making a beeline for the fridge, where my mother always kept a pitcher of iced tea, even in the dead of winter.

"No, Jessica," she said, that little pucker of worry still showing between her brows. "Something else. They don't know what it is."

"Mmm." In that moment, I was far more concerned with getting some caffeine into my bloodstream ASAP than worrying about the disease *du jour.* Those sorts of things never seemed to affect us here in Albuquerque. I wouldn't say we were exactly the city that America forgot, but if it weren't for *Breaking Bad,* I doubted most people would have spared my hometown a second thought.

From the side-eye my mother was giving me as I downed the iced tea, I guessed that the makeup I'd

carefully applied earlier wasn't doing much to hide
the evidence that I'd had, as they say, a gaudy night.
But because I hadn't been driving and was more or less
ambulatory this morning, she seemed to be giving me
a pass.

"Dad have a shift today?" I inquired, after refilling
my glass of iced tea and taking a few more gulps. Since
I felt fortified enough to eat at that point, I popped the
pitcher of tea back into the fridge and got a package of
English muffins out of the breadbox.

"Yes." She didn't exactly sigh, but I could tell she
wasn't thrilled, either.

My father was an officer with the Albuquerque
police department. Still a beat cop after twenty-five
years, too. He never had any interest in riding a desk,
liked to be out on the streets. How my mother lived
with it, day after day, I didn't know. My brother and I
generally took our father's occupation in stride, since
it had always been a part of our lives. But I knew my
father had gone through the academy after he and my
mother got married, and so it hadn't been an irretriev-
able fact of life when they were starting out as a couple.
I know she wished he was more interested in becoming a detective so he wouldn't be so much in harm's
way every day. That wasn't my father, though—even at
fifty-two, he was lean and fit, and could probably put
guys half his age through a wall if necessary.

At the time, the department was chronically short-handed, so my father picked up a lot of extra shifts. My mother never protested, since she knew he was doing it for us, putting more money in the bank, but she couldn't help worrying. Sometimes I wondered if my father knew exactly how stressed she was every time he left for work. I didn't think that would've stopped him, though, because as much as he loved her, he also loved his job and thought he was doing some genuine good.

"Well, at least it's a daytime shift," I told her, then put the two halves of the English muffin I'd just broken apart into the toaster oven.

"I know." The worry line was still there, and it seemed to deepen as she returned her attention to the TV. The talking heads had been replaced by a doctor, a woman in her late forties who probably would have been pretty if she hadn't look so tired.

"The illness manifests as a very high fever, spiking as high as 106 degrees. We're having difficulty controlling the fever, even with analgesics and ice packs." She paused, pushing a strand of dishwater-blonde hair back behind her ear. Obviously, she hadn't bothered to primp before going to make her statement in front of the cameras. "No other symptoms have been observed at this point. If you or someone in your family comes down with a fever above 103, please call your doctor or go to the local emergency room."

The camera cut to the reporter interviewing the doctor. "Dr. Leviton, any word on where this illness has come from? Is it connected to the doctors returning from West Africa?"

"No," Dr. Leviton replied at once, looking almost annoyed. "None of the victims brought in to Mount Sinai or any of the other hospitals in the city appear to have any connection. Most of them haven't even left New York during the past few months. Of those who have traveled, they've returned home from destinations as diverse as Tahiti, Paris, and Australia. Again, there doesn't seem to be any connection."

At that moment, a nurse came up and whispered in the doctor's ear. Her expression shifted from annoyance to outright worry before she said quickly, "I'm sorry—a patient needs me. That's all I can tell you right now." And she turned away from the cameras and began hurrying down the hallway almost at a run, the nurse right behind her.

The camera panned back to the reporter, who was wearing what he probably thought was a look of measured concern...but to me, he just looked scared. I wonder what the nurse had said to the doctor.

Whatever it had been, the reporter didn't mention it. He only said, "That's the latest from Mount Sinai Hospital in New York City. Again, as Dr. Leviton stated, seek medical assistance immediately if you have a fever in excess of—"

My mother turned off the TV. I arched an eyebrow at her, and she shook her head. "It's always something," she said. "I shouldn't even have turned it on, I suppose, but I was hoping to catch some weather."

"You're not worried?"

"No." She had her own glass of iced tea sitting on the counter, and she sipped from it as she watched me take the English muffin from the toaster oven and start spreading some butter on it. "Cable news always needs something to feed the monster. And unexplained diseases are a great way to keep people watching for updates."

That was something I loved about my mother—she wasn't afraid to call a spade a spade. Critical thinking was very important to her, which made sense, since she taught advanced composition and AP English at the same high school I'd attended. She made my father look like a starry-eyed dreamer.

"True," I said, munching away at my English muffin. My abused stomach was all too glad of the carbs, which should help to soak up the remnants of the tequila I'd downed the night before. Good thing I only indulged like that every once in a great while. Most of the time I was more a mixed-drink kind of girl.

"They'll play it up, and then it'll quietly disappear, just like everything else they try to make a big deal of." My mother finished the last of her tea and set the glass down on the counter. "Anyway, I'm about to go to the store. Anything you need?"

Mouth full of English muffin, I shook my head.

"Make sure you wipe down the counter when you're done," she admonished me, then picked up her purse and went out, apparently not concerned at all by what we'd just watched.

If only she'd been right. But it turned out that the worry of the doctor—and the scared-looking reporter—was not misplaced.

The next morning, the news was full of reports of people getting sick up and down both coasts, and cases had been reported in the Midwest as well...Chicago... Detroit...St. Louis. And the disease, whatever it was, hadn't confined itself to the borders of the U.S. People were sick in London and Munich and Moscow and Singapore. Hospitals were filling up.

My father sat in his wing chair in the family room and watched the news with narrowed eyes. My mother seemed to be doing her best to ignore the television, and was instead trying to worm the latest details about his football practice schedule out of my brother Devin, who was far more interested in texting with his girl-friend than watching TV or explaining why he would have practice four days this week but five the next. A senior in high school, he was hoping his record as running back for the school's team might help him to eke out a scholarship or two when he went to college next year. We were doing okay, but college was expensive—as I knew only too well, with loans piling up every semester, loans I wasn't sure I'd ever be able to pay back. Supposedly having a master's would put me on a higher rung of the salary ladder when I did have to go out into the real world, but jobs were scarcer than the college counselors wanted us poor schmucks stuck in loan limbo to believe.

"Have you seen any sick people yet?" I asked my father. I was sitting at the game table in the corner of the family room, attempting to give my paper on gender representation in gothic novels a final read-through in hard copy to catch any typos. Unfortunately, my brain was jittering this way and that, worried about the reports on the news, praying they were exaggerating and fearing they were not. I couldn't even say why I was so worried, since most of the time I ignored these sorts of reports, knowing the diseases they discussed rarely touched us here in our little corner of the Southwest. Something about the speed with which this one had spread bothered me, though. It bothered me a lot.

My father pointed the remote at the TV and turned down the volume, then shook his head. "Not with this thing. I've seen meth heads puking in back alleys and heroin addicts with the shakes because they couldn't get a fix, but this one? I don't think it's here."

The word "yet" hung in the air, unspoken, but no less ominous for that. More and more people were getting sick, and the first deaths had been reported on the East Coast. Not a lot, not yet, but although the news was trying to sugarcoat things, rumors had already begun to swirl across the Internet that no one who contracted this new disease survived. Which was crazy. Even Ebola—hell, even pneumonic plague, which had an insane mortality rate when not treated—wasn't one-hundred-percent fatal. That just wasn't possible.

"Maybe it won't," I said, although I knew even as I said them that the words were mere wishful thinking. "Maybe it'll just...blow around us, or burn out before it gets here."

"Maybe," he agreed. His eyes wouldn't meet mine, though, and I knew what he must be thinking.

I knew, because it was the same thing I was thinking. This wasn't a matter of if, but rather when.

On Monday when I arrived at school, I noticed the parking lot was noticeably less full than a university lot had any right to be this close to the beginning of the semester. And as I got out of my car and locked it, I saw that at least half the students walking around on campus wore surgical masks, the white disposable kind the news reports showed people in China wearing on days when the smog was particularly bad.

Apparently, I hadn't gotten the memo. Nothing I could do about it now...except hope that a lot of the students in the Writing 1A class I was teaching that semester had decided to bail completely.

Most of them had, except for a couple of the over-achievers. Well, at least the kind of over-achievers I'd get in a Writing 1A class, which wasn't exactly packed full with people who'd gotten 5s on their AP English exams.

I scanned the empty seats and tried not to frown, reminding myself that I'd get my T.A. stipend no matter how many butts were in those chairs on a particular day. "Okay," I said, surprised at the slight tremor in my voice, "on Friday we were just starting to get into the difference between a topic sentence and a thesis statement...."

Taylor Ortiz, who was sitting in the front row, blinked at me in apparent incomprehension. For the first time, I noticed the beads of sweat standing out on her forehead, the way she seemed to be swaying in her seat. Beneath her warm-toned skin, she looked dead pale.

"Taylor, are you all right?" I asked.

She blinked again. "Um...."

Next to her, Troy Lenz lurched to his feet. "Holy shit! She's got it!"

"Troy—" I began, maybe meaning to reprimand him for swearing in class, possibly intending to tell him to sit down, but I was fairly certain neither of those admonishments would have had any effect. All around the class, those few students who'd been brave enough to show up shot straight out of their seats, looking at Taylor as if she'd just started vomiting pea soup or something. Never mind that vomiting was not one of the symptoms of "the Heat"—the street nickname given to the disease because of the extreme fevers it caused.

"Oh, God, get away from her," a girl in the back of the class said, and before I could even open my mouth to speak again, they were all bolting for the door, a couple of them even overturning their desks in their haste.

A few seconds later, I was alone in the classroom with Taylor, who continued to look around blankly, seeming unaware that she'd managed to clear the space in about five seconds flat.

A cowardly part of me wanted to take off as well, but I told myself I couldn't do that—I was the teacher (okay, the T.A.), and I had some sort of responsibility to make sure she was all right. Besides, if she really did have the Heat, then I'd already been exposed, and there wasn't anything I could do about it now.

I approached her and put a hand on her forehead. Jesus Christ. She felt as if she was on fire from within. No wonder she was having a hard time focusing on anything. She was so hot that her brain must be cooking right inside her skull.

The university hospital was all the way across campus. I was stronger than I looked, thanks to a childhood spent hiking and walking and going to the shooting range with my father, but I knew there was no way I could get Taylor all that distance by myself.

Shaking, I went to my desk and pulled my purse out of the drawer where I always stowed it. My fingers trembled as well while I got out my phone. Thank God it wasn't too much work to dial 911.

It rang...and rang...and rang. Panic started to set in. I could feel my heart beginning to pound and my own nervous sweats starting, although I didn't think I was running a fever. Not yet, anyway.

Then, at last: "Nine-one-one, what is your emergency?"

I cleared my throat. "Hi, my name is Jessica Monroe, and I'm in Building 81 on the UNM campus. One of my students is very sick and unable to walk. I'm pretty sure she needs to go to the hospital."

"Symptoms?"

"A very high fever."

I could have sworn I heard a muttered "shit" at the other end of the line, followed by a long pause. "Ms. Monroe, we are experiencing longer-than-normal response times for ambulances due to heavy volume. We will get someone out to you, but it may be a while."

It didn't take a rocket scientist to figure out what that meant. Maybe it was lagging behind, but the Heat had finally come to Albuquerque.

I sat with Taylor, since I didn't know what else to do. She held on to the edge of her desk as if it was the only thing keeping her anchored to reality, her head first lolling this way and then that, her glassy dark eyes staring off into the distance, as if fixed on some object only she could see. It was frightening enough just being close to someone who was that sick, but even more frightening was how detached from reality she seemed to be. We Monroes were a healthy lot, and so I didn't have a lot of experience being around sick people. Devin got a horrible stomach flu one year, and we had colds and coughs from time to time, but nothing like this.

Sweat was dripping down Taylor's forehead and staining the tight T-shirt she wore. More rivulets of perspiration ran down into her cleavage, but I doubted anyone would have found the sight particularly sexy. For myself, I could only think of the millions of microbes she must be spreading in every direction each time she shifted in her seat. One time she shook like a dog, and little droplets of sweat sprayed everywhere, a few hitting me right in the face.

It took every ounce of willpower I had not to swear out loud. Belatedly, I realized that I had a partially drunk bottle of water in my purse. I doubted that would do much to help her, but at least it was something. And I had a feeling she was far past worrying about any germs I might have left behind on the bottle.

"Taylor?" I asked. No recognition in those strained dark eyes, which were still staring out at something only visible to her. "How about some water?"

She blinked. Maybe it was the only way she could answer, or maybe it was simply an involuntary reflex. Either way, it gave me an excuse to get up from the desk next to hers, to go to my purse and fetch the bottle of water. As I approached her, I could almost feel the heat emanating from her, impossibly, inhumanly warm.

What must her temperature be? I had no way of knowing, but I wondered how anyone could stay alive and conscious—even the fragile consciousness she was clinging to right now—while suffering such a high fever.

"Taylor, here's the water." She didn't seem capable of taking the bottle herself, so I held it to her lips. For a second she didn't move, only let the opening rest against her mouth, and then some lizard-brain function must have kicked in, because she latched onto it and drank greedily while I tilted the rest of the bottle's contents into her mouth. Within a few seconds, all the water was gone.

"That's all," I told her, but she didn't seem to understand, even lifting one hand to grab at the bottle when

I began to pull it away. "Just rest, Taylor. Please. The ambulance will be here soon."

That, of course, was a lie. I had no idea what "longer-than-normal response times" might mean, since I'd never called an ambulance for anyone in my life. My father might know, but even if I could get a hold of him, which I doubted, he'd probably read me the riot act for not getting out of there the second Taylor started to display symptoms. Or maybe not. He was pretty big on the whole "serve and protect" mentality.

Right now, though, I had a feeling I was on my own.

I pulled my cell phone out of my jeans pocket where I'd stowed it and looked at the time. Fifteen minutes since I'd called 911. It felt roughly ten times that. A quarter-hour response time wasn't great, but it also didn't feel too outside what might be considered normal. I might be waiting much, much longer than this. Biting my lip, I went to my contacts list and pushed the button for campus security, since I figured they might be faster than the paramedics, but the line was busy. I ended the call and tried again. Still nothing. Damn it.

As if finally registering that there was no more water, Taylor slumped back in her seat, head tilting to one side. Her body was twitching feebly. Some kind of convulsion? Again, my lack of experience with any kind of serious illness stymied me. Maybe it would be better for her to lie down, but the linoleum floor had to be far less comfortable than the chair. Since it had been a warm day, nearly eighty degrees, she didn't have a sweater or jacket that I could lay her on, and I hadn't brought one with me, either.

Never before in my life had I felt so useless, standing there and watching as the sweat rolled off her and she continued to jerk helplessly, like her body was being controlled by some unseen puppeteer. I went to the browser on my phone, thinking that maybe I could click over to WebMD or something and see if there was anything else I could do to help her, but no matter how many times I backed out of the browser app and tried to refresh it, I couldn't get the damn thing to connect. It wasn't the first time my phone had acted up like this, but in general I had good connectivity here at school. I had a feeling the phone wasn't the real problem.

But no, I didn't want to think about that. I didn't want to think about what might be going on outside the door to my classroom, what might be happening to my parents or my brother.

No, I thought fiercely. *They're fine. They have to be.*

Just when I was about to give up and dial 911 again, the door burst inward, and two men carrying a stretcher entered the classroom. *Thank God you're here* died on my lips, because they weren't wearing the usual dark jackets and pants of EMTs, but full head-to-toe yellow biohazard suits, the kind of gear I'd seen on TV on doctors and nurses treating people with Ebola.

They went straight to Taylor, extricated her from her desk, and laid her down on the stretcher. Once they were done with that and she was strapped in, one of them turned toward me.

"Name?"

I guessed they were asking about Taylor, not me. "Taylor Ortiz," I told him. "That's her purse right there on the floor. It should have her I.D. in it."

The EMT grabbed her purse by the strap and lifted it from the floor, then extracted her wallet from within. He opened it, glanced at her driver's license, and then nodded and dropped the wallet back in her purse. "You?"

"Me?" I blinked at him, then responded, "Jessica Monroe. I'm the T.A."

"How are you feeling?"

Scared. "Fine. That is, I don't feel like I'm running a fever or anything." Did that even matter? I hadn't heard what the incubation period was for the Heat, but I assumed it didn't have instantaneous onset. No disease did...or did it?

"Go straight home," the EMT said. "No contact with anyone else. If you start to exhibit symptoms, don't call your doctor. Go straight to the hospital."

"But...." The word trailed off as I attempted to gather my thoughts. Something about this didn't feel right. No, wait, scratch that—*nothing* about it felt right. I'd been exposed to someone who obviously had the Heat. Shouldn't they be quarantining me or something?

The EMT's hooded head tilted to one side as he waited for me to spit it out.

I said, "If she's sick, haven't I been infected, too? Don't I, I don't know, have to be isolated or something?"

"We don't have the facilities for that. Best thing to do is go home and stay away from other people. If you do get sick, get to the hospital. That's all I can tell you."

Then he nodded at his compatriot, and they both crouched down and lifted the stretcher, hauling Taylor out of the room. It was only after the door had shut behind them that I realized they'd left her purse behind, as if who she was didn't matter.

My phone went off then, and I looked down at the text that had just appeared on my home screen. *Due to health emergency, all classes are suspended indefinitely. We ask that all students go to their residences immediately and remain there until further notice.*

So the university's student alert system had finally kicked in.

Too bad that it was already too late.

CHAPTER TWO

THE CAMPUS WAS MOSTLY DESERTED WHEN I emerged from the classroom at a little before noon and locked the door behind me. In a way that was good, as at least I didn't have to play dodge 'em with anyone who looked infected. But there was still a long line of cars waiting to get out of the parking lot, and I sat there, worry mounting as the minutes ticked past.

What did it feel like when the Heat came over you? A sudden spike in temperature? Or was it a slow, gradual burn, until you, like a lobster in a pot, ended up boiling in your own juices?

I didn't know. And all this had happened so quickly that there hadn't been much detail on the news, either. Or maybe they'd repressed what they did know, lest they throw everyone into a panic.

At last I was able to pull out on Central, then headed west. Did I dare take the freeway to get home? All around me, the streets were choked, full of people obviously trying to get to their own homes, so I had a feeling the freeway was a very bad idea. Instead, I ended up zigzagging my way out of the downtown area, finally making it over to 12th so I could head north. A few more zigzags, and then I was back in a residential section, although still a few miles from home. There was less traffic here, although I noticed more cars on the streets than there normally would have been in the middle of the day when everyone should have been at work.

A sigh of relief escaped my lips as I pulled up in front of the house and I saw my mother's Escape parked in the driveway. No sign of Dad's Grand Cherokee, or the police cruiser he sometimes brought home. But at least my mother was here.

I scrambled out of the car, then hurried down the driveway to let myself in the back door. We almost never came and went through the front, mostly because my mother was unnecessarily fussy about the Berber carpet in the living room. Better to track dirt through the kitchen, which had abused linoleum she'd been wanting to get rid of for years.

"Mom?" I called out as I came in through the service porch, then on into the kitchen.

"Jess?" she called back. I heard feet approaching from the hallway that ran down the middle of the house. When she came around the corner, I saw that her face was dead white. She let out a little choked sob when she saw me. "Oh, thank God."

At any other time her reaction might have startled me, but not now. Not after what had just happened to Taylor Ortiz. "I'm fine," I said. "Only—"

Her brows drew together. "Only?"

"A girl in my class—she had it. The EMTs came and got her, but they sent me home. It's probably better if you don't come too close."

"Oh, God," she said, this time invoking the name in horror rather than in relief. She appeared to gather herself, voice strained as she went on, "How do you feel?"

I paused to take stock. "Okay, actually," I told her. It was true, too. Yes, I was a little shaken after being that close to someone that sick, and then having to fight my way home through hordes of panicky motorists, but otherwise, I felt fine. No fever. No chills. No sweats.

Despite what I'd just told her about staying away, she took a step closer. Motherly instinct, I supposed. She had to reassure herself that I was all right and not merely take my word for it. But because she was a smart woman, she only came close enough to see for herself that I wasn't flushed or feverish or sweaty.

After a long pause, she nodded. "I keep flipping through the stations, trying to see if someone is giving out any concrete information. What the incubation period is. How infectious the disease is. The—the mortality rate." She pulled in a breath. "And there's nothing, except that the situation is being handled and that people should stay home whenever possible. What kind of a policy is that?"

I didn't know. I would have assumed that in most cases of infection, the CDC would have send out teams to quarantine people and triage those affected, would do everything possible to keep the disease from spreading any further. Or at least, that was what I'd observed on TV when the news covered outbreaks of bird flu or whatever. But I'd seen no real government presence on my way home today, no squads of experts in biohazard gear, no blacked-out SUVs speeding down the street, no...nothing. It was as if this thing was spreading so quickly the government couldn't begin to contain it.

That thought was too frightening, though, and I quickly pushed it away. Instead, I asked, "Dad? Devin?"

She glanced away from me, her mouth tight. "I can't reach your father. I sent a text to Devin, telling him to come home, but he hasn't answered me. I called the school and got a recording that classes had been canceled and everyone sent home. So my best guess is he's taking the opportunity to have a little unsupervised time with Lori."

Lori was his girlfriend. The two had been joined at the hip since spring break last year, and I had a feeling my mother's guess was all too correct. "Did you try calling her house?"

"Of course I did. No answer. And I don't have her cell number—Devin would never give it to me. At the time, I didn't think it was worth nagging him about it. Now...."

"I'm sure it's fine," I said quickly. No point in having my mother worry any more than absolutely necessary. "If they're at Lori's house, then at least they're inside and away from other people."

"True, but...."

I knew she would fret about this until Devin appeared, whenever that was. In that moment, fury flashed through me, that he would be so selfish as to go off and bang his girlfriend or whatever while the rest of us were worried sick about him. Uttering such a thing out loud would just set my mother off that much more, though, so I only said, "Why don't you have some tea while you're waiting? I need to go up to my apartment and wash my hands and get straightened up, but I'll be right back down."

Her eyes were far away, but she nodded. "That sounds like a good idea."

I sent her what I hoped was an encouraging smile, then went out the back door and down the driveway to the detached garage. The apartment built over it was small, just a little over four hundred square feet, so there was a tiny living room, a spot under one window for a table and two chairs, a kitchenette, and then the bedroom and bath, which was so small I could reach out from the shower stall and open the door if I had to. But at least it was mine, and it felt good to escape there, to hurry up the stairs and run to the bathroom so I could turn on the water as hot as I could stand it, then let it run over my hands as I scrubbed them again and again with antibacterial soap.

As if that would make a difference. It was better than nothing, though, and I couldn't think of what else to do. My eyes stared back at me from within the mirror, wide and dark, shadowed with worry. I was pale, but I didn't look sick.

After blotting my hands on a towel, I reached up and felt my forehead. It didn't seem overly warm, but I'd always heard you couldn't really detect your own temperature by doing that. So I opened the medicine cabinet and pulled out the digital thermometer I kept there. After cleaning it off with some rubbing alcohol, I popped it in my mouth and waited.

The seconds went by with agonizing slowness. I wandered out to the living room and sat down on the futon, wondering whether I should turn on my TV, see if I could find anything worth watching. But then, if my mother had been unable to, what made me think I would have any better luck?

Instead, I stared out the window at the tree outside, a honey locust, its leaves just beginning to turn yellow. It was warm during the day, but the nights were already cold. The tree knew its time was coming.

Did I?

The thermometer beeped, indicating it was done measuring my temperature, and I pulled it out of my mouth. For the longest moment, I only held it, scared to look at what the readout might say. Finally, I forced myself to glance down.

97.6.

My breath whooshed out of me, and I dropped the thermometer on top of the coffee table. No temperature at all. On the low side, actually.

But what did that mean? Once you were infected, how long did it take for your fever to start building?

I didn't know. All I did know was that I wasn't sick. Not yet, anyway. And I'd left my mother alone long enough. Even if I couldn't sit next to her, I would be close enough so we could talk, and that would help to keep her from worrying until Devin came home. Which he would, eventually, after he'd gotten his rocks off. I loved my little brother, but sometimes he wasn't the most considerate of other people's feelings. Well, other people who weren't his girlfriend, that is.

After closing the door to my apartment but not locking it, I went back into the main house, past the washer and dryer and the overflow pantry where my mother put all the big containers of items from Costco, the sort of stuff that was "such a good deal she couldn't pass it up." What in the world we were going to do with that much tomato sauce or rolled oats, I had no idea.

She must have turned the television on, because I could hear it blathering away as I approached. "...everyone is encouraged to stay inside and away from people with obvious signs of infection. If a fever presents, take analgesics such as aspirin or ibuprofen. Ice packs are also effective. If the fever rises to above 103 degrees Fahrenheit, go to your nearest emergency room...."

I stopped dead at the entrance to the kitchen. Not because I didn't want to get any closer to my mother, but because I knew it really didn't matter whether I was infected or not.

Her body was sprawled on the kitchen floor, limp, one of her low-heeled pumps hanging half off her foot. Panic flashed through me, so quick and sudden that I could actually feel my knees beginning to buckle. I grabbed on to the doorframe for support, telling myself I didn't have time to lose it right now. After swallowing a huge gulp of air, I said, "Mom?"

No reply, but then I heard her breathing, rapid and shallow, like our old dog Sadie after a particularly strenuous walk. We'd lost Sadie last winter.

Stupid of me to be thinking of that now.

I went into the kitchen and knelt down next to my mother, reaching out to touch her shoulder. The skin under the silk blouse she'd worn to work was almost scorching, or at least it felt that way to my shaky fingers. "Mom?"

The faintest of groans. It wasn't much, but it was a sign that she could still hear me, hadn't yet retreated so far that she couldn't even react to outside stimuli.

Obviously, I couldn't leave her here. My parents' bedroom was upstairs, and I quailed at the thought of trying to move her all the way up the flight of stairs that led to the second story. Maybe I could just lay her down on the couch in the family room? At least until my father got home, and then the two of us could get her properly in bed. Even then I knew calling an ambulance was pointless. I couldn't count on anyone to come, so I figured the best thing to do was to get her as comfortable as possible.

I took her by the shoulders, and, as gently as I could, rolled her over so she was facing upward. She whimpered during this procedure, sounding so unlike herself that I felt a frightened little sob escape my throat. Luckily, she was far enough gone that she couldn't really hear me.

Telling myself that this was the best thing to do, that I couldn't leave her on the floor, I half-carried, half-dragged her into the family room and then somehow manhandled her up onto the couch. The scary thing was that she didn't even protest, didn't try to push back against me or do anything, really. It was like moving a rag doll around—a 130-pound rag doll, anyway.

But at last she was safely on the couch. I took the throw that always lay folded over one arm and spread it out across her. Another one of those little whimpers, as if she thought that would make her too hot, but knew she had to have some sort of covering. Then she subsided, eyes shut tight, chest rising and falling far too rapidly.

All of the first aid supplies were in the medicine cabinet in the upstairs bathroom, the one Devin and I used to share before I moved into the apartment over the garage. After taking another look at my mother and deciding she should be okay for a minute or so, I hurried up the stairs, moving as quickly as I could without actually running. When I got to the bathroom, I opened the cabinet, took out the jumbo container of Kirkland ibuprofen, and shook a couple into my hand. I also took out the thermometer. Yes, it was obvious my mother had a high fever...but *how* high? Past the magic number of 103?

I had to hope not.

I dashed back down the stairs. She hadn't moved, although I noticed she'd pushed the throw off her chest, down to her waist. Her blouse and skirt were getting wrinkled, but I couldn't do much about that. Another thing my father would have to help me with when he got home.

If he got home.

Don't go there, I told myself. *He'll be here. He will.*

I just didn't know what he'd find when he eventually did make it home.

The pills were cool in my palm. I realized then that I'd forgotten to get any water for my mother to take them with, so I went into the kitchen, filled a glass halfway, and went back out to the family room. She hadn't moved, was lying there twitching and shaking the way Taylor Ortiz had.

"Mom," I said softly. She didn't seem to acknowledge me, so I didn't know if she'd really heard me or not. Maybe my saying her name was to reassure myself as much as it was to let her know I was there. "Here's some water, and some pills for your fever."

I slipped my arm under her shoulders and lifted her a few inches, just enough so I could bring the water to her lips. Like Taylor, she drank greedily, gulping so much that I had to pull the glass away so there would be enough left for her to take the pills.

"Okay, first one," I told her, slipping one of the ibuprofen capsules between her lips. It just sort of sat there on her tongue, so I poured more water into her mouth. Her swallow reflex cut in, and she downed the pill without too much trouble. The second one was a little more difficult, but she did finally take it.

After that procedure, I realized I should've taken her temperature first, that the water might make the reading inaccurate. Since there wasn't anything I could do about it at the moment, I sat down in one of the armchairs, figuring if I waited a few minutes, it would probably be safe to try the thermometer.

Waiting was bad, though. If all I was doing was sitting there and watching my mother shake and shiver on the couch, then I had plenty of time to think… and thinking was the last thing I wanted to do. My thoughts chased one another around and around, worrying at each other, fretting, biting. What if my father never came home? What if Devin had fallen sick at Lori's? What if they were *both* sick?

And above all, *Why isn't anyone helping us?*

I could feel myself starting to shake, but I didn't think it was from a fever. No, I guessed it was just good old-fashioned fear with an extra helping of uncertainty. Clenching my hands together, I willed them to stop trembling. My mother was probably too out of it to really notice, but I didn't want my fingers shaking when I finally did take her temperature.

Since I couldn't think of anything else to do, I picked up the remote for the TV and switched it on, quickly lowering the volume so it wouldn't disturb my mother. As I flipped from channel to channel, I didn't see anything that was remotely reassuring. More talking heads, discussing self-quarantine procedures and dispensing advice how you shouldn't go out or come into contact with anyone if you had any symptoms, and if you did come down with a fever, to make sure you wore a mask or tied some kind of barrier over your nose and mouth when it came time to go to the emergency room. And all of them looked pale and strained, and were giving the side-eye to one another when they thought the others weren't looking, as if trying to detect signs that one of their fellow newscasters might be starting to show symptoms. On one channel, I caught a pretty young woman who didn't look much older than I sending furtive glances somewhere off-camera, as if at someone who was standing by and monitoring what they were all saying. That couldn't be good.

With all the people being sent to emergency rooms, hospitals had to be overwhelmed. I wondered how many people were sick, and how many were like me, exposed but still asymptomatic. Maybe fifty-fifty? I couldn't even begin to guess. All I did know was that I didn't see how hospitals could even begin to keep up.

Annoyed that all the stations were repeating the same useless information, I turned off the television and picked up the thermometer. My mother really didn't want to take it, but after a bit of wrestling, I got it shoved between her lips and more or less under her tongue. Her skin felt clammy and hot at the same time, which I doubted was a good sign. Maybe two ibuprofen weren't enough. Maybe I should have given her three, or even four.

Or maybe I could have poured the whole damn bottle down her throat, and it still wouldn't have done a bit of good.

Clenching my jaw, I sat and looked out the window at the trees moving in the gentle September breeze, at the sparrow who landed on one branch and cocked his head in my direction, almost as if he could see me sitting inside, watching him. The window in the family room faced out onto the side yard and the fence that separated us from the Montoyas next door. I didn't see any movement over there, which most days wouldn't have been that unusual. It was the middle of the day; both the Montoyas worked full-time, and their kids were in grade school. But the schools were closed, and it seemed as if most places of business were shutting up and sending their employees home as well.

Were they home, but ill? Or well enough, but hiding, not wanting to take the risk of being exposed? I didn't know, and I had my hands full here. If my father came home, I'd probably go over and check on them, but until then....

The thermometer beeped at me, and I gently drew it from my mother's mouth and looked at the readout. Then I squeezed my eyes shut, certain they had to be reading it wrong, that they were tricking me in some way.

I opened them again.

106.8.

Was that possible?

I supposed it had to be, since that was what the thermometer was saying. I also had a feeling that two ibuprofen might not be cutting it here. Okay, on the news they were saying to apply cool cloths, so that seemed to be the next step. Well, right after I called 911. Maybe that wouldn't do any good, but right then I was so scared by my mother's temperature that I had to at least try to get help.

After I set the thermometer back down on the coffee table, I got up and went to the kitchen, where my parents still had an old-fashioned corded phone mounted on the wall. Devin and I had both laughed at it, but my father had given us the evil eye and said that land lines were way more reliable than cell phones, and that one day we might be very glad of that old push-button phone.

I lifted the receiver from its cradle, but when I put it to my ear, all I heard was a fast busy signal, the kind you get when the phone service is out. Scowling, I jiggled the hook, then listened again. Still nothing. So much for good old-fashioned technology.

My cell phone was upstairs in my apartment, still in my purse where I'd dropped it on the floor by the door. I really didn't want to leave my mother alone, but I needed to see if the cell network was functioning any better than the land one.

After peeking into the family room and reassuring myself that she was resting as well as she could be, all things considered, I let myself out and climbed the steps to my apartment two at a time. Since I hadn't locked the door, it only took a few seconds for me to get in, pull the phone out of my purse, and dial 911.

"We're sorry—all circuits are currently busy. Please try again later."

The computer-generated voice sounded positively snotty. Somehow I resisted the urge to fling my cell phone against the wall, since I knew that wouldn't do any good. Instead, I stuffed it into the pocket of my jeans and hurried back to the house. I sure would try again later, but in the meantime, I had to do what I could to take care of my mother.

Her condition didn't seem to have worsened during the couple of minutes I was gone. That was something. I got a few dish towels out of the drawer and dampened them with cold water, then went into the family room and laid them across her forehead. Some of the moisture dripped on her gray silk blouse, leaving damp blotches. I hoped they wouldn't leave stains.

Seriously, you're worrying about a couple of stains at a time like this?

I supposed I was fixating on that, just because it was easier to worry about something like ruining my mother's clothes rather than the big-picture stuff, like how none of the phones were working. Yes, I'd heard how that could happen after some kind of disaster, but Albuquerque wasn't really prone to disasters, whether natural or man-made.

The back door slammed, and my mother started, then began twitching and shaking again. Damn. And I'd just gotten her to a place where she seemed to be more or less resting comfortably. But maybe that slamming door meant my father had come home.

I readjusted the damp towel on my mother's forehead, then got up and went into the kitchen. Devin was getting a glass out of the cupboard as I entered. He looked fine—no flushed cheeks, no sheen of sweat—and in that moment I wasn't sure whether I wanted to hug him in relief or punch him in the arm for making us worry like that about him.

"Where the hell have you been?" I demanded.

"Lori's," he replied, going to the refrigerator and getting some ice and water out of the door.

"Well, you scared the crap out of Mom. She couldn't get a hold of you—"

He shrugged. "I sent a text. Maybe it didn't go through. Anyway, they sent us home, and Lori couldn't get in touch with either of her parents, so she was freaking out. So I stayed with her."

"Oh," I said, feeling some of my righteous indignation begin to seep away. Lori was an only child, and a little coddled, so I could see why she'd be more than ordinarily upset at not being able to contact her parents. "Is she okay?"

"Yeah, her mom finally got a text through and said she was on her way home, so I thought I'd better get over here." His gaze sharpened on me, and I wondered what he saw. Lord knows, I was starting to feel kind of overloaded. "Are you okay?"

"I'm fine, but Mom isn't," I replied bluntly. Maybe too bluntly, because he almost dropped the glass he was holding.

"She's—she's not sick, is she?"

"Yes. She just got the fever about a half hour ago."

Beneath his end-of-summer tan, my brother's face drained of all color. "She can't be sick!"

Right then he didn't look like the big, broad-shouldered running back, but a scared kid. I wanted to go hug him, but lately he'd been scorning such sisterly displays of emotion, so I wasn't sure how he would react. Instead, I kept my voice calm as I told him, "She had a high fever, but I got her to take some ibuprofen, and she's resting now with some cold cloths on her head. So far, so good."

That sounded very reasonable, very steady. Never mind that I didn't really believe it. If this disease really was at all survivable, that information would've been all over the news by now. The complete radio silence on the actual facts of the disease told me that it was beyond dire...it was catastrophic.

My words didn't seem to reassure Devin. He gave me a stricken look and then went into the family room, where he stopped a few feet away from the couch and stared down at our mother. She seemed to be sleeping, but something seemed off about her face, as if her cheeks and eye sockets had begun to look sunken, far too shadowed.

No, that couldn't be right. It had to be a trick of the lighting in the room; I'd pulled the drapes almost closed so the afternoon light that was beginning to slant into the space wouldn't disturb her. Just some sort of strange optical illusion.

Only I feared that wasn't it at all.

Devin appeared to be of the same mind. He stood there, hands hanging helplessly at his sides, as he stared down at her. Finally, he whispered, "She's going to die, isn't she?"

In that moment, I was furious with him for giving voice to that thought, as if by saying it out loud he could somehow cause it to happen. "No, she's not," I shot back, my voice shaking.

"She is," he insisted, and right then I was glad that she was more or less comatose. At least that way she couldn't possibly hear what we were saying. "When I was over at Lori's house, we were on the computer, trying to get more information. A lot of the sites we went to were down, but we found one with this guy on video saying that everyone who catches it dies, and that the government is shutting down anyone who tries to spread the truth."

I recalled that one blonde newscaster, and the way her gaze kept flickering nervously to something—or someone—off-screen. FBI...or CIA...or NSA...agents, standing there and watching to make sure the reporters all said the same thing?

At any other time, that would have felt like rank paranoia. Now, though....

"That's crazy," I said, although I didn't sound all that convinced, even to myself. "No disease is one hundred percent fatal."

"That we know of," Devin shot back. Then his face twisted as he looked back down at our mother, at her strangely waxy and sunken features. "Is there anything else we can do? Like, I don't know, ice packs or something?"

"Maybe," I said. It was worth a try. Covering her in ice packs would complete the ruin of her outfit, but I doubted that mattered much at the moment.

Glad to have something to do, Devin and I went to the kitchen and got out some big gallon-sized plastic storage bags and started filling them with ice. That seriously depleted our current ice supply, but I knew the ice-maker would start chugging away in an attempt to make up the deficit.

"How are you feeling?" I asked as we zipped up the last bag.

"Fine," he said. "I mean, I feel...weird...but I don't feel sick."

That about sized it up. Weird, but not sick. The world was tilting beneath us, but neither of us knew what to do about it.

I set the bags I carried down on the coffee table, not worried about whether the cold and the moisture would mar the wooden surface. Such concerns seemed miles away from where we were right now. "I want to check her temperature again first," I told Devin, picking up the thermometer and slipping it into our mother's mouth. She squirmed a bit, but I held firm, and she subsided. We waited as the seconds went by, and when the thermometer beeped, I was pulling it out before it was even done.

When I looked at the readout, I couldn't believe what it said.

"One hundred and seven point two," I read as my stomach began to knot. So much for the ibuprofen and the cold towels.

Devin's dark eyes were practically round, they widened so much. "That's not possible...is it?"

"Well, it's possible to have a fever that high," I replied, then stopped there. It wouldn't do much good to point out that such an unnaturally high fever could result in brain and organ damage...and that there wasn't a damn thing we could do to stop it, apparently. I drew in a breath and added, "Let's get the ice on her.

Obviously, the cold compresses weren't enough."

He nodded, and I picked up the bags full of ice I'd placed on the coffee table. I wasn't even sure of the best positioning of the ice packs, but I figured she'd need one on her head, and some up against her sides, maybe on her chest....

The bag in my left hand went on her forehead, and the one in my right down on her chest. She winced, although her eyes didn't open. The bag I'd put on her chest shifted slightly, and I repositioned it. "Give me yours," I told Devin, guessing that he wouldn't feel very comfortable about setting bags full of ice on his mother's body. From the alacrity with which he handed them off, I had a feeling my guess was correct. I placed those two on either side of her waist, trying to position them in such a way that they'd get maximum contact with her torso. It was the core that needed to get cooled down. Or at least, I thought that was how it worked.

She didn't like it, I could tell—she kept shifting slightly, trying to get away from the cold, but she was so weak that her movements were ineffectual. Still, if she moved around much more than that, I'd have to find some way to secure the ice packs in place. There had to be some rope or twine or something like that in the garage.

I wondered if I should send Devin out to fetch it. He was staring down at our mother, glassy-eyed, as if not quite able to take in what was happening to her.

Then I saw the way he swayed on his feet, and a wave of cold that had nothing to do with the ice packs I'd just handled washed over me.

"Devin?" I asked, and it seemed it took him far longer than it should for him to glance over at me.

His pupils appeared to have dilated until they were so large that the black almost swallowed up the warm brown of his irises. "Huh?"

"How do you feel?" I enunciated the words carefully so there would be no chance for him to misunderstand.

"Um...weird."

I went to him and put my hand on his forehead. He didn't flinch away, which told me something was very wrong. Actually, the clammy heat against my palm told me everything I needed to know.

When I spoke, the words sounded as if they were coming from very far away, as if someone other than myself was saying them. "Devin, why don't you go upstairs and get into bed? I'll bet you're tired."

"Yeah, I am kind of tired," he mumbled, then turned with excruciating slowness and began moving toward the hallway and the staircase that led to the second floor. I prayed he'd be able to get there under his own power. My mother had been difficult enough to move. I knew there was no way I'd be able to haul 170 pounds of running back up those stairs.

But somehow he did it, putting one foot hesitatingly after the other, until at last he reached the upstairs hall and stumbled into his room. I followed, giving him his space, and when he collapsed onto his bed, legs hanging off the side, I wanted to let out a sigh of relief...but I didn't.

How could I, when I knew my brother had just been handed a death sentence?

CHAPTER THREE

I DID GO IN, AND UNTIE HIS SHOES AND PULL THEM off. Then I waited as he wriggled under the covers.

"Get some rest, Devin," I told him, and he gave me a bleary nod.

"'Kay."

Maybe he slept after that, or just plain passed out. Part of me was thinking I should go downstairs and fetch the big bottle of ibuprofen, but what was the point? I'd given some to my mother, and it hadn't made a whit of a difference. In fact, she'd only gotten worse.

I couldn't linger here, anyway—I had to go check on her. Devin seemed more or less quiescent for the moment, so it seemed safe to go back downstairs.

She hadn't moved much. The ice packs were more or less in place, except for the one on her forehead, which had slid to one side. I put it back in the proper position, feeling as I did so how quickly the ice had melted, how half the bag was now just cold water. Was that even possible?

Then again, I didn't have much experience with how quickly a 107-degree fever could melt ice. If her temperature was even still 107. It might have gone up again.

Toward the front of the house, the door slammed, and I jumped. Then joy rushed through me as I realized who it must be. Thank God.

I ran out of the family room and into the hall-way, saw my father coming toward me. The relief that spread over his face as he caught sight of me standing there, apparently safe and well, made me feel all warm and happy inside...for about a second. Then I thought of my mother, lying on the couch, silk shirt stained beyond recognition, eyes seeming to sink deeper and deeper into her head with every passing minute, of Devin passed out upstairs, the fever beginning to consume him as well, and not a damn thing I could do about it.

Something in my expression must have changed, because my father stopped dead and asked, "Your mother?"

"She's in the family room. She—" And that's all I got out, because out of nowhere I began to sob noisily, the preternatural calm I'd been able to maintain all day deserting me now that my father was here and I didn't have to be the strong one anymore.

He came to me and held me for a moment, letting me cry. No words of reassurance, though; I had a feeling he'd seen enough today to know there was nothing remotely reassuring about our situation. Then he said, "I need to see her," and let go of me.

I didn't protest. I was his daughter, but she was his wife.

When I paused in the doorway to the family room, I could see my father standing a few feet away from the couch, his head bowed. His hands hung at his sides, clenched into fists.

"I'm sorry," I said quietly. "I gave her some ibuprofen, but that didn't seem to work. Then I thought maybe the ice—" I let the words break off there. Nothing was working, and now Devin was sick, too, and right then I didn't have the ability to pile more bad news on my father. Not with that non-expression on his face, the one I'd seen a few times when he was desperately attempting to keep the world from knowing how badly he really was hurting.

He didn't move. At first I wasn't sure he was going to answer me, but then he said, "It'll slow it down, but it won't stop it."

His tone was so final that I couldn't help asking, "How do you know?"

Another one of those short, painful silences. "Because I've been out in it all day. Seeing people collapse in the street. Taking others to the hospital in my cruiser because the ambulances were either busy or already out of commission, their drivers just as incapacitated as everyone else. Even Josh—" His voice didn't exactly break, but from the way he stopped himself, I got the impression it was about to.

Josh was my father's partner. They'd been partners since, well, ever since I could remember. For my father to have seen the man he regarded as a brother come down with this terrible thing.... "I'm sorry, Dad," I said, although I knew the words were completely inadequate.

"I tried to take him to the hospital. He wouldn't go. Said he was going to die with dignity in his own house." Again I heard the faintest waver at the edges of my father's voice before he got control of himself again. "I had to carry him inside. He was already burning up. And after that, I couldn't—I didn't see the point in staying on assignment any longer. Half the force was already sick with this thing and the rest about to come down with it. I knew I had to come home. Home," he repeated, staring down at my mother's limp form.

"I'm sorry," I said again. Just words, but they did something to fill up the silence. "She seemed okay when I got here. But then...." I bit my lip, knowing I had to tell him about Devin. God, I didn't want to, though.

"Then?" he echoed.

"She collapsed. I brought her in here because I couldn't get her upstairs. And Devin...."

"He's sick, too." It wasn't a question.

"Yes. But he's up in his room. He's sleeping."

"Then he's lucky."

I wasn't sure I wanted to know what that meant. "So...what do we do now?"

"I'll take your mother up to our bed." For the first time, he shifted so he could look back at me. "How do you feel, Jess?"

"Fine," I said, the automatic response. Then I shook my head, because I knew that was a lie, and I didn't want to lie to my father. "No, I *feel* terrible. But I'm not sick."

"I understand. I feel the same way." He turned toward my mother again, gently lifted the ice packs— which were now mostly water—from her, then slid his arms under her so he could pick her up. Her arms and legs dangled, as limp as if they'd become some-how boneless, but she didn't move, didn't even make a whimper of protest. Was that a good sign, or a sign that she was slipping farther and farther away from us?

I crossed my arms and tried to suppress the shiver that went through me. From my father's expression, I could tell he wanted to be alone to lay her down in the bed they shared, to be with her now even though it was probably too late. I understood that, and yet I still wanted to run up the stairs and be with him, to not feel so alone.

As I stood there, letting my father trudge up the stairs and forcing myself to stay where I was, to give him his privacy, I heard something. The word was only a whisper at the edges of my mind, and yet it seemed to resonate along every nerve ending.

Beloved....

Going rigid, I held myself stock still, wondering where on earth that had come from. At first I thought it might have been my father, speaking to my mother, but I'd never heard him call her "beloved." "Sweetheart," yes, and "darling"—but never "baby," since she always said using that epithet only infantilized women. Such a firebrand, my mother.

Although maybe that was the wrong word to be using right now.

Anyway, their bedroom was at the end of the upstairs hall, too far away for me to have heard him unless he'd all but shouted the word. At any rate, it hadn't sounded like my father's voice. It was somewhat deep like his, but more rounded around the edges, with the faintest hint of an accent I couldn't even begin to identify.

"Who's there?" I whispered, feeling like an idiot even as the words left my lips.

No reply, of course. I was only imagining things. No one had ever called me "beloved." Hell, only one person had ever even told me he loved me. Colin, the boyfriend of my junior and senior years of college. It had taken me a while to realize his "love" wasn't the kind I wanted—he said those things to keep me placated, to keep me from noticing that he was banging at least two other girls on the side.

I'd gone to the clinic right after I dumped him and had myself tested for every disease it was possible to be tested for, and I was fine, but that experience had scarred me. I hadn't gotten past a second date ever since. Third dates were when things could start to get serious, when you might end up in the sack together. So I always made sure to end relationships before they got to that stage. No opportunities for anyone to be calling me "beloved," that was for sure.

And then I decided that the stress of the day had gotten to me, and I was hearing things. Or were auditory hallucinations another byproduct of a high fever? I didn't know for sure; apparently, I hadn't spent enough time hanging out on WebMD.

Even though I knew it wouldn't tell me anything concrete, I couldn't help putting my hand up to my forehead. No discernible change in temperature that I could tell, which meant I wasn't running a fever. No tingles or chills or any of the other telltales of my internal temperature being anything other than what it should be.

I decided that standing there and trying to determine whether I was sick or crazy wasn't helping anyone, so I went upstairs to check on Devin. The door to my parents' room was closed, and I knew better than to knock. My father would come out when he was ready. I couldn't begin to imagine what he'd seen today, and I knew he needed this time alone with his wife. It wasn't a question of if, but when; the human body just couldn't survive at temperatures like that. She should be in a hospital getting IV drips and ice baths and Lord knows what else. An economy-sized bottle of ibuprofen and some half-assed bags of ice from the freezer weren't going to cut it.

Tears began to prick at my eyes, and I blinked them away. I'd already cried once today, and I knew I'd probably have plenty more reasons to weep by the time this was all over. Or maybe by then I'd be sick, too, and I wouldn't know what was happening to me. That was one blessed thing about this entire nightmare—once people got hit by that fever, it scrambled their brains so much they didn't seem to be aware of what was happening to them. Thank God for small mercies.

I opened Devin's door a crack and saw that he had fallen into the fitful phase of the disease—twitching and jerking, his forehead sheened with sweat. Even though I knew it probably wouldn't do any good, I went to the upstairs bathroom and shook three capsules of ibuprofen out of the big bottle in the cabinet there, then pulled a little paper cup from the dispenser and filled it with water.

Just as I was approaching his bed, Devin's leg jerked out and hit my arm, causing the water to splash all down my front, soaking the knit top I wore. I muttered a curse, but he didn't even seem to realize what he'd done, and that was how I knew he must be completely out of it. At any other time, he would've burst out laughing at managing to kick water all over me.

Pulling in a breath, I did an about-face and went back to the bathroom, plucked a towel off the rack, and did the best I could to blot the worst of the moisture from my shirt. Then I refilled the paper cup and went back to my brother's bedroom, approaching with care from the side so he wouldn't catch me unawares again.

That kick seemed to have consumed the last of his strength, because he was lying on his back, one arm flopped over the side of the bed. I went to him and murmured, "Here's some medicine for you, Dev."

The water first, since that had worked well with both Taylor and my mother. He drank, and didn't protest when I dropped a pill on his tongue and made him swallow, then gave him some more water. I repeated the process two more times, giving him one last sip to empty the cup, my arm under his head to steady him. He did drink, then collapsed against the pillow when he was done.

Was any of that going to do him any good? Or was I just doing something…anything…to make myself feel less helpless?

Probably the latter, although I wasn't quite ready to admit it to myself.

Since Devin seemed to be sleeping again, I decided I could leave him for a bit. Pulling out the chair and sitting next to him felt a little too much like keeping watch over someone's deathbed, and I wasn't ready to do that yet. Also, I'd just realized I was thirsty, too—I hadn't had anything to drink since I'd come home several hours earlier.

So I slipped out of my brother's room and went back down the stairs. The door to my parents' room was still shut, and I felt a completely unworthy stab of irritation. Yes, it must be terrible for my father, but I doubted my mother even knew he was there, whereas I needed him, needed someone to talk to. But I knew I would never disturb him, so I kept going to the kitchen. Once there, I pulled a glass from the cupboard and held it up to the ice dispenser. A few cubes half-heartedly spilled out, and I guessed it was working overtime to replenish what I'd already used in my futile attempt to reduce my mother's fever.

I sat down on one of the stools at the breakfast bar and stared out the window, not really focusing on anything. Since our house was on a corner, the view included the low juniper hedges planted against the fence, and a fairly unobstructed glimpse of the street beyond. As I watched, a silver car wove its way down the street, listlessly drifting from one side of the narrow residential lane to the other, actually hitting one curb before correcting and moving toward the one opposite, like the world's biggest and slowest pinball. It finally came to rest halfway up on the sidewalk on the corner across from our property, almost touching the smooth green lawn Mr. D'Ambrosio took such pride in, when most everyone else in the neighborhood had long since given up on grass and had switched over to cactus- and evergreen-studded drought-tolerant landscaping.

No one came out of the D'Ambrosio house to check on the driver, which told me Mr. and Mrs. D'Ambrosio must be as incapacitated as whoever had been driving that Camry. In that moment, I was just glad the driver had only been going twenty miles an hour at the most. Anything else, and they could have caused a lot more damage.

Footsteps coming down the hall made me turn, and I saw my father approaching. His eyes looked red, but otherwise his face was still and calm, as if he'd made his peace with whatever was happening to my mother, to Devin...to the world.

The words made their way to my lips before I even realized I was saying them. "Is she...?"

"No." His gaze shifted to the glass of water sitting on the counter in front of me, and he gave a faint nod.

He went and got his own glass from the cupboard, and got some water as well, although I noticed he didn't bother with the ice. Afterward, he sat down next to me on one of the barstools and added, "Not yet, anyway."

"How...how long?"

"I don't know." He drank some water, and I decided I should as well, although it seemed to get jammed halfway down my throat, lodging there as if it was a solid object instead of liquid. "It...varies, from what I've seen and heard."

I didn't know why, but for some reason that bothered me almost as much as anything else that had happened so far. If a disease was going to be this evil, it should at least be predictable.

The question had been torturing me all afternoon, and now I finally had someone I could ask it of. "Dad... why isn't anyone helping? Why are we being left to deal with this alone?"

A long pause, during which he stared down at his glass of water without meeting my eyes. When he did look up, I almost wished I hadn't been watching him, waiting for his response. Never in my life had I seen such an expression of despair on my father's face. Despair...and fury.

"Because there's no one *to* help, Jess. What's happening here in Albuquerque—it's happening everywhere. New York. Los Angeles. Washington, D.C. and London and Moscow and—everywhere." His hands, his big, strong, capable hands, now somehow looked limp and broken as they rested on the counter. "There's no answer at the CDC. Tried calling in the National Guard for help, and nothing. The only good thing about the whole situation is that people are getting sick so quickly, they don't have time to get into trouble. The fever makes them incapable of violence, of looting. Most collapse where they stand. That's why I said that Devin was lucky—you got him into bed, and he's sleeping. The fever doesn't have him hallucinating and having convulsions or seizures, like I saw happen with some people today."

"So...that's it?" I whispered. "We all just sit back and wait to die?"

He scrubbed his hand over his face and glanced away from me. "I don't know. There's no way to treat this thing. Either you get it, or you don't. Or rather, I have yet to see anyone who hasn't caught it, but...you're not sick."

"Yet," I said flatly, then drank some water.

"Usually, you'd be sick by now, since you've been around infected people."

"You're not sick, either," I pointed out, and he gave a grim nod.

"I keep expecting to be, but...." Deliberately, he picked up his glass and drained the water. "I don't know. It's possible we could have a hereditary immunity. I just don't know." His fingers tightened on the glass, and for a second I thought he was going to pick it up and hurl it at the wall, do something to express the frustrated anger I saw in his eyes. Instead, he let go of it and pushed it away. "The problem is, I don't know anything."

Neither did I, except that I didn't feel sick, and my father didn't appear to have any symptoms, either. Maybe there really was something to that notion of hereditary immunity. In looks and build, I favored my mother, with my almost-black hair and dark eyes, traits she claimed came from a great-great-grandmother who was full-blood Ute, while Devin and my father were more alike, hair still dark but not as inky as mine, their eyes a lighter, warmer brown. So why my father and I were the ones with no symptoms, I couldn't begin to guess. Obviously, appearance didn't have much to do with this particular quirk of heredity.

"I don't know anything, either," I said. "But I guess I'll start with checking on Devin."

"And I'll look in on your mother." My father got up from his stool, and I followed suit.

Once I was upstairs, I could tell there hadn't been any real change with my brother. He didn't even seem to have moved, but still lay there with one arm flopped over the side of his bed, eyes tightly shut. In fact, he was so still that I went over and laid two fingers against his throat, worried that I wouldn't feel a pulse. It was there, but thready and fast, which couldn't be a good sign. His hair, cropped short for football season, was damp with sweat.

Something about that thought, the realization that he should be off at football practice right now instead of lying here, fighting a disease so mysterious and strange that it didn't even have a formal name, made the anger rise up in me again. This shouldn't be happening. He should be with his teammates, getting sweaty because his coach had made him do a hundred push-ups for being a smart-ass yet again. And an hour from now, we should all be sitting down at the dinner table together, something families hardly ever did anymore, but which my mother insisted on. I'd been skipping those meals on Tuesdays and Thursdays, since I had to teach a six o'clock class, but I tried to make it when I could.

None of that was happening, though. And it wasn't happening for Devin's girlfriend Lori, or my own friends Elena and Tori and Brittany, or—or *anyone*. All across the city...the country...the world...people were suffering and dying, and no one could stop it.

That realization made the enormity of the whole situation come crashing down on me. I let out a choked little sob and fled my brother's room, running down the stairs to the family room so I could turn on the TV, could reassure myself with the sound of someone else's voice, even if the newscasters were following the commands of people who might already be dead. I had to know a world still existed out there beyond my house, even if it was a world swiftly falling apart.

But when I picked up the remote and turned on the television, nothing came on to reassure me. Some stations blank, others showing a "please stand by" message, others with a test pattern of colored bars. My heart rate sped up as I moved from channel to channel, thinking that there had to be at least one still broadcasting, one that hadn't been abandoned.

AMC seemed to be showing a rerun of *The Walking Dead*, which had to be someone's idea of a sick joke, as I didn't think that show ever ran before nine o'clock at night due to its content. And that wasn't even the worst. Farther up the band, on a channel I didn't recognize, the screen was black, with words in stark white emblazoned across it:

And I beheld when he had opened the sixth seal, and, lo, there was a great earthquake; and the sun became black as sackcloth of hair, and the moon became as blood....

I wasn't much of a Bible reader, but even I recognized the quote from Revelations.

Making a disgusted sound, I clicked off the TV, then turned when I heard my father come to the door and lean against the frame, his shoulders slumped.

"It is the end of the world," he said softly.

That couldn't be my father—my hard-nosed, practical father, the one who made sure I knew how to shoot, how to catch a fish and clean it, how to change the oil in my car and swap out a flat tire. Nothing ever fazed him. But now some underlying steel seemed to have given way, his firm jaw somehow loose, his eyes blurred with sorrow.

"Dad?" I said uncertainly.

"She's gone," he told me, voice flat. "While we were down in the kitchen."

The words didn't seem to make any sense. Or rather, my mind refused to make sense of them, because if I understood those words, I'd know in that moment my mother was dead, and I just couldn't face that. Not yet.

For the longest moment, I didn't say anything, only stared up at him as I turned the remote I held over and over in my hand, its familiar rectangular shape suddenly alien, cold and hard. Not wanting to hold it any longer, I set it down on the coffee table.

"No," I said at last.

"Yes," he said softly. "It doesn't look like she suffered. At least, not like some that I've seen. You'd almost think she was asleep."

"Maybe she is asleep," I protested. "Maybe you just thought—just thought she was—" I couldn't say the word. Not in connection with my mother. If I said it, then it would be true, and I couldn't bear that.

He didn't bother to contradict me, only watched me. Something of the no-nonsense father I was used to was clear in those eyes. They said, *I don't want to believe it, either. But that doesn't make it less true.*

That hard knot was back in my throat. My eyes burned. For some reason, though, the tears wouldn't fall. They just remained where they were, burning like acid.

Finally, I asked, "What should we do? Should we—" I couldn't even finish the question. This would have been bad enough under normal circumstances, but at least then there was a routine to follow. You called the doctor. The doctor called the ambulance, and then eventually someone got in touch with the funeral home. That was how it worked when Grandmother Ivy—my mom's mother—had passed.

Now, though…now you couldn't even get a call through. And if by some miracle you did, it wouldn't matter, because there wouldn't be anyone on the other end to answer it.

My father wouldn't meet my eyes. "We don't need to do anything," he said, that scary monotone back in his voice. "It'll take care of itself."

And something in the way he said those words made me too frightened to ask what in the world he meant.

CHAPTER FOUR

HE WENT INTO THE KITCHEN AFTER THAT. I DIDN'T follow, but instead just stood there in the family room, my entire body feeling as if it had been encased in ice. One thought kept hammering away in my head, over and over again.

She's dead. She's dead. Your mother is dead.

I wished I could cry.

From the kitchen, I heard the clunk of ice dropping from the dispenser, the sound of liquid pouring, although not from the refrigerator door. I had a sinking feeling I knew exactly what it was.

My father was not, unlike a lot of cops, a heavy drinker. He and my mother would have a glass of wine with dinner sometimes, and I'd seen him drink champagne at weddings and have a beer after a morning of washing both his and Mom's cars, but that was about it. But there was a bottle of Scotch he kept high up on a shelf, a bottle that rarely made an appearance. One time when his partner Josh was shot in the leg while breaking up a domestic dispute. Or the time my mother found a lump in her breast and had to go in for a biopsy. It turned out to be nothing, a benign cyst, but we'd all been fearing the worst.

And now the worst had happened, although in a manner none of us could have imagined, and he was sitting at the breakfast bar in the kitchen, drinking Scotch on the rocks.

And I was too scared and shocked to even give him shit about it. If he wanted to seek comfort in a glass of Scotch rather than in me, there wasn't anything I could do about it.

Still with that horrible lump lodged firmly in my throat, I went back to the staircase and slowly went up it, each step more and more difficult, as if I were in some horrible alternate dimension that kept strengthening the gravity pulling at me with every movement. Finally, though, I made it up to the landing, then went to Devin's room.

He had shifted and was now lying on his side, half his covers thrown off. They'd probably felt far too hot, but I knew he had to stay warm. I crossed the room and grasped the sheet and blanket, hesitating as my hand paused on the comforter. Maybe that really was a bit too much, since it had been a mild, warm day, and his room wasn't anywhere close to cold yet. I could always put the comforter over him later.

As I began to settle the sheet over his shoulders, though, something felt wrong. At first I couldn't quite figure it out, and then, even as I realized what the problem was, my mind didn't want to acknowledge it. Not this. Not so soon after—well, after.

The last time I'd been this close to him, heat had fairly radiated from his flesh. Now, though, he felt cool, and when I reached down to touch his hand, his fingers were like ice, and somehow already stiff, although logically I knew it was far too early for rigor mortis to have set in.

Then again, what was logical about any of this?

I recoiled, letting go of my dead brother's hand, and backed away from the bed. As my father had told me about my mother's passing, Devin didn't look dead, just asleep. For whatever reason, his face didn't have that sunken look about it that my mother had worn. Maybe his fever hadn't burned as hot?

Not that it mattered, because he was gone, too.

A frightened little sob tore its way out of my throat, and I continued to back away, creeping out into the hallway and shutting the door behind me. I knew I should go downstairs and tell my father what had happened, but for some reason my feet took me in the opposite direction, toward my parents' bedroom.

Before I even knew what I was doing, my hand seemed to have reached out of its own accord and was turning the knob. I'd just seen death. I needed to see my mother's, too, so it would be just as real. Maybe then my brain would be shocked out of its current numb state.

The sun was beginning to set, but my parents' bedroom had a window in the western wall, so a warm, mellow light was flooding the space. It was certainly bright enough for me to see where my mother's body should be lying, propped up against the pillows on her side of the bed.

Only...she wasn't there.

My first thought was that my father must have moved her, but why in the world would he have done that? Besides, there wasn't anyplace he really could have moved her, not unless he put her in the bathtub for some reason.

On second thought, that notion wasn't so strange. He could've put her in an ice-cold bath in an attempt to bring her temperature down.

I rushed into the *en suite* bathroom, but the tub was empty. As I stared down at it, I realized that was a ridiculous notion. Even if my father had put her in the bath, I would have heard the water running, and I'd heard no such thing.

Thoughts racing, first rejecting one idea, and then another, I returned to the bedroom. From this angle, I could now see a pile of fine gray dust marring the surface of the blue and tan striped comforter, the one my father had permitted in the room only because "it wasn't too girly."

Dust? My mother would never allow dust to collect on the furniture, let alone a pile like that right on the bed.

Cold coiled in the pit of my stomach as I stared down at the strange little pile. On a dare from Devin, I'd once peeked inside the urn containing my grandmother's ashes...and they had been almost the exact color and consistency as the ashes now sitting on my parents' bed.

No, that was impossible.

Then my father's words came back to me: *It'll take care of itself.*

Was this what he'd meant? That somehow after she passed, my mother would simply crumble into a pile of dust?

No, I refused to believe that. There had to be an explanation. Otherwise....

Otherwise, this whole situation had moved from the unexplainable and tragic to the positively Biblical. Whoever heard of bodies turning themselves to ash, unless it was by some strange otherworldly force?

"You see," my father said. He must have come upstairs while I was standing there, staring down at my mother in shock. His speech sounded a little slurred, but at least he hadn't brought the glass of Scotch up with him.

"What—what happened?"

"It's what happens to all of them," he replied. "Usually within an hour of death." Rubbing at his brow, he added, "Very clean, when you think about it. Much better than having all those bodies lying around, don't you think?"

I stared at him in horror. "That's Mom lying there!"

"No," he corrected me. "That's what used to be your mother. The part of her that was really *her*—that's gone. To a better place, I have to hope, but after everything I've seen today, I'm beginning to have my doubts."

His voice was sad, but resigned. And as I looked at him, I noticed the way he wasn't completely steady on his feet, the glisten of sweat on his forehead from the last rays of sun coming in through the window. Maybe my mind had registered them earlier, but had dismissed them as effects of the alcohol. Now, though....

No. Even as my mind recoiled from the thought, I found myself asking, "Dad, are you sick?"

He gave me a sad smile. "I think I am. Finally caught up with me, I suppose." His gaze moved to the bed. "I should probably lie down, but...."

"Go to the guest room," I said. It used to be my room, but my parents had refitted it as a spare bedroom just the past year.

"I don't think so," he replied. "I want to die in here, next to where she slept."

"But—" I didn't have the strength to mention the ashes, all that remained of my mother, but from the way my father was staring at them, he knew all too well what I was thinking.

"Get her vase," he told me. "The Waterford one I bought her for her fiftieth birthday. She'd like that, I think." He reached out and grasped the doorframe, as if that was the only thing holding him up right then.

I wanted to protest, but I knew that wouldn't do any good. Besides, I didn't know how much time I had until he fell over right there in the doorway. My mother's collapse had been sudden and shocking, and Devin's not much better. So I nodded and pushed past him to run down the stairs and go into the living room, where the vase in question stood on one of the end tables.

After grabbing it, I hurried back up to my parents' bedroom, where my father—through sheer force of will, probably—was still hanging on to the doorframe. I showed him the vase but didn't stop, instead going to the bed and grasping the comforter, then tilting it so the gray dust would tip into the crystal container. During this operation, I didn't dare breathe, but the dust was surprisingly heavy and didn't puff up into the air the way I feared it might. Instead, it slipped down into the vase, filling it approximately halfway. Not letting myself think about what it held, I took it over to the dresser and set it down.

Since there was no way I would put that comforter back where it had come from, I folded it in on itself to trap any remaining dust, and set it on the floor at the foot of the bed. "Okay," I said, my voice shaking.

My father didn't seem to notice the tremor in that one little word, but only pushed himself off from the doorframe and then staggered over to the bed. After pausing to kick off his shoes and remove his belt, complete with holsters and badge, he fell down onto the mattress. That seemed to have taken the last of his strength, because his head fell back against the pillow at once, and his eyes shut. Incongruously, I noted how heavy and thick his lashes were, lying against his flushed cheeks.

"Dad?"

He lifted one hand. "Just tired. I took some ibuprofen on the way up. Not going to do any good, but I didn't want you to have to get it for me."

My heart was breaking. I could feel it...literally feel it. One piece torn away for my mother, the next for Devin. And when my father went, did that mean my heart would finally shatter once and for all, gone to dust like everyone else in the world?

Cramming my fist into my mouth to push back another one of those ragged sobs, I went out to the hallway and staggered over to the carved wooden balustrade on the landing. I wrapped my fingers around the rail and hung on as if for my life. No fever scorched its way through me, but I felt as weak as though my temperature was 110 degrees.

Beloved, it will all be over soon.

That voice again. It had to be a hallucination, some strange coping mechanism my brain had cooked up, but still I found myself replying out loud.

"Does that mean I'm sick and will soon be dead along with everyone else?"

No. That is not your fate.

"What is my fate?"

Silence. Apparently my subconscious or whatever it was that had created the soft, reassuring baritone didn't quite have the balls to tell me what my future held. Not that you needed to be a fortune-teller for that. Raging fever, and a pile of dust somewhere. Should I go out on the family room couch, or hike my way back up to my apartment when the time came? That seemed like a lot of unnecessary effort. After all, no one was using the spare bedroom.

I went into the bathroom to get a drink of water and saw the big bottle of ibuprofen sitting on the counter, the cap still off, as if my father hadn't possessed the strength or will to put it back on again. Fingers shaking, I picked it up and twisted it onto the bottle, then put the ibuprofen back in the medicine cabinet. I didn't want to leave a messy house behind.

Messy for whom, I didn't know. From what my father had said, it didn't sound as if anyone was getting out of this alive.

The thermometer was lying on the top rack in the medicine cabinet. I already knew I wasn't sick, but I needed the external reminder. I took it out, opened the bottle of rubbing alcohol, and wiped down one end of the thermometer. Then I stuck it in my mouth and waited.

98.1. Up a little from the last time, but still below normal.

I rinsed it off and put it away. Then, moving so slowly I felt as if I were dragging my feet through mud, I went back to my parents' bedroom, half expecting to see a pile of dust there. To my surprise, my father's eyes opened when I came into the room. They were bright with fever and had those telltale dark circles beneath them, but they seemed lucid enough. Maybe he wasn't as far gone as he had thought.

"Dad, I could try some ice—"

A very small shake of his head. "No. Once you have it, you're done." His eyes shut, and I could see how his big frame was wracked with shivers, even though he'd pulled the blanket up to his chin. "I'm sorry."

"Sorry?" I repeated, wondering what he had to be sorry for. "None of this is your fault."

"No—not that." He shifted under the covers, then opened his eyes again. "Sorry that we'll all be gone, and you'll still be here."

Something in his words chilled me. In that moment, I could see how dying along with everyone else might be preferable to being left in a world with no one to talk to, no one to even know I'd somehow managed to survive. Voice brittle, I replied, "Oh, I'm sure I'm not long for this world, either."

"Fever?"

"No."

He closed his eyes. It seemed as if he didn't have the strength to keep them open and focused on me for more than a few seconds at a time. "You're immune, Jess. Don't know how...or why...."

That is not your fate. Despite the stuffiness of the room, I shivered as I thought of those words, spoken gently by someone who wasn't there.

"Write down what's happened. Maybe...there'll be someone left to tell."

I nodded, then realized he couldn't see me. "I will."

"Might as well put that English degree to some use."

Oh, Dad. Even at the end, he had to make a joke. "All the commas will be in the right place. I promise."

No reply. He could have simply fallen asleep, but I didn't think so. Unlike my mother and Devin, he'd pushed all the way to the end, burned the candle until no more wick was left.

Somehow I put one foot in front of the other, walking slowly until I reached his side of the bed. A finger against his throat, telling me that he had gone, had left this world and was with Mom and Devin. I had to believe that. I'd break apart otherwise.

Since his eyes were closed, I didn't bother to pull the sheet up over his face. Soon it wouldn't matter anyway. He'd be a pile of dust, as no doubt my brother was by now as well.

I didn't recall going downstairs, but the next thing I did remember, I was standing in the kitchen, staring down at my father's half-drunk glass of Scotch. The ice had mostly melted, shifting the color to a pale gold. Without thinking, I lifted the glass and brought it to my lips, poured the liquid within down my throat. It burned, but not as much as I had thought it would.

What did it matter that my father had drunk from that same glass? According to him, I was immune. The thing that had killed him couldn't touch me.

At last I could feel tears pricking at my eyes, stinging like acid, but I knew I couldn't let them fall. If I did, I knew they would never stop. What was that old song, about some girl's tears drowning the world? That would be me, if I wept now. Then again, maybe that wouldn't be such a bad thing. Maybe a river, an ocean of tears, would wash away all this death, all the dust of people's lives left behind.

Maybe. In the meantime, I had something I needed to do.

My parents had always loved the big oak tree in the backyard. In the summer, they hung a hammock there, and had a pair of Adirondack chairs they would drag out underneath it so they could sit in the shade and drink iced tea and plan the yearly family vacation, or maybe just a long weekend, so we could do something fun like go hiking up around Angel Fire or visit the museums in Santa Fe, or take the long trip down to Carlsbad Caverns.

All those things we'd done together as a family. Well, I'd make sure my family was together in the end, even if I couldn't be with them. It was the only way I could think of to say goodbye.

My father kept all the gardening tools in a shed next to the garage, since the garage itself was full of camping equipment and tools and the usual crap any family of four tends to accumulate over the years. I went to the shed and got out the shovel, then headed back to the oak tree, staking out the spot where those Adirondack chairs usually sat.

It wouldn't have to be a very deep hole. After all, I was only burying dust, not bodies. The ground was not as hard as I'd feared, mostly because my father had given the old oak one of its bimonthly soakings with the hose only this past weekend. I dug and dug, dirt flying out around me, only stopping when it looked like I was about to hit a big tree root. The hole was far larger than it needed to be, but better that than the opposite.

I leaned the shovel against the shed, then went into the kitchen to wash my hands. After that, I got a clean glass from the cupboard and filled it with water, then drank slowly, deliberately. I knew what was waiting for me upstairs.

There was enough room left in my mother's Waterford vase for the dust my father left behind, so I poured it in on top of my mother's remains. Going back to Devin's room seemed far more difficult, for some reason; maybe it was that I hadn't really been able to say goodbye to him. At least my father and I had shared those last few words.

The sight of the dust didn't shock me anymore, but it was still awful enough to know that my brother had been lying in the same spot only an hour earlier. His MVP trophy from the previous football season seemed about the right size, so I did the same thing I had with my parents' remains, using the bedclothes as a funnel to pour the dust into the receptacle I'd selected. That dust was a dark, cloudy gray, fine as silt, and seemed oddly liquid as I tipped it into the trophy.

I took Devin downstairs first, carefully setting the trophy down on the breakfast bar before returning to the second story to retrieve the Waterford vase. They went into the ground in reverse order, my parents' dust poured into the hole first, followed by Devin's. Grimly, I retrieved the shovel and began piling the dirt back on top of the dust, holding my breath in case any should plume up during the process. At last, though, the hole was more or less filled. I dragged the shovel back and forth, smoothing the surface, attempting to make it as level as possible.

Now was the time to say a few words, but nothing seemed to come to mind. I couldn't even remember the Lord's Prayer, or more than the first few words of the Twenty-third Psalm.

"*The Lord is my shepherd,*" I began, then shook my head. What came next? The lines were all jumbled together in my head, nonsense syllables that sounded like something straight out of "Jabberwocky." And what did it matter, anyway? We weren't a religious family; we went to Christmas Eve services some years and some years not, maybe Easter. I'd gone to Sunday school when I was really little, but my parents hadn't even bothered with that when Devin came along.

For the longest time I stood there under the oak, the sun disappearing altogether, deep dusk falling upon the yard. Then I moved, and the motion-sensor light mounted to the side of the garage flashed on.

"I love you all," I said finally, then set the Waterford vase and the football trophy on top of their grave.

After that, I went back inside and shut the door behind me. It seemed to echo in the unnatural stillness of the house, and I realized it was hardly ever this quiet—someone always had the TV on in the background, or there was music playing, or somebody talking on the phone. Now the quiet pounded against my eardrums, and I realized how big a three-bedroom, two-thousand-square-foot house could feel when you were the only one in it.

The only one in the world....

The thought whispered through my mind, and I did my best to ignore it. Surely if I were immune, and not just having extremely delayed-onset symptoms for some reason, that meant other people had to be immune, too. How many? I couldn't begin to guess. I didn't know the mortality rate of the disease. Even if 99.9% of the population was dead, that would leave around a thousand people still alive in the greater Albuquerque area, if I was doing my mental math correctly.

I turned on the overhead lights in the kitchen, then went through the house, turning on all the lamps. Maybe that wasn't the smartest thing to do—maybe advertising my presence would do more harm than good. But I couldn't sit there in the dark, not after everything I'd been through that day. Besides, when I peeked out through the curtains, I saw mine wasn't the only house on the street that was all lit up. Most likely the others just had their lights on because no one was around to turn them off, but it did make mine seem less conspicuous.

"Are you there?" I asked of the darkness. Even a voice that was only a product of my imagination was better than this deep, deep silence, the kind of quiet you should never hear if you lived in a big city.

No reply, of course. My gaze shifted to the remote control, still lying where I'd last dropped it on the coffee table. I didn't want to turn on the television, not after what I'd seen the last time around. Would it all be static by now, or would that one station still be showing blaring red text with more quotes from Revelations?

I was too much of a coward to pick up the remote and find out.

But there was still the stereo, and all the CDs my parents wouldn't get rid of, despite Devin and me telling them all that plastic just took up space and that they should just rip all their music off those CDs and then play it through Apple TV or something. And now I had to be grateful for their stubbornness, because that meant I could get up and choose something to blot out the silence. My father liked country, but old country, like Hank Williams and Willie Nelson and Patsy Cline, and my mother preferred classical. That sounded better to me right then, so I found her favorite, Rachmaninoff's Second Piano Concerto, and put that on.

It actually was better, with the sound of an orchestra and Vladimir Ashkenazy on the piano drowning out that awful stillness. Or at least it was better until I realized that no one would ever play that piece live

again, that there would be no more symphony orches-
tras or Arcade Fire concerts or anything, ever again.

"Oh, God," I gasped, pushing myself up from the
couch and running into the kitchen, where I turned on
the faucet and splashed cold water in my face. As if that
could begin to help. It was all too big to comprehend,
so awful and enormous that I could literally feel the
horror of it beginning to sink in, like some noxious
chemical seeping into my skin.

And then it was as though strong, invisible arms
wrapped around me, bringing with them a soothing
warmth. Unseen lips brushed against my hair, and I
heard the voice again.

Be strong, my love. Be strong for just a while longer.

Just as suddenly, the presence was gone. I held on
to the tile of the kitchen counter, feeling the cool surface beneath my fingertips. In that moment, I truly
wondered if I'd lost my mind.

What other explanation could there be?

CHAPTER FIVE

MORE BECAUSE I KNEW I SHOULD EAT SOMETHING than because I had any appetite at all, I gathered myself enough to put a few slices of wheat bread in the toaster. Once they were done, I buttered them and set them on a plate, then headed back out to the living room, where Rachmaninoff still played to the empty space. Just as I was setting my plate down on the coffee table, the lights flickered and went out, and the CD slurred to a halt. Silence reigned once more.

Heart slamming painfully in my chest, I waited a second, then another. Surely this had to be just a glitch. In a second or two, the power would come back on.

But it didn't. How could the power plants run, with no one left to manage them?

The blackness was absolute. From my camping days, I knew how dark, how *very* dark, our desert skies could be. This seemed worse, though, because this wasn't the expected dark of a night out under the stars. I was in the heart of Albuquerque, New Mexico. It wasn't supposed to be like this.

Luckily, my mother loved candles, and so there were already a pair of pillars in wrought-iron sconces on the mantel, and another pillar candle sitting on a metal leaf-shaped dish on an end table. She kept a long-handled lighter in one of the coffee table's drawers, so I reached in and fumbled around for a few seconds before locating it. As soon as I pulled it out of the drawer, I pressed the button to activate the flame. That pushed back on the darkness a little, and it got that much better when I lit the candle on the table next to me. Then I had enough illumination that I could get up and light the candles on the mantel.

From there I went into the kitchen and found the sugar cookie–scented jar candle sitting on the breakfast bar, and lit that as well. Upstairs—well, I'd worry about that later. At least now I wasn't blundering around in total darkness…and the candle flames weren't bright enough that they would be seen through the drapes and blinds, all of which I quickly closed.

All the same, I knew there was one thing I really needed to do.

On the ground floor was a study that my parents shared, although in reality it was mostly my mother's space, housing her desk and computer and several shelves full of books. On the opposite wall, though, was my father's gun safe.

I knew the combination. He'd trusted me with that, just as he trusted me to be responsible when we went shooting and to clean the guns I used and follow all the safety rules he'd taught me. I wasn't sure if Devin had known the combination, although I somehow doubted it; my father hadn't given me that information until I turned twenty-one. And even though I might be the only person left alive in Albuquerque, no way was I sitting alone in this house without some means to protect myself.

The lock turned easily, of course. My father took as good care of the safe as he did the guns inside. There were a lot, too—in addition to his service Glock, he owned an AR-15 rifle, two shotguns, a small .22-caliber hunting rifle, a Ruger, a Beretta, and my favorite, the Smith & Wesson .357. Sort of an old-fashioned gun, but my accuracy had always been good with it. Besides, with a revolver, you didn't have to worry about the gun jamming.

I set the candle I'd brought with me down on my mother's desk, then opened the safe. Hanging from one of the sleeves on the door was the .357, and on the shelf directly opposite the gun, boxes of spare ammo.

My father wasn't exactly what you'd call a survivalist type, but he did believe in maintaining his supplies. If necessary, I could waste a lot of bad guys before I ran out. Not that there were probably any bad guys left. This was more for my own peace of mind than anything else.

After lifting the S&W from where it rested, I pushed the latch forward to release the barrel, then moved the latch outward. As I'd suspected, the chambers were empty—my father didn't believe in leaving loaded handguns lying around, even in the safe. One by one, I dropped the bullets into the chambers, then closed the gun back up.

Habit made me shut the door to the gun safe as well, and make sure the lock was fully engaged. Maybe I was the only person left alive in Albuquerque...and maybe not. No matter what the reality of the situation might turn out to be, I didn't think it was a very good idea to leave a fully stocked gun safe accessible to just anyone.

Picking up the candle with my free hand, I went back out to the living room. My toast was stone cold by then, but I made myself eat it, and then drank some more water. I set the gun down on the coffee table, within easy reach should I need it.

And then I leaned against the back of the couch and shut my eyes, wondering what the hell I was supposed to do next. My entire family was gone—I had two grandparents still living, but I had no reason to believe they hadn't suffered the same fate as my parents and brother. Three cousins and an aunt and uncle, all on my mother's side; my father was an only child. Could this strange immunity that seemed to be protecting me have somehow sheltered any of them? Uncle Jeremy and Aunt Susan also lived here in Albuquerque, so it wouldn't be that hard to try checking on them tomorrow, after the sun came up. No way was I venturing outside in the dark.

Maybe it wasn't the best idea—a fool's errand, as my father might have said. But it was the only thing I could think of to try. There were my friends, too... Tori and Brittany and Elena. I had no reason to believe they hadn't suffered the same fate as everyone else, but again, I would never forgive myself if I didn't try to find out what had happened to them.

There is no point. They're all gone.

"Oh, really?" I snapped into the candlelit darkness. "How are you so sure of that?"

Because they weren't immune.

"But I am."

Yes.

"Why?"

No answer—not that I'd really expected one. It seemed as soon as I asked the hard questions, the voice quickly decamped. Only my subconscious, trying to convince me not to put myself in harm's way? I wouldn't be surprised. Nevertheless, I knew what I had to do the next day.

The next day, a bright sun rose on an empty world. I couldn't bring myself to sleep upstairs, not even in the untouched guest bedroom. Too much death up there, too many reminders of everything I'd lost. Instead, I'd fetched some spare blankets from the linen closet and spread them over me so I could sleep on the living room couch. That, more than anything else, was a sure sign of the apocalypse, since my mother would never have allowed her new sofa to be sullied by someone sleeping on it when she was alive. But the living room faced out on the street, and I reasoned I'd better be able to listen for any signs of life or activity on the road by sleeping there, rather than back in the family room, which was toward the rear of the house.

I got up off the couch, rubbed the kink in my neck, then cautiously pushed the curtains aside so I could get a glimpse of what was going on in the neighborhood. Not much; the sprinklers were on at the D'Ambrosios' house on the corner opposite ours, but I knew that didn't mean anything, since they were on an automatic timer. As I watched, they seemed to shut themselves off, the bright green grass of the yard glinting in the morning sun. Otherwise, everything was completely still.

No, scratch that—I saw the Munozes' shepherd mix nosing around in the grass in front of their house across the street. She was a wily critter and got out at least once a week, but now I guessed it was because she was hungry. Luckily, she was a sweet dog and knew me. The power was out, and we had some leftovers in the fridge that might as well get eaten before they spoiled.

I let the curtain drop and went to open the front door. The morning air was cool, but carried with it the smell of smoke. Something in the city was burning. Here, though, we seemed to be safe enough, at least for the moment. I'd worry about the fire later.

Crouching down slightly, I called out, "Dutchie! Dutchie!" Hector Munoz had been a professor of Spanish literature at UNM, and I think Dutchie's original name had been Dulcinea. The Munozes' little girl, Jaclyn, couldn't pronounce the name, though, and so Dulcinea had sort of degenerated into "Dutchie." A sharp, knifing pain went through me, though, as I thought of little Jaclyn and her big brown eyes and her endlessly asking "Why?"

I had a feeling she wouldn't be asking any more questions.

The dog lifted her head and looked over at me, one ear cocked slightly. No one was completely sure of Dutchie's heritage. Best guess was part German shepherd, part border collie, and part Lord knows what, but she was a beautiful dog, with a silky black and tan coat, and one blue eye and one brown eye. The blue eye seemed to focus on me particularly.

She gave a little shake and then trotted obediently over to me, pushing her head against my knee and giving the faintest of whines. Poor thing had to be hungry.

"You want some breakfast?" I asked her, and both her ears went up. Just like our old dog Sadie, who'd passed last winter. Debates had still been raging at my house as to when would be a good time to get another dog...not that it mattered now.

But Sadie had had an extensive vocabulary when it came to anything food-related, and it seemed as if Dutchie was the same way. She padded after me as I tucked the revolver into my waistband, then went into the kitchen, got a bowl from one of the cupboards, and poured her some water.

At least, that was what I intended to do. When I turned the tap, however, nothing happened. A few drops sputtered from the faucet, but that was it. So the water was gone, too.

That fluttery feeling of panic returned, and I forced it down. When we were at home, we got our water from the dispenser in the refrigerator door, but we always kept a couple pallets of bottled water in the pantry for road trips or even just running around town. I wasn't going to die of thirst anytime soon.

I fetched one of the water bottles and poured its contents into the bowl. Dutchie began slurping it up greedily, so while she was occupied, I got out a plate and then retrieved one of the covered storage bowls in the fridge, the one with the leftover roasted chicken from the weekend. Taking out one of the chicken legs and shredding it onto the plate relaxed me a little, made me focus on something other than the dry tap. If I attempted to turn on one of the burners on the stove, would it light? Or was the gas out, too?

Most likely. Which meant there would be no heat. Yesterday had been warmer than normal, but I'd heard that temperatures were supposed to start dipping toward the end of the week. Conditions might become downright uncomfortable.

Oh, like they're so wonderful right now, my brain mocked me as I bent down to give Dutchie the plate of chicken. She immediately abandoned the water and wolfed down the bits of chicken leg, then looked up at me with pleading eyes when she was done.

"There's no more, you little pig," I said with some affection, reaching to scratch her behind the ears. Her fur was soft and silky, and infinitely reassuring. Somehow everything didn't seem quite so bad if I could have Dutchie with me.

She whined, and I remembered we still had some dog treats up on the highest shelf in the pantry, left over after Sadie died. I got out the step stool, then climbed up and retrieved them. Dutchie watched the entire procedure, tail wagging, and I gave her one of the biscuits.

"Better?" I asked.

No reply, of course, but I figured the way she was hunkered down on the kitchen rug, munching on the biscuit, tail wagging, told me everything I needed to know.

All right. So I had some companionship. Now I had to take care of myself. My appetite was still nowhere in evidence, but I helped myself to some of the leftover chicken as well, then had a piece of bread and butter, washed down with water from another bottle I took from the pallet. Obviously, a shower was out of the question, but I took some of the water and splashed it on my face. It helped a little.

Carrying the half-full bottle of water, I went out the back door, Dutchie following me, and headed up to my apartment. Everything looked so normal there, so unchanged, and I realized I hadn't been there since my parents—since Devin—well, *since*. It was no sanctuary, though, no place where I could hide from what had happened.

That wasn't my reason for being here, though. I set the gun down on the coffee table, got out of my clothes from the day before and stuffed them into the hamper, and then pulled on fresh jeans and socks, and a waffle-weave henley shirt I wore sometimes when I went hiking. My hiking boots were tucked into the far corner of the closet, and I got them out as well and laced them on. I had no idea what I might encounter today, so it seemed smart to be wearing comfortable, serviceable clothes, the kinds of things that wouldn't get in my way.

Speaking of which—

I headed into the bathroom, brushed my hair, and pulled it back with an elastic band. Afterward, I brushed my teeth, being as sparing with the bottled water as I could. No point in wearing any makeup, but I put on some colored lip balm because the weather was dry, and they felt parched.

During all this, Dutchie sat in the middle of my tiny living room and watched me. After I had extracted my wallet from my purse and slipped it into my pocket, then tucked the S&W back into my waistband, I paused and asked her, "Am I crazy for doing this?"

She cocked her head to one side, mismatched eyes shining. Apparently, she didn't have an opinion on my preparations, but was probably hoping for another dog biscuit when we got back to the kitchen.

"Okay," I told her. "I'll see what I can do."

Tail wagging, she ran out the door as soon as I opened it, then practically galloped down the stairs. From what I could tell, she wasn't exactly pining for her former masters. Or maybe she was just so happy to see someone—anyone—that she was willing to be their new best friend, no matter what.

Once we were back in the kitchen, I gave her another dog biscuit, then hesitated at the key rack by the back door. If I was really going to venture out into deserted Albuquerque, I didn't think my little Honda was the best choice in vehicles. My mother's Escape had all-wheel drive, but I knew my father's Grand Cherokee was the sturdiest car we owned.

My hand shook as I took the key with its leather fob from the rack. My father loved that SUV—washed it every week, changed the oil regularly, conditioned the leather seats, the whole thing. He'd never let me or Devin drive it, and even my mother was only allowed behind the wheel if her own car was in the shop for something. But my father was far past caring about the Cherokee, and I knew it was my best bet for getting where I needed to go.

There is no point, the voice in my head said sadly.

"There is a point," I retorted. "I need to know if they're alive or dead."

You already know the answer to that.

"No, I don't. Not for sure."

Your heart does.

I didn't want to believe him. In fact, I refused to believe him. Voice tight, I asked, "All right—where do you think I should go?"

The answer was immediate. *North.*

"North?" I repeated in some incredulity. "You do know that winter is coming, right? If I have to get out of Albuquerque, it would make a lot more sense to go south, to Alamogordo or Las Cruces." Or Roswell, I added mentally. Maybe I can go there and stick my thumb out, see if the aliens might give me a ride right out of here.

North. The voice sounded implacable.

"Well, I'll take that under advisement," I said lightly. "For now, though, I have some friends and family to check on."

It is a mistake.

"Then it'll be *my* mistake. Come on, Dutchie."

Had I already descended to arguing with the voices in my head? It sure looked that way.

The dog trotted after me as I went out the back door and over to the driveway. Good thing I'd decided on the Cherokee, as it was blocking my mother's car anyway. I went around to the passenger side and opened the door. Dutchie didn't even need an invitation—she jumped right inside, eyes shining, ears up. Her claws slipped a little on the leather seat, and I winced. I had to hope that my father really had gone on to a better place, one where he couldn't see his prized SUV getting scratches on the seats and, no doubt, dog hair everywhere.

I walked slowly around the back of the vehicle, watching, listening. Since the D'Ambrosios' sprinklers had shut off—or, more likely, run out of water—besides the cawing of a few crows as they circled overhead, the neighborhood was completely still. Again, that silence made the skin on the back of my neck prickle, and I hastened to the driver-side door, then got in.

The sound of the engine turning over seemed ear-piercingly loud after all that quiet. At the same time, the radio turned on in a burst of static, and I quickly shut it off, knowing that there wouldn't be anything useful on the radio, any more than there had been on the television. My father had probably been scanning the bands as he came home, looking for a report that would tell him what was going on. Something. Anything.

I paused to slide the gun out of my waistband and into the glove compartment before backing the Cherokee out into the street. On the seat beside me, Dutchie had her head up and was sniffing the air, even though the windows were all the way up. I rolled down the one next to her so she could stick her nose out, then slowed before we'd gone even halfway down the block. I knew what I would find, but I had to check.

The front door to the Munozes' house was locked, but when I went around back, I discovered that the side door which led to their service porch was halfway open. The reason why presented itself soon enough—there was a pile of gray dust just inside, right in front of the dryer. I had a feeling, though, that whoever had gone out there had been looking for more ice, as the

Munozes had an upright freezer tucked into one corner, away from the other appliances.

Grimacing, I stepped over the little pile of dust, glad that I'd left Dutchie inside the car. "Professor Munoz?" I called out. "Jaclyn? Maria?"

No answer, of course. In the living room, I saw the reason why—a pile of dust on the sofa, a smaller one next to it. I couldn't know for sure whether it was Maria Munoz or her husband who had expired in the laundry room, or who had been sitting on the couch next to their daughter. I supposed it really didn't matter. They were gone. No wonder Dutchie had started wandering the neighborhood, looking for someone to take care of her.

When I got back inside the Cherokee, I leaned over and gave the dog a fierce hug. "I'm here, Dutchie," I said. "I won't let anything happen to you."

She licked my cheek and let out a whine, but a questioning one, as if asking whether I was okay.

No, I really was not okay, but I couldn't let myself start to lose it now. I straightened, gave her ears a quick scratch, and then started up the SUV, moving down the street so I could get out onto Rio Grand Boulevard and head over to my friend Elena's house, as she was the one who lived closest to me. After that it would be Tori's, and then my Aunt Susan and Uncle Jeremy's house. And after that....

Well, I'd see how much more I could take after that.

It was slower going than I'd expected, mainly because a lot more abandoned cars choked the streets than I'd thought there would be. In my mind, I'd imagined more people would have made it home before they expired, but that didn't seem to be the case. I had to weave in and out of the stopped vehicles, several times being forced up on the curb to make my way around the blockage. And everything so silent, so still, save for the ceaseless cawing of crows overhead.

No carrion for you to eat, you bastards, I thought as I eased the Cherokee off yet another curb.

And in a way, I had to be thankful for that. The Heat might not have killed me to start, but if there had been millions of corpses left behind once the disease had done its work, typhoid fever or cholera surely would have finished the job.

I turned into the residential section where Elena lived, glad to see there were fewer vehicles blocking the streets here. But still I saw no sign of life anywhere, not one person stepping out of a house to flag me down, to let me know at least one other soul had survived the plague that had swept over the world.

Unlike my house, which always had a full driveway and my car parked at the curb, Elena's looked pristine. Then again, her family had more money—her father was a lawyer—and their house had a three-car garage.

It wasn't unusual to see no real evidence of anyone being home.

I stopped the Cherokee, then reached into the glove compartment and retrieved the revolver. Dutchie looked at me, wide-eyed, as if wondering what in the world I needed with a gun.

"Good question, Dutchie," I said, but I tucked it into my jeans anyway. "You stay here."

She wagged her tail and didn't try to get out of the car as I exited the vehicle. That was one damn good dog.

After looking around quickly and not seeing anyone, I went up to the front door of Elena's house. Ringing the doorbell was no use, since the power was out all over town. Instead, I knocked, then waited.

No answer, but I hadn't really been expecting one. I put my hand on the latch, and, to my surprise, the door swung inward. It seemed logical enough that the last person to come home had been so ill they hadn't bothered to lock the door behind them, but it unnerved me nonetheless. Swallowing hard, I made myself enter the house.

It was a big Santa Fe–style faux adobe, with tile floors and wood-beamed ceilings. My footsteps echoed through the two-story foyer as I moved toward the center of the building. Something sweet and smoky tickled at my nose. Incense. Elena's mother was a devout Catholic. Maybe she'd burned the incense as she prayed to God to save her, save her family.

Unfortunately, God didn't seem to be listening lately.

The house had built-in art niches, one of which held a shrine to the Madonna. I saw a pile of gray dust immediately in front of it and knew it must be Gabriella Cruz. Limbs trembling, I made myself walk past it, go through the rest of the ground floor: the great room with the kitchen and family room combined, the formal dining room, the living room. No sign of Elena or her father. Which didn't mean all that much. There was still the upstairs.

Pulse pounding painfully in my throat, I mounted the steps. The house had four bedrooms, one of which was an office. In there I found another pile of gray dust, which I guessed must be Eduardo Cruz, Elena's father.

Her bedroom was on the opposite side of the upstairs hallway, two doors down. Truth be told, I'd always envied her that room, with its own bathroom and the little sitting area off the balcony. It felt like a room for a princess, compared to the boxy twelve-by-twelve space that had been mine all through childhood and high school. No wonder Elena had never been too worried about moving out. "I'll go from here to my husband's house," she used to say with a laugh, and the rest of us had pretty much believed her. No one could really imagine Elena trying to scrape by in a tiny one-bedroom apartment, just for a spurious sense of independence.

And it was on the wrought-iron bed, with its filmy topping of mosquito net and matching white embroidered comforter, that I found the third pile of gray dust. For the longest moment, I just stood there, staring down at it, remembering my friend's quick, flashing smile, the annoying way she absolutely could not get through a movie without offering her own running commentary on it. How she'd quietly slipped a wad of money into my hand one day during our senior year so I could get the prom dress I really wanted and not the bargain gown my mother was pushing me into, because "in five years you're just not going to care what you wore."

But I still did care...although mainly because of what Elena had done to help me out, and not the dress itself.

You see? the voice said, its tone quiet and sad. *There's no point in you doing this. You can't save them. They're already gone. Mourn them if you must, but your path lies northward.*

I wished then that the voice were real, that it was attached to a real body, so I could grab it by the shoulders and shake it for being so thoughtless. "That's not the point," I said, my own voice trembling. "I need to know...and I need to say goodbye."

It remained silent then...wisely so. I reached out and touched the twisted wrought iron of one of the bedposts, and whispered, "Sleep well." Then I turned away and walked down the hall, descended the steps, and went out the front door, shutting it quietly behind me.

Dutchie's tail thumped happily as I got back in the Cherokee, but I didn't say anything, only reached out to pet her, to feel her silky fur beneath my cold, cold fingers. For a long moment, I just sat there, the key still in my hand, the gun digging uncomfortably into my waistband. Finally, I reached back and pulled it out, returning it to the glove compartment.

Uncle Jeremy and Aunt Susan next. Could I do it? Could I go to the house where I'd spent Thanksgiving and Christmas—Susan was my mother's sister, and they traded holidays so no one family would have to do all the work—and walk in to see my uncle and aunt reduced to dust, and my cousins as well? Well, two of them, anyway. My cousin Shane was in college in California, at Stanford, to be exact, and so he wouldn't be around. He would have died far away from his family.

If *he died,* I reminded myself fiercely. *He could be immune, too. You don't know.*

No, I didn't know. I just wasn't sure how I would ever find out.

Even so, I put the key in the ignition, then turned it, pointing the vehicle north and east, toward Sandia Heights. It was a longer jog than the one from my house to Elena's, but up here the streets didn't feel quite as crammed with abandoned vehicles. There was plenty of evidence of unexpected death—cars crashed into walls, into trees, into one another. And as I gained some height, I could now see that the smoke I had smelled earlier seemed to be coming from the city center. Downtown itself, maybe, or the university. I couldn't tell for sure from this distance, and it didn't really matter. That was miles from where I was now, miles from my house. It might spread that far, but I had a feeling I'd be long gone by then.

As I drove along Academy Road, I passed a PetSmart and saw the strangest sight. All kinds of dogs were converging on the store, and right out in front I saw several of them tearing into big bags of dog food, then beginning to feast. More dogs came to join them, but there was no fighting over the food. In fact, I even saw a big pit bull mix move to one side to let a fluffy little dog—a Maltese, I guessed—come in next to him and start eating.

"What the—" I said aloud, and Dutchie swiveled her head in my direction.

The animals will be taken care of, the voice told me.

I'd been so caught up in my own losses, and so relieved to have Dutchie by my side, that I hadn't even stopped to think what would happen to all those thousands of ownerless pets left with no resources, no one to watch over them.

"They'll be taken care of?" I demanded. "By whom?"

They will not suffer. They are innocents.

This whole situation was getting stranger by the minute. The way all the bodies of the dead had dissolved into dust seemed to tell me something greater than a single rampaging strain of microbe was at work here, and now, seeing the way the animals were all cooperating, hearing the voice reassure me they would be fine—well, I didn't know what to think.

"Is this a judgment?" I asked. "Some sort of punishment?"

Silence.

"Who's doing the punishing?" I demanded, voice shaking. "And why wasn't I punished along with everyone else?"

Again no answer.

I drove on, knowing I would receive no reply to my questions.

CHAPTER SIX

My aunt and uncle's house looked intact, Uncle Jeremy's Beemer in the driveway, a little garden flag with an autumn leaf design flapping in the breeze as I got out of the Cherokee. The rest of the neighborhood looked similarly peaceful, but I knew better than to trust that outward appearance of tranquility. I knew what it hid.

Unlike Elena's house, the front door here was locked. I wished I could take that as a sign to turn around and go, but that would be the cowardly way out. Instead, I headed toward the back, to the entrance that opened on the patio. Their backyard wasn't landscaped with grass and trees like ours, but was completely paved over except for some plantings along the edges, with a pergola to protect the area to one side where they had the patio furniture and the barbecue. My hiking boots seemed overly loud as I walked across the flagstones and tested the back door.

Locked. I knocked, then waited. Nothing.

I knocked again, calling out, half in a whisper, "Uncle Jeremy? Aunt Susan?"

No reply, but, to be fair, I wasn't sure if I'd been loud enough for anyone to really hear me inside. Maybe I'd kept my voice down because I wanted an excuse not to know.

I tried peeking inside, but the blinds were closed almost all the way, and so I couldn't really see anything. The planter next to me was bordered with large rocks; I wondered if I should pick one up and smash a window in. Even if by some miracle someone was alive inside, I didn't think they'd get too angry about me breaking a window to check on them. At least, I hoped they wouldn't.

Bending down, I wrapped my fingers around one of the rocks. At the same time, the voice thundered in my head, *Behind you!*

I whirled, rock still in one hand. Standing a few paces away was probably the last person I'd expected to see—Chris Bowman, who lived next door to my aunt and uncle, and who I had always found extremely creepy. He was a few years older than I but still lived at home, and more than once I'd heard my aunt say "what a shame" it was that his parents had to deal with him, but I never was able to find out exactly what she meant by that. I'd always assumed Chris maybe had a substance abuse problem, or possibly mental health issues. Frankly, I didn't want to get close enough to him to find out, as it seemed that every time my family came to visit, he'd have some excuse to be outside, watering the flower border or getting the mail—anything so he could stand there and watch me with his pale eyes until I disappeared inside my aunt and uncle's house.

Back then, his behavior hadn't worried me too much, because I knew if he actually tried anything, my father would have made sure it never happened again. But now, with the whole world dead except for me and Albuquerque's biggest creep?

My fingers tightened around the rock I held, but I kept it behind me and hoped he hadn't noticed as I picked it up. Hard to say, because I hadn't even heard him approach. He was wearing his typical costume of baggy jeans and an oversized T-shirt—this one emblazoned with a Captain America shield—and his high-topped Converse apparently hadn't made any sound as he crossed the flagstones of the patio.

"Chris?" I finally managed, because one of us had to say something, and it seemed he was content to just stand there and stare at me with those weird pale blue eyes of his.

Finally, his mouth curved in a smile. His teeth were slightly yellowish, as was his skin and hair. Everything about him seemed vaguely yellow, except his eyes. "You're immune," he said, and made the oddest sound, like a choked little giggle.

The hair on the back of my neck stood up. "Maybe," I replied. "Or maybe I just haven't gotten sick yet."

"No, you're immune." His pale gaze raked me up and down, and I tensed. The clothes I wore were anything but revealing, and yet the way he was looking at me made me feel as if I wasn't wearing anything at all... that he'd spent way too much time imagining what I looked like naked. "Just like me."

I wanted to retort, *I am nothing like you,* but something held me back. Yes, I had that rock in my hand. Belatedly, I realized that was all I had, since in my haste to get out of the car and up to my aunt and uncle's front door, I'd left the gun in the glove compartment of the Cherokee. Shit.

"This is perfect," he went on, his tone almost dreamy. "Everyone gone except you and me. Just the way I always wanted it."

Jesus Christ. I could feel the sharp edges of the rock biting into my fingers and palm. If I threw it, would it be enough to knock him out, or at least put him off balance enough for me to bolt to the car? I had no idea. Normally, I'd say I was pretty strong...but was I strong enough?

"Um, Chris," I said, figuring that ignoring his comment seemed safest in that moment, "what about your parents? Your neighbors on the other side?"

An expression of annoyance crossed his lumpy features. "I *told* you. They're all gone. Everyone on the whole street. I checked." A pause, and then he added, "Your aunt and uncle, too, and your cousins. I went in and looked, then locked the door when I came back out. I figured no one else would be going in there." The annoyed look morphed into one of sly knowing. "So you won't need that rock to break in. Why don't you give it to me?"

I didn't reply. He frowned, taking a step toward me, eyes fixed on my face, greedy, hungry. A pale pink tongue darted out to moisten his lips, and I felt my stomach heave.

Now, Jessica!

Without stopping to think, I whipped my arm around and hurled the rock at Chris's head with all the strength I possessed. It hit him square in the temple, and he let out a shocked cry, eyes wide and disbelieving, then backed away from me as blood began to pour through the fingers he put up against the wound.

That was the only opening I would get, I knew. I tore out of there, bolting as if someone had just shot off a starter pistol at a track meet. Behind me, I could hear Chris cursing, calling me a bitch and worse— but he was also coming after me. And though he was soft-looking and most likely out of shape, he was also almost a foot taller than I, which meant his legs could cover the ground a lot more quickly.

If I looked back, I'd be lost. I could only continue to pound my way toward the Cherokee, one hand scrabbling in my pants pocket for the key as I ran. My fingers closed around the fob, and I hit the "unlock" button while I was still a good twenty feet away. The lights flashed, and from the passenger seat I could hear Dutchie bark—not a friendly bark of greeting, but a sharp, strained one, as if warning me.

A cold, clammy hand caught hold of my bicep and spun me around. Chris's washed-out blue eyes, even more blindingly pale now that they were circled by bright red blood flowing down from the gash in his head, bored into me.

"You're going to regret that."

"Chris, please—" I thought I'd been scared before, watching my family die, wondering when the fever would rise up to consume me as well, but that was an entirely different species of fear from what I was experiencing now. This was far more personal, in a way, because I knew all too well what Chris Bowman wanted from me.

"Shut up." His fingers tightened on my arm, and he began to pull me toward him. Overcome by panic, I struggled against him, tasting the sourness of bile in my mouth, knowing if he touched me in a way that was any more intimate than this, I would be sick. I drove my knee upward the way my father had taught me, and I hoped I could catch Chris in the groin, but he seemed to guess what I had planned and kicked out at me, catching me in the shin and sending me flying to the ground, where I hit the sidewalk with a jolt, pain lancing up through my wrists as I jammed down into them with almost all my weight.

Tears of pain and fury leaped to my eyes, but I couldn't lose it now. I started to crawl toward the SUV, only to feel Chris's hands on me again, this time around my waist. I kicked back at him, but he let go of me with one hand so he could catch my ankle and flip me over.

Then he was looming over me, his horrific blood-stained face getting closer and closer. I knew what he was going to do, and I knew I wouldn't be able to stop him—he was bigger and stronger, and just plain crazy, and I now had at least one, if not two, sprained wrists.

And then...then it was as if a pair of invisible hands caught hold of him, pulling him away from me, flinging him backward as if he weighed nothing, was only a child's toy someone had left out on the lawn. He hit the trunk of the palm tree in my aunt and uncle's yard with a sickening crunch, then slid down, his head hanging at a strange angle. Was his neck broken? No way was I going to get close enough to find out.

I didn't even realize I was saying the words out loud until I heard them coming from my mouth. "What the—"

The voice sounded stern and sad. *Do you see now why I did not want you to come here?*

"Point taken," I panted, and got shakily to my feet. Both my wrists were aching, and I hoped I'd be able to get the Cherokee home. Not that I had much choice. It was the only safe haven I knew.

Wincing, I dug the key out of my pocket and climbed into the SUV, trying to maneuver with my elbows so I wouldn't have to bend my wrists any more than was strictly necessary. Dutchie whined and tried to lick my face.

"I'm okay, sweetie," I told her, more for her sake than because I really believed what I was saying.

Trying to put on the seatbelt would have been excruciating. Besides, with all the wrecks littering the roads, I wouldn't be driving much above twenty-five miles an hour anyway. Somehow I managed to get the car started, then bit my lip in pain as I put the Cherokee in gear. At least I'd been parked at the curb and not in the driveway, so I didn't have to worry about backing out or anything.

The throbbing ache in my wrists prevented me from thinking about anything except getting back to the house. I drove slowly, grinding my teeth whenever I had to maneuver around abandoned cars by going up on the curb. Every jolt and jounce felt magnified a hundredfold.

Finally, though, I made it back to my street and eased the car into the driveway, then turned off the engine. I knew there was no way I could reach across and open the passenger door from the inside, so I slid out and went around the front of the SUV. Dutchie bounded out the second she was free to do so, and I retrieved the gun from the glove compartment before shutting the door behind her and clicking the lock button on the remote.

Limping, since I'd realized in that moment just how much my right knee hurt as well, I went in through the back door and locked it behind me. Then I headed to the front of the house to test the lock there as well. All was as it should be, but I couldn't stop shaking.

Dutchie sat in the living room and watched as I secured the house. Then she tilted her head toward the clock over the fireplace, as if to say, *It's lunchtime, you know.*

Despite everything, I couldn't help giving a rusty chuckle. "Soon, Dutchie. I need to take care of me first."

We had a very well-stocked first aid kit in one of the cupboards in the service porch. It hurt just to reach up and get it down, but I made myself do it. First I attended to the superficial scratches on the palms of my hands, gritting my teeth as I swabbed them with alcohol pads, and then I wrapped both wrists with Ace bandages. They still ached, but not as badly. My knee was banged up, but I hadn't torn my jeans, so I figured any bruises I'd gotten would heal on their own.

Afterward, I limped into the kitchen and got Dutchie some more chicken. Besides the leftover dog biscuits, there was also a partial bag of dry dog food in the pantry that I could feed her, but I figured I might as well get rid of the perishable stuff first.

Then it was some water for me, and a makeshift sandwich of wheat bread and butter and the last of the strawberry jelly. My hand shook as I lifted the sandwich to my mouth, but I made myself eat anyway. That burst of panic, of terror, had used up a lot of my reserves.

The silence in the house seemed to press on my ears. I noticed the voice had been suspiciously quiet since I'd returned.

Finally, I set down my water bottle and snapped, "All right, you want to tell me what the hell *that* was all about? How can a pasty creep like Chris Bowman be immune when everyone else is dead?"

No reply at first. Then it was as if someone sighed quietly, far back in my mind. *We cannot control who is immune, only what happens to them after they have survived.*

"'We'?" I demanded, figuring I'd ask the most pressing question first. "Who is 'we'?"

The resulting silence was so drawn out that I was fairly certain I wouldn't get a reply, that I'd asked exactly the wrong question. Finally, the voice said, *That is not important.*

"It's important to me." I hurt all over, and I was tired of the sense I'd begun to have that something huge was behind all this, something I wasn't sure I'd ever be able to understand. "Who are you?"

This time the answer came back almost at once. *I am not at liberty to say.*

That answer only made the impotent rage within me burn all the hotter. This last evasion was about all I could take at the moment. "What the hell is this—a White House press conference?"

You are upset. This is understandable. But tell me— have I not done whatever I could to protect you?

I recalled how Chris Bowman had been torn away from me by invisible hands, thrown up against that palm tree as if he weighed nothing, even though he was six feet, two inches of solid pudge. "Was that you?"

My only wish is for your safety. That is why you need to leave this place and go north.

So we were back to that again. I had to admit, after this morning's events, I was a little more open to the idea of getting the hell out of Albuquerque and not looking back. Part of me—the stubborn part—still wanted to go to Tori's house, to see for myself what had happened to her and her family. But I also knew I was putting myself at risk every time I set foot out the door. A great deal of the population had vanished during the previous three days, but not all of it...and it was those remnants I had to worry about.

"All right," I said wearily. "I'll think about it."

Maybe I was only talking to myself. Right then, I didn't want to think too hard about the whole insane situation.

That afternoon I dozed a little, and when I woke up, I actually felt better. My wrists didn't ache as much, and the abrasions on my hands already looked completely scabbed over. What the hell? Was this part of the "voice"—I didn't know how else to think of him, or it—watching over me? Did he have some way of making me heal far faster than I normally would?

At any other time, I would have dismissed the notion as crazy, but so many insane things had happened since Monday that I couldn't reject any of them outright. Maybe my particular immunity brought with it certain other benefits, although I couldn't begin to think how that worked. I'd always been a healthy person, so I bounced back from bumps and bruises and sprains fairly quickly—but not this quickly.

Putting that conundrum aside to ponder at a later date, I decided to take stock of what I had in the house, and what else I would need in the way of supplies. We had a good deal of camping gear, so I was set when it came to sleeping bags and Coleman lanterns and all that sort of stuff. The first aid kit was stocked well enough for ordinary scrapes and bruises and strains, but I wondered if I should hit up a few of the local pharmacies and get myself antibiotics, some kind of painkillers, cough and cold medicine...a decent supply of my birth control pills. Not that I was expecting to get laid anytime soon—Chris Bowman's bloodied face flashed into my mind, and I shuddered—but the pills did help to keep my periods manageable. And that was another thing. I'd need sanitary supplies, enough to last me for a while. Making do with rags the way they did in the bad old days was not something I wanted to face quite yet.

Night began to fall again, and I moved around the ground floor, lighting candles. I still didn't want to go upstairs, for some reason felt safer here on the couch. I fed Dutchie the last of the chicken, and snacked on a couple of granola bars, trying to ignore how much my body ached for something more substantial. I wasn't quite at the point of being willing to kill for a cheeseburger, but I could see myself heading down that road in a couple of days.

I spoke into the stillness of the house. "So if I'm supposed to head north, where exactly am I going? Santa Fe? Taos? Colorado?"

Go north, and I will guide you where you need to go.

"That's not an answer."

It's all the answer you require.

"You're a real pain in the ass, you know that?"

Something that might have been a chuckle. *I have been told that on occasion, if not in those precise words.*

"But you're still not going to tell me where I'm going."

No.

Well, at least he was being honest. I'd begun thinking of the voice as "him," although it still could have been merely a product of my fevered imagination, of a mind that couldn't handle all the death and destruction around it, and so had slipped into a nice, cozy form of psychosis.

Maybe so, but that didn't explain the way Chris Bowman had been torn away from me, as if some invisible giant had grabbed him and thrown him across the yard.

Telekinesis? Some kind of delayed-onset *X-Men* action?

Okay, now I was beginning to sound ridiculous even to myself.

"All right," I said. "I'm convinced. Mostly because I'm not sure that creeper doesn't know where I live...if he's still alive." A pause then, while I waited for the voice to break in and tell me that oh, yes, Chris Bowman was dead, and I needn't worry about him any longer.

But I heard no such thing, just a silence that began to echo in my ears. Great. So apparently Mr. Bowman wasn't exactly down for the count.

I took in a breath and plunged ahead. "And anyway, staying here is starting to sound less and less attractive. I'll head out in the morning after I get some more supplies."

You won't need them.

This was said flatly, as if he didn't expect me to contradict him. "Well, sorry, but since you won't tell me where I'm going or how long the journey is going to take, I need to be prepared. And that means getting a few things. I'll be careful."

The way you were careful at your aunt and uncle's house?

Bristling, I replied, "Okay, I was caught off guard. That's not going to happen again."

No reply. I wasn't sure whether that meant the voice had run out of arguments to give me, or whether it was simply tired of me throwing up roadblocks. I decided to take its silence as tacit agreement with my plan. And really, it shouldn't be that big a deal. The Walgreens I frequented was less than a mile from my house. I'd pack everything else I needed in advance, then go there on my way out of town. Surely the voice couldn't have any real problem with that?

It probably could, but unless it woke me up in the middle of the night to tell me everything I was doing wrong, I was going with it.

Falling asleep that night was difficult. The silence rattled me; every creak and sigh of the house contracting as the night air grew colder made me startle, thinking Chris the Creeper had returned to finish what he'd started outside my aunt and uncle's house. Well, the joke would be on him—I had the revolver right next to me on the coffee table, and had gotten the shotgun from the gun safe and was lying with it propped up against the arm of the sofa near my head. He'd be a red smear on the wall before he had time to blink.

But the guns didn't reassure me as much as I'd thought they would. Maybe it was more that I'd begun to pick at what the voice had said to me, how he'd said that "we"—meaning him and others like him, I supposed, whatever or whoever they were—hadn't controlled who lived and who died of the Heat, but that they did have some say in what happened to the survivors. That was a frightening thought. True, everything he'd done so far seemed to have been for my benefit... but why?

I realized he hadn't called me "beloved" for a while. Was that an oversight, or had all my questions and my ignoring of his advice annoyed him enough that I wasn't quite so beloved anymore? The thought bothered me a little...but not as much as contemplating what it might mean to be the beloved of some incorporeal being who spoke to me only in my thoughts.

If he was even real. I really could just be imagining the whole thing. After all, there were accounts of mothers going ballistic and lifting trucks off their toddlers or whatever. Wasn't it possible that I'd been the one to fling Chris Bowman away from me, and my mind had just embellished the event so it seemed as if some kind of supernatural force was involved?

I didn't know. And the worst part was, I had no one to talk to about my situation, except a disembodied voice that might or might not be merely a figment of my imagination. For most of the day, I'd managed to push to one side the pain of losing my family, my friends, but now as I sat there in the dark, one candle flickering on the coffee table, it all seemed to come back in a rush, like a great, gaping wound in my middle where my heart had been torn out. I was twenty-four years old, but right then all I wanted was my mother. I wanted her to hug me and tell me it was all going to be okay.

And then I felt him there, as I had earlier, like a wash of warmth moving over me, strong arms around me, the touch of an unseen mouth against my tumbled hair. *Ah, beloved, you do not believe me now, but it will get better. Sleep now, and leave the pain for another day.*

I opened my mouth to speak, but I found I didn't have the strength to form any words. Instead, darkness washed over me, taking me along with it. In that moment, I knew I lacked the strength to fight the inevitable.

CHAPTER SEVEN

DUTCHIE'S GROWLING WOKE ME. I STARTLED awake, sitting bolt upright and blinking against the darkness. Only it wasn't completely dark, as the pillar candle still burned bravely in its dish on the coffee table. Thank God for that, because the dog was sitting in front of the door, teeth bared in a snarl, a deep, bone-rattling growl rumbling within her throat.

Without thinking, I pushed back the blankets that covered me and grabbed the shotgun. Yes, the .357 had great stopping power, but I knew anything I hit with that shotgun would go down and stay down. Well, except for the parts that got splattered on any nearby walls. And if I did somehow manage to miss, that Remington would make a pretty decent club.

My heart was hammering away in my chest, but I made myself go to the peephole in the front door and attempt to peer out. Fat lot of good that did—the night outside was pitch black, with not a hint of a moon. I couldn't even see the rose of Sharon bushes on either side of the doorway.

But the whole time Dutchie didn't stop growling, although as I backed away from the door, shotgun still clenched in my right hand, she moved as well, padding toward the back of the house.

Great. The front door was much bigger and heavier than the back door. Anyone sufficiently motivated could kick in the door off the service porch.

I had a feeling that if he was still ambulatory, Chris Bowman would be feeling really motivated right around now. Maybe I was just being paranoid, since I had no idea how he could have even found me. We weren't exactly what you could call listed in the phone book; cops tended to be circumspect about that sort of thing. Then again, Chris seemed like the type who might have mastered the finer points of hacking into secure databases, and considering his apparent obsession with me....

Shit.

Dutchie trotted ahead of me. Her ears were up, nose pointed directly toward the service porch at the rear of the kitchen. And that was when I heard it, too—a faint scratching noise coming from the back door. If I hadn't known better, I would have thought it was one of the other neighborhood dogs trying to get in. But after seeing that whole "peaceable kingdom" bit at the PetSmart up in Sandia Heights, I knew Dutchie wouldn't be growling like that if it was simply another dog on the other side of that door.

I'd already loaded the shotgun before I lay down to sleep, so all I had to do was pump it to bring a shell into the chamber. Even though I could feel my heart still wailing away in my chest, I managed to call out in what sounded like a reasonably steady voice, "Whoever that is, back away. I'm armed, and I will not hesitate to shoot."

There. My father would've been proud, if he'd been around to hear that.

No reply, of course. Dutchie sat down on her haunches, then looked up at me and gave a questioning whine. It seemed obvious she thought she'd done her job in warning me that something was out there, and now it was my turn to do something about it.

Not unreasonable of her, but no way was I going to reach out and open that door. If I had to stay here all night with the shotgun pointed at the back entrance to the house, I would.

That odd scratching noise started up again. I gritted my teeth, wondering if I should send off a warning shot. But all that would do was mess up the back door, and what if that scratching noise was coming from an ambitious rat or something? I'd look like an idiot, and worse, I would've completely compromised my home's security.

I dragged out the step stool and sat down on it, shotgun still pointed toward the back door. Dutchie stayed where she was, although she did send me an inquiring look over one shoulder. I shook my head at her, and she settled down in a sphinx-like position, still at attention, snout in a direct line with the doorknob. In that moment, I wondered whether I should even be trusting Dutchie's instincts. Obviously, she was a very good dog, but she wasn't *my* dog. I didn't know if she was a great watch dog or the type to go off half-cocked at every random sound. Yes, there was something outside, but it didn't necessarily have to be anything threatening. For all I knew, it could have been a branch from the willow bush just outside the back stoop scratching on the doorframe or something.

But then the door creaked open, and my breath caught in my throat. Standing there was Chris Bowman, face puffed and bruised, pale eyes glaring at me. Something glinted in one hand, reflecting the faint light from the jar candle I'd left lit in the kitchen.

Lock picks. Son of a bitch. Trust a maladjusted bastard like Chris the Creep to know how to pick locks.

Slowly, I got to my feet, the gun still trained on him. "Get out, Chris."

His eyes were still fixed on my face, as if he hadn't even registered the Remington pump-action shotgun in my hands. "No. We're the only survivors. We're meant to be together."

My finger was resting on the trigger. Just the slightest squeeze, and he'd be splatter on the doorframe. Could I kill someone, though, just like that? Before, when I'd thrown the rock at his head, I'd only meant to slow him down, to give myself enough time to get safely away. The shotgun was an entirely different story.

"I don't want to hurt you, Chris," I said, forcing my voice to remain steady, just as I willed my hands not to shake as I gripped the shotgun. "The two of us being immune? It's just an accident of biology. It doesn't mean anything. So please, go back home."

For the first time, he glanced away from my eyes, down at the gun I held. A look of almost comical confusion passed over his puffy features. "But I *want* you."

My stomach twisted, and right then I was glad I hadn't eaten anything more than that bread and jelly sandwich a few hours earlier...or whenever it had been. I wasn't wearing a watch, and of course the digital clocks on the appliances in the kitchen had died along with everything else when the power went out.

"But I don't want you, Chris," I said, and right then my voice did contain a betraying tremor that I hated, although I couldn't do anything about it. "I told you,

I don't want to hurt you. But I will. My dad was a cop, and he taught me how to use this. And I will."

During this little speech, Chris's eyes grew narrower and narrower, as if he was finally processing my rejection of him. His lip curled, and he said, "You don't have the guts," right before he lunged at me.

Without thinking, I let my finger jerk on the trigger. At the same time, it was as if a powerful hand had grasped the barrel, pointing it away from Chris so all I did was blow a hole in the ceiling, destroying the combination light/fan fixture there and raining drywall everywhere. I blinked, sure the creep was going to come after me, now that I'd missed so heinously, but instead something seemed to grab him by the neck, squeezing so his eyes began to bulge and his feet scrabbled helplessly against the linoleum of the laundry room floor.

A few gurgling moans came from his throat, and then once again he was flung away from me, this time with so much force that he flew across the backyard, hitting the corner of the garage before tumbling in a heap into the irises that still half-heartedly grew there. Shaking, I tightened my hold on the shotgun and started down the back steps toward him, only to hear the voice say,

Stop, Jessica. There is no need.

I paused on the bottom stair. "That—that was you?"

Yes.

"And he's—"

Yes. I did what I should have done back at your aunt and uncle's house.

My breath seemed to go out of me in a whoosh, and I found myself sitting down hard on the step, the concrete cold even through my jeans. Thank God at least I'd gone to bed fully dressed, except for my hiking boots. I looked over at the gun I still held.

"I wouldn't have missed, would I?"

No. You would have killed him, had I not pushed the gun away. I did not want that on your conscience.

So...a being who would go out of his way to protect me, but didn't think twice about killing someone else. Not that Chris Bowman was exactly a wonderful specimen of humanity, one worth saving.

"Are you an angel?" I asked abruptly.

Another of those low chuckles. *Hardly. But you are safe now, so you should go back inside and try to sleep.*

"You seriously expect me to sleep after that?"

Yes. You are safe now. No one else knows of your presence in this house. You can sleep here, and then leave tomorrow morning.

I knew I'd exhausted all my arguments. After pushing myself to my feet, I glanced over toward where Chris Bowman's body lay, twisted and limp in the ruin of what was once my mother's prized bed of irises.

I will take care of that. Go to sleep, Jessica.

Bowing my head, I nodded, then went back inside and locked the door. Even though the voice had told me I was safe, I still took the step stool and wedged it up under the knob of the back door. Maybe it was a foolish gesture, but it made me feel a little bit better.

Dutchie looked up at me and wagged her tail, teeth showing in a doggy smile. "Okay," I said. "You get a treat for the warning." I got out a dog biscuit and gave it to her before heading back to my makeshift bed on the living room couch, where I leaned the shotgun up against the sofa's arm once more. Maybe I wouldn't need it, but I knew I'd sleep better if it was there.

Assuming I slept at all, of course.

I did, finally, and awoke to bright sunshine peeking around the edges of the living room curtains. The clock above the fireplace was battery-operated, and so had no problem telling me that the time was ten minutes until eight.

When I'd laid my head down on the sofa pillow the night before, I had no idea I'd sleep in that much. The confrontation with Chris Bowman must have taken more out of me than I thought. Speaking of which....

After pushing the blankets covering me off to one side, I rose and padded in sock feet to the back door. The step stool was still there, shoved up under the door-knob. I removed it and set it to lean against the wall, then opened the door and looked outside, toward the garage. The bright morning sunlight clearly revealed the clump of smashed iris plants where Chris Bowman had landed the night before, but his body was gone. No blood, no nothing.

If I looked more closely, would there be a pile of ashes half hidden among the blade-like iris leaves? But no, he'd died from severe head trauma, not the Heat. The body had been simply...taken away.

Deciding it was best not to contemplate exactly how that had happened...or what had been done with him...I went back inside and poured Dutchie some fresh water from one of the bottles in the pantry, and gave her a good helping of dry dog food. She wolfed it down, tail wagging the whole time, so obviously she hadn't been irrevocably scarred by the events of the night before.

I wasn't sure I could say the same for myself, but I had other things I needed to focus on. The day before, I'd told the voice I would pack up and leave this morning, so that's what I needed to do—assess what I would take with me, based on how much I could fit into the Cherokee. With the back seats folded down, I really could haul a good deal of gear, so I didn't think space would be too much of a problem.

More bread and butter for breakfast, supplemented with some dried apricots I found smashed into one corner of the pantry. My mother had been a very organized woman, but Devin was a source of chaos that could defeat even the most orderly person. I started stacking what was salvageable on the breakfast bar: the rest of that bag of apricots, a pile of granola bars, an unopened bag of blue corn chips, the remnants of the dry food and the dog biscuits for Dutchie. That would get us started, and I figured I could always stock up on a few more things in the food section of the Walgreens.

Truly, you do not need that much. The voice sounded almost amused this time.

"Well, until you're telling me how far I'm driving, I'm going to over-pack," I said, setting the half-used flat of bottled water next to the dog food.

Jessica, do you not like surprises?

"Not particularly, no." I surveyed the meager pile and thought I really wasn't overdoing it by anyone's standards. True, I could start piling up the economy-sized cans of tomato sauce and beans my mother had bought at Costco, but I could get that stuff anywhere if necessary. It wasn't as if there was going to be a lot of competition for the enormous stockpiles of canned food left behind by the mostly deceased people of New Mexico.

Well, I think you will like this surprise.

Since that reply just annoyed me—what was I, five?—I made a noncommittal sound in my throat and headed out the back door, up to my apartment. This time, Dutchie didn't seem too inclined to follow me. I guessed the reason why when I saw her nose around the backyard, then squat to pee. The second move-ment, so to speak, would probably follow shortly, but I didn't see any need to hang around for that.

Like an idiot, I'd left the door to my apartment unlocked, but, as far as I could tell, Chris hadn't made it up here. It was possible that he'd detected the faint glow of the candles from inside the main house and realized that was where I'd bunked down. Just as well, because I didn't know if I could have brought any of my belongings with me if I'd known he'd pawed through them.

In my closet I had one of those airline-regulation hard-sided suitcases, the kind with wheels, as well as two largish duffle bags. I filled one of the duffle bags with underwear and bras and socks, along with a cou-ple of sleep shirts. The other duffle bag got shoe-carry-ing duty—which turned out not to be much, since I only packed my trail shoes, a pair of knee-high boots with rubber soles, and one pair of flip-flops. And... well, I didn't see where I would ever wear them again, but I didn't want to leave behind my pretty black flats with the scallop detail, or the high-heeled sandals with the jeweled embellishment. Maybe I could just take them out from time to time and fondle them. I loved those sandals.

I filled up the remainder of the duffle bag with my toiletries, although I left behind all the hair-prep tools. What was the point, when there was no more electricity? Maybe if I got really bored I'd invent a solar-powered blow dryer, but in the meantime, that was a whole lot of stuff I didn't need to drag along.

I took the same no-nonsense approach with my clothes: jeans and T-shirts in both short- and long-sleeved varieties, a flannel shirt I'd inherited from my ex-boyfriend (he was an ass, but that shirt was soooo soft), the all-weather anorak I used when going on hikes. If I really was going north, I'd need some protection, so I added my dark green plaid cashmere scarf and lined leather gloves to the pile, along with the black knitted cap that Elena had once complained made me look like I was about to hold up a liquor store.

Getting it all to fit was a challenge, although leaving out the anorak helped. I could always lay it down in the back of the SUV. When my gaze traveled back to the closet, where all my "fun" clothes still hung, looking a bit forlorn and abandoned, it lingered on the black dress I'd worn out for drinks on my birthday. All right, I knew there was no reason I'd ever need to wear that dress again, but I loved the way it fit, the way it seemed to follow all the curves of my body without clinging too much. But it was made of knit fabric and wouldn't take up that much room.

Off the hanger, it did roll up into a surprisingly small ball. I tucked the dress into a corner of the suitcase and then zipped the thing closed. A sound outside on the landing made me start, but it was only Dutchie, coming up to investigate what I was doing.

"Just about done," I told her, lugging the suitcase off the bed and picking up the lighter of the two duffle bags, the one with my underthings in it. I'd come back for the other duffle bag and my coat.

The dog ran ahead of me down the stairs, tail wagging. It seemed she knew what these preparations meant—that I'd be going in the Cherokee soon, and that meant she'd be going along as well.

I set the luggage down by the breakfast bar, then returned to my apartment and gathered up the rest of my things. Sitting on the small side table next to the couch was a wedding photo of my parents, my mother with impossible big '80s hair but looking beautiful even so, and next to it a snapshot taken last year of the whole family at a football game, Devin wearing his shoulder pads, sweaty and grinning proudly. My heart clenched when I looked at their faces, and yet I knew I couldn't leave them behind. What if I began to forget what they looked like?

Fighting back tears, I shoved the pictures, frames and all, into my oversized purple purse; I wasn't sure why I was bringing it, since the backpack I was taking with the rest of the camping equipment was a lot more practical. But that purse seemed to be the last reminder of the "old" me I had—the cell phone, useless now, although a few days earlier I would have said I couldn't have lasted more than a few hours without it; the tube of lip gloss; my wallet; stubs from movies I'd seen over the last few months; a pen and some tissue, because my mother told me I should always carry a pen and Kleenex.

And my keys. I went out onto the landing, closed the door behind me, and then locked it. I couldn't really say why, as I doubted any survivors—if there were more besides me and the late Chris Bowman— would bother coming all the way back here to loot the apartment. Our house was one of the more modest ones on the street; there were plenty of better pickings elsewhere.

But that thought only served to depress me, as if the things my parents had worked so hard for had turned out to be worth very little in the end. The first stinging pinpricks of tears told me I'd better abandon that line of thought, as I still had a lot to do.

And maybe, just maybe, I'd feel better once I was gone and away from the place that now only served to remind me of everything I'd lost.

In the end, the Cherokee was full but not filled. I put two bottles of water in the cup holders, patted the passenger seat so Dutchie would know it was time to get in, and shut the door behind her. After that, I climbed in behind the wheel and closed my own door.

All the exertion had made my wrists start to ache again, but only slightly, which just proved some sort of supernatural healing must be going on. Not that I was going to argue. Heading out into the world while even partly incapacitated wasn't a very good idea.

So...had my unseen guardian speeded up my healing process so my injuries wouldn't slow down my departure?

I didn't know how I should feel about that.

No point in brooding over it now, though. I was just glad that I was able to back out of the driveway without my wrists or hands hurting too much. Today, although the sky was mainly blue, I could see clouds beginning to drift in from the northeast. I hoped they didn't indicate some kind of weather was on the way; bad enough that the voice expected me to head out of town in a direction of his choosing without having to handle driving in heavy rain as well.

He—or it—had been conspicuously silent so far this morning. It could simply be that he had no reason to intervene while I was packing, since I was already doing his bidding by prepping to get out of Albuquerque.

The local Walgreens was around a half mile from my house. Its parking lot backed up to a middle school, and it felt stranger than strange to get out of the SUV and not see a bunch of kids running around on the soccer field and the track. At least it was far enough away that I couldn't tell if those fields had little piles of gray dust scattered around on them. No, I realized they probably wouldn't, as the schools had been closed down fairly quickly...not that it had made much of a difference in the end.

As I approached the drugstore, I saw that the front doors had been smashed in. Glass was strewn everywhere. My hackles went up, and I almost reached back and pulled out the Glock, which I'd tucked into my waistband. The whole incident with Chris Bowman had put me more than a little on edge, and I'd decided to drive with the gun on me. The S&W was way too big for that, though, so I'd gone with the Glock. It would still flatten someone, especially if I hit them with multiple rounds.

But as I entered the store, glass crunching under my hiking boots, it seemed the place was deserted enough. Dark, too—I supposed I should have been expecting that, but in my mind's eye the Walgreens was always brightly lit, blazing with fluorescent illumination. I paused by the checkout counter, which was close enough to the door that I could see what I was doing, and plucked one of the keychain flashlights off the display there. Not as good as my father's Maglite, which was buried deep in the cargo area of the car, but it would do.

I turned on the flashlight, grabbed a cart, and made my way to the back of the store where the pharmacy was located. All around me, I could see evidence of looting—empty shelves, racks overturned, aisles filled with discarded bags of Doritos, rolls of toilet paper, kids' toys. My heart sank. If so much had been taken, what would be left for me to collect?

As it turned out, not a heck of a lot.

There were still some generic medications left in the first aid aisle—ibuprofen, allergy remedies, sore throat lozenges. I grabbed boxes haphazardly and threw them into the cart I'd picked up at the front of the store, figuring something was better than nothing. All was chaos behind the pharmacy counter. I didn't know if all those items had been taken by people who were sick and trying desperately to alleviate their symptoms, or whether any survivors had realized there was a lot of heavy-duty stuff here just ripe for the picking.

Pretty much anything with an opiate in it was gone, I realized as I ran the flashlight's beam over the shelves. I could forget about easing the pain of armageddon with a little Oxycontin. All of the high-powered stuff was gone, except for one bottle of codeine-laced cough syrup high on a shelf. I took that, figuring it might come in handy.

The antibiotics were also ransacked, although I found a couple of bottles of tetracycline. Old school, but it would still work just fine for an infected wound or a bout of bronchitis. They got added to the growing pile in the cart.

A lot of the medications had names I didn't even recognize, so I passed all those by. What I really wanted was the birth control pills, and I found those when I went around a corner, on a set of shelves that were a little disorganized but mainly intact. It made sense; most people probably weren't thinking of family planning when they were being beaten down by the modern-day equivalent of a Biblical plague.

A small sigh of relief escaped my lips when I found the Ortho-Novum, and I gathered up every little packet they had. Enough to last me for a year, from the looks of it. After that, well...I'd worry about that then.

Like you're really going to be alive a year from now.

I pushed that thought out of my head. Two days ago, I was sure I'd be dead along with everyone else, and yet here I still was. Never say die.

That had been a favorite phrase of my mother's. How woefully inappropriate.

Mouth tightening, I moved the flashlight I carried over the shelves once more to make sure I wasn't missing anything. The problem was, I didn't get sick all that often, and even when I did, regular over-the-counter stuff worked just fine for me. I could be leaving something valuable behind here and wouldn't even know it.

You can't take everything, I told myself. Anyway, it was creepy in here, blundering around in the dark with only a single small flashlight to relieve the gloom. Better for me to just cut my losses and get out. It wasn't as if there wouldn't be more drugstores between here and...wherever I was going.

That thought reassured me somewhat, so I stepped out from behind the counter and made my way two aisles over, where the feminine products were located. I didn't pay attention to brand or type, but just tossed boxes of tampons and packages of maxi pads into the cart until I was almost out of room. That should do me for a while, and I still needed to see if anything edible had been left behind.

I began walking toward the far left of the store, where I knew the food was located. Anything in the refrigerated case would be spoiled—and I was glad the doors were all shut, as otherwise the smell probably would have been nasty as hell—but there could still be chips and crackers and cookies, probably some beef jerky and other things of that ilk as well.

Not the healthiest of diets, but sometimes you had to take what you could get.

Figuring I should try to pick up some food for Dutchie as well, I stopped at the aisle where the drugstore usually stocked dog treats and a few brands of dry and canned food—not the stuff I would have chosen to feed her under ideal circumstances, but it would have been better than nothing. However, for some strange reason, those shelves were completely picked over. I even skidded on some scattered pellets of dry food before I regained my balance and glanced down to see that a big bag of Purina had been torn open, its contents scattered across the floor.

Muttering a curse, I left that aisle and went to the snack food section, which was in slightly better shape, and started gathering up what I could. By the time I'd dropped a couple of packets of beef jerky and a box of Ritz crackers on top of the pile in my basket, it was full, and I figured I needed to get going. It was almost noon, according to the watch I'd fished out of my nightstand and strapped on my wrist. A while back I'd almost stopped wearing watches, since I could just look at my phone, but now the watch was the only thing telling me what time it actually was. Yes, I had the clock in the Cherokee, but that only helped when I was driving.

I'd just passed the checkout counter—trying to quash my very real sensation of guilt over walking out with a bunch of stuff I hadn't paid for—when a shadow filled the doorway. Almost without thinking, I reached back for the Glock tucked into my waistband. Yes, Chris Bowman was still dead and gone, but all sorts of predators could still be out there. Or at least as many as the Heat had allowed to survive.

Then my eyes adjusted, and I saw the shadow was that of a man, probably in his late forties, smiling at me nervously.

"I'm sorry I startled you," he said, seeming to take note of how I remained rooted in the spot where I'd stopped by the checkout. "It's just—I haven't seen anyone else alive for two days. I thought I was the only one."

"There are a couple of us, I think," I responded. He looked pretty harmless, with his thinning dark hair and worried eyes, but I was still wary. "I never heard anything about the mortality rate. Everything went so...fast."

He nodded, his gaze traveling to the cart in front of me and then back up to my face. I stiffened, worried I'd see the same sort of predatory stare that Chris Bowman had given me, but this stranger only seemed relieved that he wasn't the only living person left in Albuquerque. "It was 99.8 percent. Or at least that was what the reports said."

"Reports?" I asked. "What reports?"

"Not on the news," he said. "I worked in the emergency-management bureau downtown. Those were the latest figures we got before everything just...stopped. By then there were only two of us left out of a team of twenty-seven, and Lydia died soon afterward. There was no way to let anyone know...not that there was anyone left to know, I suppose."

"There were a few of us." I had to stop then, the enormity of it threatening to overwhelm me. With a mortality rate like that, it meant there were maybe two thousand people left in Albuquerque. That sounded like a lot, until you realized there used to be almost a million people living in and around the city center. "But you're right—I suppose it wouldn't have made much of a difference. It's not as if we could have stopped it."

"No," he agreed, his features drooping even more.

"So…." I went on, not sure where I was supposed to go from here. It was pretty clear that the voice meant for me to leave Albuquerque alone, but now that I'd met a survivor, could I simply leave him behind? He appeared to be harmless. "Do you live around here?"

The man gave a vague gesture over his shoulder, toward the west. "Off Chavez Road."

That wasn't too far from where we stood. No wonder he'd come foraging over here. "Your first time out and around…after?"

A nod. "I didn't know if it would be safe, but I started to run out of things, and this was the closest store…."

"There's plenty left," I assured him. "The looters kind of tore the place up, but they didn't steal all the Doritos. I'd probably go to a grocery store if you really want something decent to eat, though."

"That was my plan after this, but I could walk here, so I figured I'd come here first." For the first time his eyes took on a certain glint, one I wasn't sure I liked. "That your Cherokee out there?"

There wasn't any point in denying it. For all I knew, he'd seen me pull up and get out of the SUV. "Yes."

"Leaving town?"

A flicker of unease went over me. "I was thinking about it," I hedged.

To my surprise, he didn't seem that put off by my reply. "That might be a good idea. It might be safer where there aren't as many survivors. People are going to get desperate."

They already have, I thought, recalling the way Chris Bowman had broken into my house. Then again, that was a special case of one highly obsessed nut job. The survivors in Albuquerque would probably be a lot more interested in getting supplies than getting into my pants.

"So what are you going to do?" I asked, trying to shift the conversation away from me and my plans.

"I'm not sure. I figured food was the first step. After that?" He shrugged, then offered me a faint smile. "Right now, it's just kind of good to hear another voice."

I almost agreed with him, except I had been hearing a man's voice in my head for the past few days. So what if the jury was still out as to whether that voice was real or not?

"Well, I don't want to leave my dog sitting in the car too long," I said, since it seemed to me that the man wouldn't mind standing here and chatting all day, if it meant he didn't have to be by himself.

He looked startled by the *non sequitur,* but then nodded. "Oh, of course. It is starting to warm up. You have a good day." The way he said it made it sound as if he wasn't sure such a thing was possible anymore.

Since there wasn't much else I could do, I smiled slightly, then moved toward the exit. For a second or two, I was worried he might put out an arm to stop me, but he only stepped out of the way and headed into the store.

I allowed myself a small sigh of relief before going to the Cherokee and unlocking it, then quickly unloading the loot from my cart into the rear cargo area. From the front seat, Dutchie whined, but I wasn't sure why. It was a little warm in the car, but nothing too bad—I'd made sure to crack the windows before I locked up the vehicle.

When I turned around, though, I almost dropped the car key. The stranger was standing there, holding a pistol pointed straight at me. His expression was no longer mild, but greedy. Not the kind of greed I'd seen in Chris Bowman, though. This man's gaze wasn't fixed on me, but the SUV I'd just closed up.

Without blinking, he said, "Give me the key. Now."

CHAPTER EIGHT

AT FIRST I COULD ONLY STAND THERE, GAPING AT him. From the way he held the gun, a small .22, I could tell he didn't have much experience. One part of my mind began to coolly calculate whether I was fast enough to get that Glock out of my waistband before he fired on me. My father had taken me to the indoor range many times, and shooting up in the hills around town even more, and he'd made me practice pulling the gun from a holster as well as the waistband of my pants. I knew I had far more experience than the man who faced me. But... was it enough?

Stalling for time, I stammered, "W-what?"

"You heard me." He waved the pistol in what he probably thought was a threatening manner. "I don't want to hurt you. I just want the car."

"But—" I kept my hands out where he could see them, knowing that he was probably nervous enough just handling the gun that he might do something really stupid if I made any sudden movements. "There are plenty of abandoned vehicles all over the city. You don't need mine."

"Yes, I do." His gaze shifted from the rear door of the Cherokee to my face, and I could see the desperation in his watery brown eyes. "I don't have to hunt for the key, and it's a four-wheel drive loaded with supplies. I doubt I'm going to find anything better."

Well, when he put it that way.... "It needs gas, though. Do you know how to siphon gas?"

His bemused expression told me he didn't.

"Look," I went on, knowing there was no way in hell I was going to let him have my dad's SUV, "it's been a horrible week. I get that you feel desperate. But you don't need to do this. There are plenty of alterna—"

BLAM! The pistol went off—not pointed at me, thank God, but somewhere over my shoulder and just above the roof line of the Cherokee. Even so, I jumped enough that I could feel the backs of my thighs hit the SUV's rear bumper.

"I'm not negotiating," he said. The look on his face shifted from confused to crafty. "But maybe you could come along. You say you know how to siphon gas?"

I actually hadn't said that I did, but the truth was, my father had showed me and Devin once, when Devin ran out of gas while driving Mom's Escape. It wasn't that difficult, really, as long as you selected a vehicle without a locking gas cap. In the back of the Cherokee, along with the rest of my supplies, was a long rubber tube I'd brought along for that very purpose. With the power out, it would simply be easier to siphon gas from abandoned vehicles rather than attempt to switch the pumps at a gas station over to manual.

"Maybe I do," I hedged, my pulse beginning to escalate.

"You seem like you might be...useful," the man said, and this time his watery gaze remained fixed on my face. It was clear his thoughts were beginning to run in other directions than merely stealing my car.

Dude, I could put you through a wall, I thought, but that inner remark was more bravado than anything else. Yes, he looked like the quintessential wimpy office worker. On the other hand, he'd still managed to sneak up on me, so I wasn't about to underestimate him.

Since I couldn't trust myself to speak without giving myself away, I only shrugged. At the same time, I let my hands drop to my sides, my right hand beginning to move slowly backward, toward the reassuring weight of the Glock in my waistband. Thank God the shirt I was wearing hung loosely enough that the man didn't seem to have noticed he wasn't the only armed person in this little convo.

He stepped closer. Now I could smell the stink of perspiration and fear on him. Maybe I hadn't had a decent shower since before the Heat began, either, but at least I'd tried to wash up as best I could, and made sure to put on deodorant before I got dressed each morning. I couldn't say the same for this useless specimen of humanity.

Were only the weak, the crazy, or the unscrupulous left? And if that was the case, what the hell did that say about me?

I decided I'd think about that later. In the meantime, I had bigger things to worry about. I needed to get away from this guy. Shooting him was not a particularly appealing prospect, but I would if I had to.

No wonder the voice had been urging me to get out of Albuquerque. I wished I hadn't dragged my feet quite so much about that. If I'd left straight away, as he'd told me to do, I would never have run into Chris Bowman...wouldn't be standing here now, with this milquetoast former bureaucrat holding his puny .22 on me and thinking he was Dirty Harry.

And where the hell was the voice? He had saved me from Chris the Creep twice, but was conspicuously absent at the moment. Did he think I could handle this guy on my own?

Time to find out, I supposed.

"Oh, I'm very useful," I snapped, reaching the rest of the way so I could pull the Glock out of the waistband of my Levi's and point it straight at the stranger's face.

He blinked and took a step backward. The gun wavered in his hands, and then he tightened his grip. "You didn't need to do that."

"Well, I kind of did, since you were holding a gun on me." Unlike him, I didn't move, didn't blink. "By the way, my father was a police officer. He made sure I knew how to shoot this thing. So don't think for a second that I'm holding this gun up for show, because I'm not. I know what I'm doing. The best thing you can do is back off and go find a car someplace else. There are thousands in the city up for grabs right now."

No response at first. His mouth opened and closed once, making him look like a fish on a hook. I got the distinct impression he didn't know what he should do—shoot, or turn tail and flee. That made him all the more dangerous, in my eyes, because I really didn't know how he was going to react. I doubted he was someone who'd been inclined toward criminal acts in his past life. But he'd been pushed to the limit by all the death he'd seen, and that made him volatile. Unpredictable.

"Please," I said softly. "Just go."

The gun shook in his hands. I remained motionless, the Glock still pointed directly at his face, my stance square and solid, just the way my father had taught me. Then I saw him twitch, and thought,

Oh, shit.

A *bang,* louder than I'd anticipated. Smoke puffed out from the chamber of the .22, and I knew the bullet was going to hit me. How could he miss at such close range?

Time slowed down, or possibly my thought processes sped up. I wasn't quite sure, but it was almost as if I could see the silvery-gray shape of the bullet speeding toward me. My entire body clenched, waiting for the shock of impact. At the same time, my finger clenched on the trigger of the Glock, and it went off with a much more impressive *bang* than the one that had issued from the .22. My ears began to ring. That was the first time I'd ever shot a gun without wearing earplugs, and damn, it was louder than I'd expected.

Two things happened then—first, it seemed as if the air in front of me shimmered, and the bullet the stranger had fired at me bounced away as if it had hit a pane of bulletproof glass. He had no such protection, however, and the shot I'd fired hit him in the chest, sending him flying backward, blood beginning to run down the front of the sweat-stained dress shirt he wore.

His head hit the pavement with a sharp *crack,* and I winced. But even as I did so, I realized I was all right. It should have been me lying there on the ground with dark blood trickling from my chest, but it wasn't.

Are you ready to leave now? the voice asked. For some reason, he sounded tired. Well, that made two of us.

I finally lowered the gun. "That was you?"

I told you I would protect you.

"Couldn't you have stopped him before he fired at me?" It seemed the voice was falling down a bit in the omnipotence department.

I cannot see everything. Your fear called me to you, just as it called to me last night when that creature broke into your house. When I saw what was happening, I put up the barrier to keep the bullet from touching you.

Just like that. What kind of powers did the voice control, to be able to construct an invisible shield that would deflect a bullet?

Obviously something far, far beyond anything I'd ever heard of.

But then, I'd already sort of gathered that.

Pulling in a breath, I flipped the Glock's safety back on, then stuck the gun into my waistband once again. After that, I looked over to where the stranger lay groaning on the asphalt. From the amount of blood that had pooled beneath him, I guessed he didn't have much longer to live. Should I be feeling guilty for that? I didn't know. At the moment, all I felt was a sort of bone-deep weariness...and the day wasn't even half over yet.

I approached him, then crouched down near his head. His eyes flickered open and fixed on me, plead- ing and scared. "I didn't want to do that," I said quietly.

"You should have just left me alone. There's plenty in this city for everyone."

A strangled sound came from his throat, possibly one of protest. I couldn't tell for sure, since he was obviously beyond forming actual words.

Although I knew I'd acted in self-defense, hadn't even squeezed the trigger until he'd shot at me, it was still hard to see him like this, knowing I couldn't do anything for his pain. "I'm sorry," I said at last, then straightened up and headed back to the Cherokee. The best thing I could do now was get the hell out of here.

I got in the car, shut the door, and pulled out of the parking space. As I drove away, I didn't look back.

Head north, the voice said once I was a few blocks from the Walgreens. *Get on the freeway.*

"Are you kidding?" I asked, hands tight on the steering wheel. Right then, I wasn't sure whether I had a death grip on the thing because of all the vehicles choking the roads, or because I was still shaking from that confrontation back in the parking lot. Maybe a little bit of both. "The freeway is going to be worse than the surface streets."

No, it isn't. Trust me.

Considering he'd just saved me from a speeding bullet, I decided to trust him.

The closest on-ramp was at Paseo del Norte, so I headed in that direction, keeping my speed below twenty-five miles an hour, and sometimes even slower than that, depending on how congested the street around me was. When I got to the on-ramp, I actually had to drive onto the shoulder to get around two vehicles that seemed to have crashed head-on into one another. Now it was impossible to tell whether they'd both been trying to get on the freeway at the same time, or whether the drivers had been so ill that they'd basically plowed into each other at the worst possible spot.

After that, though, the connector was clear enough, and I eased up onto I-25, keeping my speed down. The voice had been right, though—yes, there were still abandoned vehicles here, but they tended to have either crashed into the center divider or drifted over to the shoulder. The middle two lanes were fairly clear, although I still had to slow down from time to time to get around a car or truck that had stopped in the center of the highway.

In fact, the going was easy enough that I thought it safe to risk opening one of the water bottles so I could get a drink. My throat was parched, and I drank half the contents of the bottle without even stopping. In the passenger seat, Dutchie cocked her head and looked at me.

"I'll take care of you when we stop, girl," I told her. Along with the camping gear, I'd stowed a set of collapsible dog dishes in the back of the Cherokee, relics of the times when we used to take Sadie on day trips with us. My father never got rid of anything—which was why none of our cars ever actually lived in the garage—and I'd found the dishes when I was scrounging some of the other stuff.

Dutchie wagged her tail, then sort of collapsed onto the seat, curling up in a smaller ball than I would have thought possible. Up until then, she'd been sitting up and looking out the window, but, truth be told, once you were on the freeway, the sights and smells really weren't that interesting.

"So where are we going?" I asked of the general air around me. Judging by his delayed reaction to the man who'd assaulted me back at Walgreens, the voice wasn't necessarily around at all times. In this case, since I was asking a direct question, I had to hope he was close enough that he would hear me and respond.

North.

"Besides that," I snapped, irritated now. I'd done what he asked—Albuquerque was dropping farther and farther behind me, since I'd started out from the more northern end of the city sprawl anyway. At this point, I really couldn't see the reason behind the continuing games of evasion. "It's a little early for ski season."

That is all you need to know for now. I will tell you when it is time to get off the freeway.

I might have growled. But since I knew there was no point in pressing the issue, I took another swig of water and kept my gaze focused on the road. I actually hadn't been about to run out of gas; the tank was nearly full. I'd just hoped that lying about the gas situation would convince the stranger at Walgreens to choose some other prey. So much for that brilliant idea.

At any rate, I knew I wouldn't have to stop for gas for some time. Maybe not at all, depending on how far I was going. What I had in the Cherokee right now was probably enough to get me to the Colorado border, although I sincerely hoped I wasn't going quite that far.

So I continued to drive north on the freeway, pushing my speed closer to forty miles an hour as I left Albuquerque behind, and the vehicles littering the road gradually grew fewer and farther between. Not to say that the highway was completely empty, but it was open enough that I felt safe going a little faster. Wherever I was headed, I wanted to get there as quickly, albeit as safely, as I could.

An hour passed. Dutchie slept in the passenger seat, and I could feel my stomach begin to growl. If I'd been thinking clearly, I would've gotten some of the food out of the back and brought it up here with me, but shooting someone at point-blank range does tend to rattle your logic centers a bit. Ever since I'd left Albuquerque, I'd been telling myself that there was nothing else I could have done, that he'd shot at me first...but those kinds of reassurances only go so far when you're trying to wrestle with the realization that you'd killed someone earlier that day.

It was not your fault. The voice was soothing, its earlier weariness apparently gone. I must have been really broadcasting my angst, because in general, the voice only answered direct questions and didn't respond to my inner thoughts. *He forced the issue. You should not blame yourself.*

I knew that intellectually. But I also knew that killing, even in self-defense, carried its own weight of emotional consequences. When I was in high school, my father had shot someone while on duty—a drug dealer who'd drawn a .38 Special when he was pulled over for running a red light. My father didn't have much choice but to shoot. Even so, he was in counseling for months after that, coming to terms with what he'd done. Taking a human life was not something to be dismissed lightly. And how much heavier was the burden of doing something like that when so few people were even left alive?

I wasn't sure, but at the moment it felt pretty damn heavy.

The world has changed, the voice told me. *So you must change with it.*

"So I'm supposed to not care?" That didn't sound right at all. What was the point of surviving all this, if the only way to do it was to become a person I didn't like very much?

I did not say that. But there are certain realities you must face. There is nothing wrong with killing, if that is the only way for you to stay alive.

In other words, I shouldn't feel bad about acting in self-defense. Maybe someday I'd get to that point, but at the moment I'd had too many shocks in too short a period of time. I really just wanted to curl up in a ball somewhere and pretend the world didn't exist for a while.

Here, the voice told me. Take the turnoff for 84 north.

"Santa Fe?" I asked in some surprise. For some reason, I'd thought I'd be going much farther than that.

Yes, Santa Fe.

Well, thank God for small favors. I did as instructed and pulled onto the highway, which was more that in name than anything else, since in reality it was just a four-lane road cutting through town, with shops and schools on either side. Here I had to slow down again, as there was a good deal of stalled traffic once more. Not enough that I couldn't get around it when necessary, even if I had to pull up onto the island at the center of the street, but it was still nerve-wracking.

Then turn here, on Cerillos.

So we were heading into the heart of the town? I knew Santa Fe, although not intimately; my family had come here from time to time, mainly when my mother was tired of camping and hiking, and wanted us to get some culture. And I'd visited the town with Elena and Tori a couple of times, generally when Elena borrowed her parents' timeshare so we could get out of Albuquerque and let our hair down for a few days. Even then, though, I hadn't been the one driving. We always took Elena's car, because she had a Porsche Cayenne, which was a lot more impressive than my eight-year-old Honda or Tori's Ford pickup.

But I did know enough to realize if I stayed on my current route, I'd be heading toward the old town square and the touristy areas around it. Sort of a strange choice, if the voice was really that intent on keeping me out of population centers.

I slowed even more, as the road was getting narrower, and I knew I was about to enter the maze of one-way streets that twisted around Santa Fe's central square. Oddly, there weren't as many abandoned vehicles here. But this was a touristy area—maybe everyone had bugged out for home as soon as the infection began to spread.

And now down Alameda.

"So I'm not going to the center of town?"

No.

"Is it far?"

Not that far.

Good, because I knew I was going to need a bathroom fairly soon. I just had to hope that my destination included those sorts of civilized comforts, even if I wouldn't be able to flush after the first time.

I angled the Cherokee down Alameda, stopping every so often to go up on the curb to avoid yet another abandoned car. Luckily, the south side of the road ran along an open greenbelt, so there were no businesses located there, which meant no parked cars, either. To either side, the trees were brave with fluttering leaves of yellow and orange, but no one was around to admire their autumn finery, and I was too focused on my route to give them more than a passing glance.

The street continued in this way for some time, until I was out of the downtown area and in a more residential district, still heading steadily eastward. Since the voice had given me no further commands, I kept going.

And right here, it said, just when I thought I was going to be on Alameda forever.

I turned as instructed, moving onto Canyon Road. As I did so, I couldn't help wondering just where the heck I was going. This was still a residential area, but with the houses spaced farther apart. The upside was that I didn't have nearly as many stray cars to maneuver around.

Follow the curve, the voice said then.

Veering off to the left, I found myself now on Upper Canyon Road. It narrowed further, but even in my current focused state, I couldn't help being impressed by some of the compounds I passed. They had high adobe walls that seemed to stretch on for a full block. Just the kind of thing for people with fat wallets and a serious need for privacy.

The road wound on and on, steadily rising. It became more rutted, littered with gravel. I slowed down, although I didn't think it was quite time to engage the four-wheel drive. There was still pavement under my tires, albeit pavement that hadn't been very well maintained.

Eventually, though, even that rutted and gravelly pavement disappeared, and the road turned to dirt. I brought the Cherokee to a crawl, put it in neutral, and then engaged the four-wheel drive. After I felt it catch, I sped up again, but cautiously, knowing I should keep it around twenty-five for safety's sake.

Even up here there were scattered home sites, and I wondered if I would be told to turn off at one of them. But then the voice said, *This road,* indicating a dirt track that branched off from Upper Canyon, heading even farther into the hills.

I slowed down a little bit more, jolting and bouncing along the unpaved surface, which now was only wide enough to allow a single car through. Good thing

I probably didn't have to worry about someone coming this way from the other direction.

Dutchie, who'd been dozing for the past hour or more, blinked and got to her feet, pressing her nose to the window. She left quite a smudge, and I winced. Even though I knew my father was far past caring about what happened to the Cherokee, I still couldn't help experiencing some discomfort at knowing the SUV wouldn't exactly be in showroom condition by the time I got to my destination...whatever the hell that might be, out here in the middle of nowhere.

The track kept snaking farther and farther back into the hills. At least I'd had some experience driving off-road, so the rocky, rutted surface beneath the car didn't bother me too much. What did bother me was how far away from civilization this place must be. Had the voice lured me out here to....

To what? I asked myself with some scorn. *If he wanted to kill you or do anything else, he could have done it already. What would be the point in sending you out to the back of beyond like this?*

No point at all that I could tell.

Which didn't mean much.

At least the voice couldn't seem to hear my interior monologue. A minute or so later, it said, *Here.*

Another dirt track, even narrower than this one. It split off from the main road—if you could call it that—and wound up the side of a hill. Around the crest of that hill, I thought I spied a flash of shimmering gold leaves. Aspen trees?

I turned where the voice had directed, crawling along. Nothing about this hill seemed all that different from all the others I had passed. It was studded with juniper trees and yucca, with dry yellow grass in between. Yes, there was something of a road, but leading to what?

A few minutes later, I had my answer. Almost hidden until you came upon it, a compound of some sort was built just below the top of the hill. From what I could see, there was a main building and several smaller structures clumped around it. A high adobe wall appeared to circle the entire property. There was a metal gate with, of all things, the same Zia sun symbols as seen on the New Mexico flag adorning its four quadrants. At the moment, that gate stood wide open.

I brought the Cherokee to a stop. The voice said, *It is all right. There is no one here.*

"Why is the gate open?"

I opened it for you.

Not sure what I should do about that particular statement, I swallowed, then nudged the gas. The SUV moved forward slowly, and in a few more seconds, I was inside the compound. Almost as soon as the rear bumper had cleared the gate, it closed behind me.

"You again?" I asked, hoping I'd kept most of the worry out of my voice.

Yes.

Since there was nothing else to do, I took a quick survey of my surroundings. There seemed to be a large house, built in the typical Santa Fe style with sheer walls of thick adobe and a flat roof. Aspen trees surrounded it, their golden leaves fluttering in the afternoon breeze. Just past the house was an outbuilding that appeared to be a large garage with four bays, and beyond that something that looked like an extensive greenhouse.

Everything was very tidy, very neat, except for some fallen aspen leaves on the ground. Here, the driveway was crushed gravel, which crunched under the wheels of the Cherokee as I slowly inched it toward the garage. When I approached, the door to the bay farthest on the left rolled up and out of the way.

This time it wasn't entirely unexpected, but I still felt the skin along the back of my neck prickle as I pulled into the garage. The bay was quite wide, almost big enough for two cars, so I had plenty of room to park and then climb out. It was scrupulously clean, the walls finished. Overhead, a light bulb glowed.

I blinked at it, wondering if I was imagining things. Or maybe that was just more of the voice flexing its power. "Is that you?" I asked.

No. Look out, past the house.

I did as instructed, ignoring Dutchie's whines to be let out. She could hang on a minute longer. As I paused at the entrance to the garage, I saw that the property was very large, probably at least four or five acres, all enclosed within that high adobe wall. The other structure I'd glimpsed was in fact a greenhouse, but beyond that was a small solar farm, and beyond that still I spied a windmill whirling away.

"There's power here?" I had to fight the words past the lump in my throat; crazy how the mere thought of having electricity could get me so worked up.

That, and so much more. Come—let me show you.

I nodded, but then hurried over to open the passenger door. Dutchie sprang out, tail wagging, and promptly christened the place by squatting down on a patch of grass next to the garage. Despite everything, I couldn't help grinning and shaking my head.

But then I turned away from her so I could follow the flagstone path that led from the garage to the front door of the house. It was painted blue, and shaded by a long colonnaded façade, with heavy wood beams supporting the roof. Again, typical New Mexico architecture, but it looked heavy and solid. Safe.

I put my hand on the latch. The door was unlocked, and swung inward.

It was all I could do not to let out a gasp. The house was, as Elena might have put it, amazeballs.

Red tiled floors. Wooden viga ceilings overhead. A kiva fireplace in one corner. Big, heavy ranch-style furniture. Navajo rugs.

I stepped inside, Dutchie on my heels, then carefully closed the door behind me. My footsteps echoed off the shining floor as I moved farther into the house. It was the sort of place I might have seen in a magazine, with doorways of sculpted adobe, Mexican star lights made of pierced tin hanging in the entry, every piece seemingly selected for one particular spot and that spot only, unique and beautiful.

"What is this place?" I breathed, after I'd recovered myself enough to move from the living room into the dining room, which was dominated by a copper-topped table big enough for twelve and sturdy chairs of dark wood with leather seats and nail-head accents. Landscapes of the area around Santa Fe hung on the walls.

It was built by a real estate developer from Phoenix who wanted to make sure he would survive the end of the world in comfort. Unfortunately, his plans did not take disease into account, only war and civil unrest.

What was I supposed to say to that?

Shaking my head, I went into the kitchen, which was roughly twice the size of my little over-the-garage apartment. I heard a faint humming noise and wondered what it might be, then realized it was the refrigerator. Strange how only a few days without those sorts of background noises could render them unfamiliar, alien.

I had to know. I walked over to the refrigerator and opened the door. Inside, it was stocked with items that wouldn't spoil easily—cheese, sausage, lunch meats. A six-pack of Kilt Lifter ale sat on the bottom shelf. When I peeked inside the freezer section, it seemed as if it was full of other similar "guy food" sorts of items: frozen pizza, tamales, taquitos. A box of Hot Pockets. A couple of bags of frozen chicken breasts from Trader Joe's.

Dutchie cocked her head, tongue lolling out. I wondered if she'd gotten a whiff of the cheese or sausages in the deli section of the fridge.

"It looks like the owner just stepped out," I said, my tone only partly accusing. "Are you sure no one's been here?"

Quite sure. The developer died two days ago, and the man he hired to watch over this place passed away yesterday, only three days after the last time he checked in here. You'll find more food in the pantry, and a storeroom in the basement with canned goods, flour, sugar...that sort of thing. The greenhouse has tomatoes, lettuce, carrots, strawberries, and more.

Basically, pretty much anything I would need to keep on living for a good deal longer. And while doing it basically in the lap of luxury.

"How did you find this place?" I asked. I sort of doubted it was the kind of property that popped up on Trulia.

I knew you would need a sanctuary. So I...looked around.

A sanctuary. Yes, that was what this place felt like. More questions bubbled to my mind, but I wasn't sure the voice would answer any of them.

And in the end, what did it matter? I was here, and I was safe. No one left alive even knew this place existed, and I could hide here for...months. Years, probably. Never mind that I didn't really want to contemplate what it would be like to be out here for years and years with only a disembodied voice and a dog for company.

Well, I didn't have to think about that now. I had other things to do.

"Come on, Dutchie," I said. "Time to unpack the car.

"We're home."

CHAPTER NINE

In the kitchen cupboards, I found brightly colored Fiesta ware, and heavy blown-glass tumblers and goblets that I thought must have come from Mexico. I poured water—yes, the taps worked, thanks to a well out back that was powered by the windmill—into a bowl for Dutchie, and then tipped some of the Blue Buffalo dry food I'd brought from home into another bowl. She set to, lapping at the water greedily, crunching away at the dog food. I could tell she thought she was home, too. At some point I'd have to see about replenishing her food supply, but that could wait a while. Based on the amount of kibble left in the bag, she'd need some more in about a week. In a pinch, I could defrost some of those frozen chicken breasts and cook them up for her, but it would probably be smarter to head into Santa Fe and go for-aging there for some real dog food.

For the moment, though, I was content to explore the rest of the house. It was very large, probably at least four thousand square feet, although I'd be the first to admit that I wasn't very good at judging those sorts of things. But there were three bedrooms, as well as an office, a sitting room, and a family room, in addition to the living room and kitchen. Off the back of the house was another covered patio, and surprisingly lush plantings of various native trees. In a secluded corner, a solar-powered fountain bubbled away. It felt tranquil, sheltered, so far removed from the horrors I'd seen in Albuquerque that I might as well have been on another planet.

Here, I thought I might be able to heal.

After I'd taken care of Dutchie and put all my things away, stowing the guns on a shelf in the master bedroom closet, I treated myself to a long, hot shower. And it was hot, thanks to the solar water heater. The storms I'd feared might be moving in had never mate-rialized, and the day was sun and shadow, but with enough sunlight to keep everything in the house run-ning. I soaked in that shower, letting the water run over me, allowing it to wash away the terror and fear and tragedy I'd left in a place I could no longer think of as home. I would never be able to forget any of it, but now, for the first time, I thought I might be able to focus on what lay ahead, instead of what was behind me.

The softest rugs in the world had been laid down over the tile in the bathroom, and I got out and dried myself off, using the equally soft towels hanging from the rack. If the owner of this place truly had been a real estate developer, it was obvious that he'd spared no expense in outfitting his survival getaway. I had to wonder if he'd actually ever been here, or merely hired people to build and decorate the place to his specifications. Something about it did feel...well, not exactly soulless, because it was too warm and inviting for that, but staged, maybe, as if an interior designer had done all the heavy lifting in making the decorating decisions. And had the developer intended to bring someone with him to share the world after the apocalypse, or had he planned to live in all this luxury alone?

Whatever the case, it was certainly far, far more than I ever could have expected might be awaiting me at the end of my journey. I blotted my hair, found a hair dryer in one of the drawers in the vanity area, and experienced the luxury of actually being able to blow-dry my hair, something I'd thought I'd never be able to do again. I put on clean clothes and my flats, since I wasn't planning to go hiking anytime soon. The next day, I'd roam around and explore the property thoroughly, but for now I was content to cocoon indoors.

When I emerged into the family room, the voice asked, *Are you feeling better now?*

"Much," I replied, although I couldn't help wondering how much it could see. Had it been spying on me in the shower?

No, that was ridiculous. And it had been polite enough to wait to address me until I was in one of the more public areas of the house.

"I'm going to make some dinner," I added. "You want anything?"

Another one of those sounds that might have been a chuckle. *No, thank you. But do enjoy exploring the kitchen.*

In that moment, it seemed as if the voice had gone again...if it could ever be said to actually be *here* in the corporeal sense of the word.

I went on into the kitchen, where Dutchie greeted me with a thumping tail. Had she been here the whole time, waiting to see if I would come back and make some people food?

Apparently so, because the second I opened one package of sausages, her tail began wagging even more fiercely.

"This is not for dogs," I told her in the severest tones I could muster, but she only smiled up at me and cocked her head. Well, that had never worked on my old dog Sadie, either.

I could have nuked the sausages, but for some reason it felt better to rustle out a skillet and cook them the old-fashioned way. The savory smell filled the kitchen, and my stomach rumbled. After digging around in the freezer, I located some frozen home-style potatoes and added them to the mix. Yes, I really needed some fresh fruit or vegetables, but right then I was suddenly too tired to bother with going out to the greenhouse. It could wait another day.

What I did find, tucked under one of the counters, was a wine refrigerator. "Thank you, Mr. Real Estate Developer," I breathed, looking at the gleaming bottles, all chilled to a perfect fifty-four degrees. Not that I knew the first thing about wine, but I did know about needing a drink, and boy, did I need one.

I selected a Black Mesa Montepulciano. I had no idea what a Montepulciano even was, but it sounded exotic. Probably far too exotic for my prosy meal of sausages and potatoes, which were still happily sizzling away on the stove top, but I doubted anyone from *Wine Spectator* magazine was going to drop in and grade me on my wine pairings.

There was a drawer seemingly dedicated only to wine openers and related gadgets—stoppers, little metal collars with padding inside to keep wine from dripping down the side of a bottle after it had been opened. I'd never been able to manage a waiter-style corkscrew, but there was also one of those "jumping jack"–style openers, and I selected that and went to work on the wine bottle, keeping an eye on the potatoes and sausages the whole time.

The sound of a cork coming out a wine bottle has to be one of the happiest sounds in the world, and I thought I could use a little happiness right then. I pulled one of the heavy blown-glass goblets out of the cupboard and filled it approximately halfway. Everything I'd read and heard said you were supposed to let wine breathe, but I wasn't going to bother with that. I took a sip and closed my eyes. No, I hadn't been much of a wine drinker, had always ordered mixed drinks or tequila shots when I was out with my friends. Now, though, I started to understand the appeal of wine, the smooth darkness of it on my lips, the gentle warmth it seemed to spread through my limbs.

I allowed myself another sip, then went back to the stove so I could turn over the sausages and stir the potatoes around a little. They were basically done, so I scrounged in the cupboard for a plate and dumped everything onto it. Dutchie's tail began to wag frantically, and I couldn't help smiling.

"Okay, we'll see if there's anything left over," I told her, then got out a knife and fork, picked up my goblet of wine, and went into the family room. No way was I going to be the only person sitting down at that massive copper dining room table.

But the family room was a much cozier space, and I settled myself on the couch and placed the plate of food and my wine glass on the coffee table. A flat-screen TV hung on one wall, although it wasn't going to do me much good unless the real estate developer had a stash of DVDs hidden somewhere. He probably did, but in that moment I was too hungry to worry about it. As with so many other things, I'd go exploring later.

There was also a kiva-style fireplace in one corner, with a nice stack of wood in a basket next to it. After I was done eating, I thought I might light a fire and allow myself to simply sit here for a while, quiet, letting my food digest. Hell, maybe I'd even drink that whole bottle of wine. After everything I'd been through, getting drunk sounded like it might not be a half-bad idea.

But no...I knew I wouldn't do that. Just the glass, and maybe half of one afterward. The voice had reassured me I was safe here, and had closed the gate to the compound behind me, but until I'd slept a few nights unmolested, I wasn't about to let my guard down like that. Dutchie had proven to be a good watchdog, and I had a feeling a place like this had some decent built-in security, but even so, being careless seemed like a good way to get myself killed.

Instead, I drank the wine slowly, taking small sips in between bites of my food, until my glass was empty and my plate almost so. There were a few potatoes and the end of one sausage left, and I put the plate down on the floor so Dutchie could have the rest of it. Who cared if that wasn't the most hygienic thing in the world to do? She was deliriously happy about getting some table scraps, and as far as I was concerned, she'd earned them.

Once she'd polished the plate clean, I picked it up, as well as my wine glass, and went back to the kitchen. The plate went in the dishwasher, and I poured enough wine into my goblet to get it to a little below the half-way mark. In the drawer with all the other wine accoutrements, I found a stopper, so I jammed that into the open bottle, figuring I'd finish it off the next day.

And although I was bone-tired, sitting in front of the fire didn't seem so appealing after all. I might as well get more of a handle on this place that was now supposed to be my home. Going back to the family room, I discovered that the large carved cabinet placed up against one wall did in fact hold the real estate developer's Blu-Ray collection. Most of it was fairly typical new-release stuff, with some action classics thrown in. There was also an entire shelf of porn, and I just had to laugh when I looked at it. It was pretty obvious what he'd intended to do with at least some of his time after surviving the zombie apocalypse, or whatever.

I closed the cabinet with one hand, lifted the wine goblet with the other so I could take a drink, and wandered off down the hallway that led to the bedrooms and the office. That was the space which really

interested me the most. After flicking on the light—
and marveling at how easy that was—I went into the
room and took a quick survey. Again, the furniture here
was dark distressed oak, a perfect match to the haci-
enda-style feel of the rest of the house. One wall was
mainly window, covered in wooden shutters. Against
another wall was a large desk with what looked like a
brand-new iMac sitting on it.

There was also a gun safe. I set down my wine
glass on the desk, then went over to the safe and tested
the lock. I suppose it was silly to think that the thing
would have been open, but I couldn't help experiencing a stab of disappointment when the doors wouldn't
budge. My father had trained me not to leave guns
lying around, and although I was sure they would be
fine where I'd put them on the shelf in the closet, I'd
feel even better if I could lock them up.

Sitting next to the desk was a file cabinet, and I
opened that, quickly rifling through its contents. This
was a trove—I found manuals for the computer, the
drip setup in the greenhouse, all the appliances, the
security system. That seemed to feed into the iMac,
so I touched the space bar on the keyboard, waking
it up from its sleep. Thank God it didn't seem to be
password protected; I was able to find the security pro-
gram easily enough, which brought up a feed from a
number of cameras. At the moment it was showing a
grid of all nine of them, although it appeared that I

could also expand one image and then rotate through them if I preferred.

Not that it mattered one way or another, as far as I could tell. By then it was completely dark, and the cameras didn't show much of anything. I supposed it made sense not to have security lights blaring around the exterior of the house and the perimeter of the property; that would only serve as a beacon to show that someone was living out here. And actually, after I toggled around a bit, I realized that no lights were needed, as the cameras switched into infrared mode in the dark. Pretty high-tech.

How much had the developer spent building this place? I couldn't begin to guess, but it had to be at least a million dollars. And all for nothing...well, at least where he was concerned. I was more than grateful that the house existed, and that the voice had found it for me, but it still seemed somewhat ironic that so much money had been spent to defend against something which ended up having no defense.

That thought sobered me, and I picked up my goblet and took a large swallow of wine. Dutchie had followed me in here, settling down on the floor in a little ball. There was something almost resigned about her posture, as if she knew that once a human being started mucking around on a computer, they were going to be useless for a good number of hours.

But that wasn't why I'd come in here. I only wanted to know what the room held, and now that I'd seen the kind of security that was protecting this place, I felt a good deal better. Had the system been on when I got here, and the voice had simply disengaged it to allow me to enter, or had he switched it on once I was safely inside the compound? He'd clearly intended for me to come here all along, so I had a feeling it was probably the former. There hadn't been much chance of someone accidentally stumbling across this place, but even so, better safe than otherwise.

Among the manuals was the guide that had come with the gun safe. I flipped through it with one hand, sipping from my wine glass at the same time. When I got to the last page, I saw that some numbers had been written down along the edge of that leaf. The combination?

Only one way to find out.

I put down the wine glass and went over to the safe, then slowly spun the dial around to match the sequence of numbers I'd found inside the manual. There was a soft click, and the door opened outward.

Even though I'd grown up around my father's arsenal, I couldn't help letting out a gasp at what I found. There was—well, an arsenal worthy of holding off an entire horde of zombies. Shotguns and rifles and a parade of handguns, along with box after box of ammo.

The problem wouldn't be defending this place if necessary, but deciding which gun to use to do it.

Well, that and trying to squeeze my own meager collection in here.

I closed the safe, reclaimed my wine glass, and finished the rest of it with one swallow. After that, I took the empty glass with me and performed a quick inspection of the other rooms. Nothing out of the ordinary, just bedrooms decorated with the same taste and flair as the rest of the house. Another bathroom, not quite as luxurious as the one in the master suite, but still large enough that two people could comfortably brush their teeth in there or perform other bathroom prep as necessary. It seemed sort of a shame to waste all this space on me, but truthfully, so far I hadn't come across any survivors I'd be willing to share this house with. Yes, there had to be some good people who'd made it through the Heat unscathed. I sure hadn't seen them yet, though.

Suddenly feeling even more tired, I headed back to the kitchen so I could rinse out my wine glass and set it on the counter. For the first time, I noticed a door off to one side; I opened it and saw it concealed the laundry room, which was large and well laid out as well, with a state-of-the-art washer and dryer combo, as well as plenty of storage and a separate wash tub for scrubbing out stubborn stains, or whatever. Inside the cupboards I found what looked like a lifetime supply of detergent, along with all the spare towels and sheets for the various bathrooms and bedrooms. It seemed clear that the developer hadn't been worried about the appliances using up too much of the power the solar farm produced.

Well, if he hadn't worried about it, then I wouldn't worry, either, when the time came. Right now I had enough clothes to last me another week, so laundry wasn't exactly a concern.

The master bedroom had its own kiva fireplace, and I decided it would be better to have a fire there. Having a fireplace in my own bedroom felt deliciously decadent, and the thought of having the flames there to warm me through the night seemed extra appealing.

So I brushed my teeth but didn't worry about my face, since I'd taken a shower only a few hours earlier, and then got some logs from the basket on the floor near the hearth and made a stack the way my father had shown me. There was a lighter on a shelf nearby, so I used that to get things going. Dutchie watched all this with some bemusement, but once the fire got crackling away and began to spread its heat through the room, she let out a contented little sigh and curled up on the rug, her eyes closing almost immediately.

I know how you feel, Dutchie, I thought. Even so, something in me was reluctant to turn off the bedside lamp, as if, once I had done so, I'd never be able to get the light back. Silly, I knew. It wouldn't even be fully dark with the lamp shut off, as the fire was certainly adequate to illuminate the room.

Still, I sat there on the bed for a long time, looking at the glow of the lamp on the bedroom's warm terra-cotta-painted walls, at the gold leaf detailing on the wall where the door was located. Everything felt cozy and quiet and safe, and yet for some reason I couldn't bring myself to reach over to the lamp and turn the knob. Finally, I got up off the bed, went to the closet, and retrieved the Smith and Wesson revolver from the shelf. I laid it on the table next to the bed, then took a deep breath and shut off the lamp.

It wasn't dark. The room danced with firelight, and wasn't even completely silent, between the crackling of the logs and Dutchie's soft snores. I settled my head against the pillow, breathing in the indefinable scent of clean linens. Had the caretaker put fresh sheets on the bed when he'd come by a few days earlier? It certainly seemed that way.

But I didn't want to think about that, because then I'd think about how he was dead, and the man who'd built this house, and Elena and Tori and my aunt and uncle...my mother and father. Devin. Even as I tried to push those thoughts away, I could feel the telltale lump in my throat that meant I was dangerously close to bursting into sobs.

Don't cry, I told myself. Don't. *It won't bring them back. All you can do is keep living, so there'll still be someone around to remember them.*

At first glance, that notion might not have seemed very reassuring. Somehow, though, it did calm me, and I found myself falling asleep, succumbing at last to the weariness of the day and the softness of the bed in which I lay. The last thing I heard was a soft *pop* from the hearth as a log split and settled down on top of the others.

I'd never been much for dreaming. That is, I knew I must dream, because everyone did, but I hardly ever remembered any of those dreams. I was never the one recounting in excruciating detail my crazy dreams about flying or driving my car up the side of a building, or whatever. And I certainly never had *those* kinds of dreams, the kind you awake from all hot and bothered.

But I did that night.

I dreamed I lay in that bed, with the warm glow of the fire flickering against the walls and the comforting scent of wood smoke in the air. The strange thing was, I dreamed that I slept, and that I awoke to strong arms around me, holding me close, and someone kissing me. In my dream, I didn't think that was strange at all. I opened my mouth to this dream man, tasted the sweetness of his lips, felt him release me from the embrace so he could caress my body, even as I reached over to touch him, to feel his arousal.

And it seemed so natural for him to press me down into the bed, to push himself into me so that we were moving together, my legs wrapped around him, driving him farther into me. This was all done in complete silence; only when the orgasm hit did I finally cry out, but softly. And he said nothing at all, although I could feel the climax shudder through him as well. We stilled, lying in bed, our breaths filling the silence. Then his lips brushed against my cheek, and I heard him whisper, *Beloved*.

I sat up in bed then, heart racing, and pressed my palms flat against the mattress. Shaking, I put one hand to my chest. Unlike in the dream, I was still dressed, wearing the sleep shirt I'd put on before I went in to brush my teeth. My mouth tasted of mint, not...him. And I could tell that no one had touched me. Things didn't...feel...any different.

Just a dream. A horribly vivid dream. In a way, I could even understand it. I was feeling alone, and the voice had been my only real companion for the past few days. All right, I had Dutchie, but that wasn't exactly the same thing. Was it so strange for my subconscious mind to turn that disembodied voice into a sort of dream lover, someone to make me feel as if I weren't the only person left alive on the planet?

Maybe not, but I still felt shaken to my core. I pushed back the sheets and blankets and duvet, then crawled out of bed and went to the bathroom. There, I splashed water on my face, trying to calm myself, and telling myself I should be glad that I was someplace where I had the luxury of running water.

That no-nonsense thought did help me to regain my composure somewhat, and I headed into the bedroom after that, pausing to put another couple of logs on the fire and stir it up a bit with the poker before finally returning to bed. Through all of this, Dutchie had slept peacefully, apparently not discommoded at all by my wandering around.

I got back in bed, then pulled in a deep breath, and another. After everything I'd been through, was I really going to let a dream rattle me? I told myself that I needed to let it go, that everything would be fine.

I just wasn't sure whether I believed those reassurances or not.

CHAPTER TEN

I SPENT THE NEXT FEW DAYS REALLY GETTING myself accustomed to the property and everything on it—the greenhouse, the solar farm, even the garage, which was hiding a Polaris ATV in the farthest bay. When I found that, it somehow made me miss my father even more. He'd always wanted one, but a vehicle intended solely for off-roading was a luxury that just hadn't been in the family budget.

As the voice had told me, there was a good deal of food stored in the basement. Scratch that; there was enough food down there to satisfy the most rabid prepper, shelf after shelf of canned goods and staples such as flour and sugar and cooking oil, and enough spices that I could probably bake something different every day for the next year and still not use everything up. In fact, the basement was so extensive that I got the impression it was actually bigger than the house itself, spreading beyond the walls of the structure directly above it.

The greenhouse was set up on a drip system, one supplied by the same well that gave the house its water. I found a good deal of produce that was at its peak or even just past it, so I harvested that as best I could, eating what needed to be consumed right away and putting the rest in the refrigerator. On the bookshelves in the office, there were a number of reference books on all sorts of topics of interest to the homesteader or survivalist—home canning, sewing, weaving, butchering...even how to make your own bullets. In fact, I found the molds for that very activity down in the basement, along with a quantity of black powder and other supplies. I had to hope none of it would explode and send Dutchie and me sky-high one day.

Although having every conceivable supply on hand should have made me feel better, in truth it only depressed me. I thought of being here so long that I would have to start canning food or sewing my own clothes, of having to go out in the ATV to hunt deer or elk. Even though my father had taken me hunting a few times, I'd never had the heart to pull the trigger. Maybe if I were starving I'd feel differently about the whole thing, but until then I couldn't conceive of killing something so beautiful.

The one thing the compound didn't have was dog food. I wasn't sure what to make of that; maybe Mr. Real Estate Developer wasn't a dog person, although you'd think he would've factored dogs into his survival plan, just because they were good to have around in case things got dicey. Whatever the reason, I was down to about a day's worth of dry food left for Dutchie, which meant I needed to go foraging.

For some reason, the voice had been fairly scarce the past couple of days. I wondered at its absence, thinking that maybe it believed its work was done, since it had gotten me here safely. All the same, I thought I'd better telegraph my plans, let it know I was leaving the compound for a few hours.

"Dutchie's almost out of food," I said as I got the shotgun out of the gun safe. I already wore a gleaming Ruger in a holster on my hip, said armament courtesy of the trove I'd found within that safe. Possibly it would have made better sense to take along a gun I was more familiar with, but I couldn't resist the chrome-plated allure of that Ruger. My father would have known how much it cost, but I didn't have a clue. A lot, that's for sure.

Silence met my announcement, so I went on, "I'm going down into Santa Fe for a few hours. Can I assume the coast is clear?"

Nothing again, and I frowned. But since I'd seen more clouds massing up to the northeast, I didn't want to dilly-dally. Maybe twenty minutes in and twenty minutes out; I'd actually seen a PetSmart down a side street as I was making my way along Cerrillos Road when I came into town, so at least I wouldn't have to waste a lot of time looking for a pet store. Having no cell service and no way to look anything up on the Internet definitely made what should have been easy tasks a lot more difficult.

With a shrug, I closed the safe and locked it, then headed out to the kitchen. I really didn't need anything else in the way of supplies, although the chilliness of the nights even now, in early October, told me that the cold-weather gear I'd brought along might not be sufficient for a full-blown Santa Fe winter. Well, if I had time to poke around, I'd see if I could find something.

As I was getting ready, I debated whether to bring Dutchie along, and then decided against it. She was safe here, and I knew I'd move faster if I didn't have her along. Besides, I needed someplace to stow the shotgun. I wasn't sure if she'd take kindly to being relegated to the back seat so the shotgun could...ride shotgun.

I patted her head, got her some fresh water, and then told her I'd be going out but would be back soon. Since she'd gotten used to me coming and going between the house and the garage or the kitchen and the greenhouse, she took this announcement in stride, lapping up some of the water I'd just poured before she settled down on the rug in front of the oven. That was one of her new favorite spots, which made things sort of difficult when I was trying to cook.

Smiling, I went out the back door and made my way along the flagstone walk to the garage. In my explorations, I'd found the remotes for the garage and the front gate, so technically I didn't need the voice to let me in and out. Still, I couldn't help wondering where he'd gotten to.

With a shrug, I opened the garage door, then climbed into the Cherokee. I leaned the shotgun against the passenger seat, checked the fuel gauge, and backed out, glad that I wouldn't have to worry about getting more gas anytime soon. This place felt like it was out in the middle of nowhere—and it was—but I doubted it was more than five miles one way from here to the city center. I could go back and forth at least twenty more times before I had to bother with fueling up.

The dirt track hadn't improved any since the last time I'd driven over it, and I gritted my teeth as I bounced and jounced along at a steady twenty miles an hour. It was a relief to hit the actual road, even though it wasn't in the greatest shape, either. But at least here I could increase my speed to thirty, slowing occasionally to go around an abandoned truck or car.

Nothing had changed. I wasn't sure why I'd expected it to, except I supposed that was a normal, human thing to think—the world around us had never been static, people and cars coming and going, shifting their positions. Here, though, there were no more people left to change anything. Or rather, so few of them probably remained that it would take some doing to run into any of them. I was a little hazy on the population of Santa Fe before the Heat laid everything waste, but I had a feeling there couldn't be more than a hundred or so people left in the general area, if even that much.

Eventually, I backtracked my way to Cerrillos, then drove some distance down the street before I spotted the PetSmart off to my left. I turned—going wide to avoid a Ford Explorer sitting right in the middle of the intersection—and pulled into the store parking lot. There weren't that many vehicles here, most likely because people had been thinking about other things than feeding their pets when the doomsday disease swept through town.

When I went inside, my father's heavy police-issue flashlight in one hand, I was relieved to see that all the live small animals—the rats and mice and gerbils, the birds and lizards and snakes—had apparently flown the coop. How they'd gotten out, I had no idea, unless this was another example of "being taken care of," as the voice had assured me back in Albuquerque. There was evidence of the food being tampered with, but although anything within reach of a large dog's muzzle seemed to be either gone or half-eaten, there were still bags and bags on the upper shelves. I got a shopping cart and loaded it up, took it to the Cherokee, and dumped the bags there, then repeated the process until my arms ached and I wouldn't be able to see out the back window if I kept it up any longer. That would be enough to see Dutchie through the winter, and after that—well, I'd just come foraging again.

I also grabbed a miscellany of dog treats and dog toys from the displays at the front of the store, and wedged those in and around the big twenty-pound bags of dog food. Dutchie was definitely going to be one spoiled doggie, but I thought she deserved it.

During this whole process, which I estimated took me about twenty minutes or so, I didn't see any evidence of anyone else being around. True, a pet store probably wasn't the sort of place where survivors hung out, but I felt myself relax a little. Maybe this was why the voice had let me alone—it had known I had nothing to fear on this particular trip.

Humming to myself, I got back in the SUV and pointed it northward, back along the way I'd come. When I got to the intersection where I should have turned on Alameda to head back up into the hills, though, I found myself slowing down, and then cutting left so I could drive up Don Gaspar.

Almost at once, I heard the voice in my head. *Jessica, what are you doing?*

Relief flooded through me. So I hadn't been completely abandoned. "I want to see."

See what?

"The center of town. I want to see if it's all right."

Why should that matter?

"Because it matters," I said, an edge of irritation in
my voice. "It was a cultural center. Lots of museums,
historical sites. What can it hurt to look?"

Silence for a few seconds. *You may not like what
you see.*

Ice etched its way down my spine, but I attempted
to ignore it, instead asking, "So where the hell have you
been, anyway? The Bahamas?"

He didn't answer directly, but said, *You missed me?*

Did I want to admit that I had? Probably not.
Hedging, I replied, "Well, I love Dutchie, but she's not
the world's greatest conversationalist."

I heard one of those low chuckles. *You may be right
in that.*

Despite what he'd just said about my not liking
what I would see, I couldn't help smiling. That smile
faded abruptly, though, as I came around the corner to
Santa Fe's famous plaza. In good weather—and even
not-so-good weather—the plaza was usually full of
people, whether tourists, musicians, vendors, or locals
out to get some air. I'd expected it to be empty. What
I hadn't expected to see were the obvious signs of

looting, of storefronts smashed in, merchandise scattered across the sidewalk.

Mouth grim, I parked the Cherokee in a place that would have been heinously illegal a few days earlier, straddling the curb at the intersection of Palace Avenue and San Francisco Street. There really wasn't anyplace else, as cars still lined the streets, their meters run out long ago. I didn't bother to look and see if there were piles of gray dust inside those cars. If their owners had died outside, the wind would've blown their remains away days earlier.

"I don't understand," I said. "Why would people loot here? Food or medical supplies I can understand, but expensive jewelry and art?"

I don't know for certain. Perhaps they were attempting to assert some control over their environment as everything was falling apart.

That was one way of looking at it. My hiking boot hit something that clinked against the sidewalk, and I looked down to see that it was a heavy gold cuff bracelet studded with sapphires and diamonds. I thought I even knew which store it had come from, because it was a place where Elena and Tori and I had pressed our noses to the window and gawked at the wares inside, trying to figure out how anyone would pay almost fifty grand for a pair of earrings, even if said earrings were huge drops of tanzanite and diamond that looked as if they should be at the Academy Awards, not a shop window in Santa Fe.

Without thinking, I bent down and picked up the bracelet, then slid it onto my wrist. It was cold against my skin; the day had turned cloudy and dark, the temperature dropping with it. I even thought I felt the first spatter of a raindrop or two against my face.

Or maybe those were tears.

I saw other items scattered around—a lone earring, a trinket box of carved stone. For some reason, I began to pick them up, gathering everything I could find and then taking it into the nearest store, a shop that seemed to have specialized in high-end western gear. It had been hit, too, but not as badly as the jewelry stores.

Again the voice asked, *Jessica, what are you doing?*

"What does it look like I'm doing?" I asked angrily. "I'm cleaning this up."

A long pause. Why?

"Because—because someone loved these things once. Someone made them, and someone chose them to sell in their store, and I don't want them lying all over the place like garbage. They deserve better than that." As I spoke, I realized that tears were running down my cheeks, dripping bitter salt into my mouth.

When it spoke again, the voice was very gentle. *My dear, they are just things.*

"I know that!" I raged. "But I also know they're the only things *left!* So I'm not going to leave them here!"

Silence again. Then, *Jessica, do not distress yourself so. I will take care of it.*

I don't even know how to describe what happened next. A wind came swirling out of nowhere, seeming to come in and pick up all the detritus in the square—baskets and rugs and loose bits of jewelry and hats and paintings and pots, everything that had been scattered on the ground during the looting. It coalesced into a cloud of debris, snaking through the air and rushing into the open door of a shop, then slamming it shut.

Blinking, I stared at the streets around me, saw how they were clear of everything except a few scattered leaves, all evidence of chaos gone as if it had never existed. Somehow, I managed to find my voice. "That—that was you?"

Yes.

"But...why?"

I do not like seeing you in distress.

What could I possibly say to that? I swallowed, my throat dry. The air around me was still once more, heavy and cold. Again I felt the stinging touch of rain sharp against my face.

"Thank you," I managed at last.

Go home, beloved.

I nodded, then made myself turn around and go back to the Cherokee, to climb behind the wheel and turn the key in the ignition. Perhaps there was more damage beyond the plaza, but I didn't want to look. I'd seen enough for one day.

The trip home was uneventful, though, and in a way it felt good to busy myself with hauling all those bags of dog food out of the back of the SUV and storing them in the basement, save for one that I shoved into a corner of the pantry. I also got out a chewy treat and gave it to Dutchie, who wagged her tail ecstatically and settled down on her rug to start masticating.

It wasn't until later, when I'd put away the Ruger I hadn't needed and similarly stowed the shotgun, then sat down to catch my breath, that I stared down at the heavy gold bracelet on my wrist. How much was it worth?

Wrong question, in this time when a pound of beef was probably worth a lot more than a pound of gold. The more accurate question to ask would be, *What did this cost?*

I didn't know. I'd had a small collection of costume jewelry and a few pieces of Native American work, mostly turquoise. When I packed my belongings and left Albuquerque, I hadn't brought any of it along, save the small silver hoops I was already wearing. Just hadn't seen the point.

But this thing, which should have been adorning the wrist of some movie star on the red carpet? Who knows. Probably as much as the Grand Cherokee had cost my father when he bought it brand new.

I twisted the bracelet around and around, and then became aware of something sharp sticking into my left hip bone. Puzzled, I reached into the pocket of my jeans, thinking that maybe I'd stuck something in there earlier and forgotten about it.

My fingers closed around two cool, heavy objects. I drew them out, then opened my hand to see what the hell they were.

For a second or two, I just stared down at them. Then, because I couldn't think of what else to do, I began to laugh.

In my hand were the tanzanite and diamond earrings Elena and Tori and I had admired on our last trip to Santa Fe.

I didn't bring up the subject of the earrings. How could I? That would mean I'd have to ask how the voice knew I'd seen those earrings and fallen partly in love with them, even though I'd known I would never in a million years be able to afford something like that.

No, I'd stowed them in the drawer of my nightstand and tried to put the incident out of my mind. And since in the days that followed, I didn't need to leave the compound, I didn't hear from the voice much. If I was trying to find a certain item, like a screwdriver, I'd ask where it might be located, and the voice would always answer. Otherwise, though, it seemed to be leaving me alone again, allowing me to find some equilibrium in my new life here.

There was, surprisingly, enough to keep me busy. As I'd promised my father, I wrote down as much as I could about the way the Heat had come to Albuquerque, and what the city had looked like when I left. That was a spare and painful narrative, though, and so I also wrote down random memories, just so I wouldn't forget them—the surprise party my father had thrown my mother for her fiftieth birthday. Devin's touchdown at the homecoming game last year. The crazy artist who'd approached me on one of our girls' Santa Fe trips and told me I had an amazing face and that he wanted to paint me. Things like that...bright pieces of a world now gone forever.

In addition to all that, I tended the plants in the greenhouse and puttered around the house and took Dutchie for long walks, which also helped me inspect the perimeter of the property. The wall was in perfect condition, as far as I could tell, and a good barrier against wild animals, of which there were plenty in the area. I could hear the coyotes calling at night sometimes, and one time the snarl of a cougar or bobcat. Needless to say, I hadn't ventured out to investigate, although Dutchie had gone nuts, growling and barking as she moved from window to window, presumably following along as the wild cat moved along the wall that bordered the property.

But none of those animals had gotten close enough to trigger the security system, which was why I almost had a heart attack one afternoon, about ten days after I'd come to Santa Fe, when all of a sudden the house was filled with a shrill alarm. I'd been sitting in the breakfast nook in the kitchen, keeping one eye on the book I was reading and another on the loaf of bread I had in the oven. Bread-making was a new venture for me, but really, what else did I have to do with my time?

I shot a quick glance at the timer and saw the loaf still had around a half hour to go, then bolted from the kitchen so I could bring up the security feed on the computer in the office. After I jiggled the mouse to wake up the iMac, I saw the grid with its images from all nine security cameras, including the one at the front gate.

Someone was standing there, staring up at the house. From the way his mouth was moving, it sounded as if he was calling out, but the security system didn't have audio, only video. And because it was a chilly day, threatening rain just like the time I'd had my meltdown in the plaza, all the windows were shut.

Should I ignore him? Wait it out and hope he would go away? If he'd meant to sneak in and wreak havoc, he probably wouldn't have been shouting for attention at the front gate. Still....

This was the first living soul I'd seen in two weeks. The camera didn't show a huge amount of detail, because the sun was at his back and all I could see was his silhouette, but I hadn't seen any evidence of a gun or any other weapon. Not that that meant much.

Deciding to compromise, I got the shotgun out of the gun safe and then headed out the front door, Dutchie tagging along at my heels. She hadn't barked yet, but maybe that was only because she hadn't yet caught a whiff of the stranger.

I walked down the driveway and paused about six feet from the gate. Because the drive sloped up the hill toward the house and the garage, I had something of a vantage point, could see that this unwelcome visitor was a young man probably around my age or maybe a few years older. Black hair pulled back into a ponytail, warm brown skin, black almond-shaped eyes. Definitely Native American.

And...gorgeous. Like, the kind of gorgeous I would've had a hard time not staring at if I'd been in a club or out with my friends at a restaurant or the movies or the mall. Having someone who looked like that turn up on my doorstep, when I hadn't seen anyone since the man I'd shot outside Walgreens?

Well, let's just say it was a little overwhelming.

But not so much I forgot that I was here alone, sitting on top of a stockpile of supplies that were a damn good incentive for murder, as far as I was concerned. I hefted the shotgun so he could see it, but didn't bring it up to eye level.

"Who are you?" I demanded, while Dutchie sat beside me, wagging her tail. So much for looking intimidating.

"Jason Little River," he said, eyeing the shotgun but clearly attempting to keep a pleasant expression on his face. "My friends call me Jace."

"So, Jason," I said, emphasizing his full name, "how did you find this place?"

He paused, clearly a little disconcerted by the hostility in my tone. "The tire tracks," he replied, pointing at the rutted road that led to the compound. Since it had started raining on the way back from my last trip into town, the tracks I'd left were fairly defined. Damn. I hadn't even thought of that.

But those obvious tire tracks didn't explain everything. "You still had to get a good way out of town to even see where this road started."

"True. I had a friend who lived on Upper Canyon. I came here to Santa Fe—well, I came here hoping he might still be okay. Stupid, I know." Jason paused, gaze lingering on the shotgun before returning to my face. "And when I went to his house...." Under the heavy backpack he wore, the kind of metal-framed thing serious hikers used, his shoulders lifted. "No one there, of course. I was sort of walking around, trying to figure out what to do next, and I saw the tracks on the road going up the hill past his property. I figured I might as well check it out. The tracks seemed too fresh to have been made before...well, before."

I didn't bother to ask him what he meant by "before." For all of us survivors, our lives would forever be divided between "before" and "after." "You say you came here to Santa Fe. Where from?"

"Taos. I lived on the pueblo there." A disarming grin, one that under different circumstances might have made my knees melt. "Well, part-time. I also had an apartment in town. You?"

It was on my lips to say I was the one asking the questions here, but that sounded awfully rude, even under the current circumstances. "Albuquerque."

His eyebrows went up. "How'd you manage to get here, of all places?"

I hefted the shotgun. "I don't think that matters. I'm here now."

He didn't miss the way I'd shifted the gun, just enough to show I wasn't thrilled by his questions. "Hey, it's okay. It's just—I haven't seen anyone for almost two weeks. I'm probably a little off."

You and me both, honey. Relenting a little, I asked, "So no one was left in Taos?"

A shadow seemed to pass over his face, but his voice was level as he replied, "No one in the pueblo. When I went into town, I didn't see anyone, except one woman lurking around one of the hotels. She took one look at me and ran off screaming." He shrugged. "Since I could tell she wasn't open to conversation, I didn't bother to go after her. She could have been armed."

"And you weren't?"

Again I saw his eyes flicker toward the gun I held. "No. Well, not besides this." His hand went to his hip, where I could see he wore some kind of leather scabbard, about the size to conceal a hunting knife.

"Let me see it."

From this distance, I couldn't really hear him sigh, but I could tell his patience was starting to run thin. Holding my gaze, he undid the snap that kept the knife in place, then pulled it out of its sheath. As I'd thought, it was a big piece clearly designed for hunting, with a serrated edge. My father had owned one not unlike it.

"And that's all?" I asked.

He nodded, then went on, "Hey, I have a peace offering."

"What?" Saying my tone was guarded would have been an understatement.

"I'm going to get something out of my backpack," he said, laying the knife down in the dirt in front of him. "Okay?"

"Depends what it is," I told him.

A grin, one that showed off a dazzling set of white teeth. I had a feeling he'd used that smile to good effect a number of times in the past, but I had to make it seem as if it wasn't affecting me, even though I could feel a not-unpleasant shiver go through me at the way the smile lit up his dark eyes.

"I think you'll like this."

He unslung the backpack, setting it on the ground before unzipping it and spending a few seconds going through its contents. His back was to me, so I couldn't see exactly what he was doing. Almost at once, though, he turned around. In each hand he held a wine bottle.

"Very nice, but I've got a pretty stocked cellar up there," I said, jerking my chin back toward the house.

"Ah, but this is La Chiripada cabernet sauvignon. New Mexico wine. You have any of that?"

I really didn't have any idea. Besides the wine refrigerator in the kitchen, I'd discovered another trove in the basement, cases and cases of wine, most of it from California and France, from what I could tell, and some odd bits from South America and Arizona. I hadn't noticed anything from New Mexico, but then again, I hadn't exactly been looking for it, either.

As I hesitated, not sure how to respond, I heard the voice in my head.

He is safe.

"What?" I murmured under my breath, hoping the stranger wouldn't notice me muttering to myself.

He is safe. There is no reason to keep him out.

"Wait...you actually *want* me to let him in?"

Yes.

To say I was flummoxed would be an understatement. Here it seemed the voice had done everything to keep me safe, to have me avoid other survivors because of the dangers involved, and now he wanted me to allow a strange man to simply walk into my sanctuary here?

"What happens if he *isn't* safe?"

He is safe. I promise you.

Even with the voice stating his opinion so flatly, I couldn't help hesitating. True, he had always protected me, argued with me when I wanted to do things he found too dangerous. So I supposed I should be trusting his judgment here.

I sent a sidelong glance in the stranger's direction. He was still standing there, a bottle in each hand, a half hopeful, half anxious expression on his face. There was something so goofy about the combination, so oddly adorable, that I found myself relenting.

"All right," I muttered to the voice. "You'd just better not be playing supernatural matchmaker here or something, or we'll be discussing this further."

No answer to that. I hadn't really expected one.

Not quite allowing myself to sigh, I transferred the shotgun to my left hand and began walking to the gate. There was a manual release there, since obviously I hadn't brought the remote with me.

"Okay," I told Jason. "I've never had La Chiripada."

The look of relief that passed over his face was also adorable, and erased some of the strain I'd seen in his features. "Great. Thanks. I appreciate this. Really." He began stuffing the wine bottles into his backpack, then hefted it onto his shoulders. After that, he shot me a questioning look. "And your name is?"

"Jessica," I told him as I pushed the button to open the gate. "Jessica Monroe."

Another one of those blazing smiles, "Well, Jessica, I am very pleased to make your acquaintance."

CHAPTER ELEVEN

W<small>E</small> <small>HEADED UP TO THE HOUSE AFTER THAT,</small> Dutchie dancing around Jason, tail wagging and tongue lolling as if her long-lost best friend had just come home.

"I hope you're a dog person," I told him as we went in the front door.

"I am, actually. There were always a lot of dogs on the pueblo. I didn't have one of my own, since I was living in an apartment about half the time, but—" He broke off, pausing a few paces inside the entryway. His expression was so awestruck that at first I thought he was impressed by the house, which didn't surprise me too much. It was pretty impressive. But then he said, "Is that *bread?*"

"It is," I said, adding, "and I hope I haven't just burned it."

I jogged into the kitchen, Dutchie tagging along at my heels, since of course the kitchen was her favorite room in the house. Jason followed at a more sedate pace, probably because of the backpack he carried.

But when I peered into the oven, the bread looked perfect, golden brown and with just the right amount of loft. The timer said I had exactly thirty seconds to go. So I grabbed some potholders and pulled out the pan, setting it on the stove top to cool.

By then Jason had shrugged off his backpack and leaned it up against one of the cupboards. "That's amazing."

"What is?" I asked, turning to face him.

"The bread. This." He waved a hand, as if indicating the kitchen and the house beyond. "It's like—it's like it never happened."

Again, I didn't have to ask what he meant by "it." "Someone definitely put a lot of work into this house. I was lucky to find it."

A pause, during which I wondered if he was going to ask again how I had found it...and what the hell I should say in response to such a question. Instead, though, he inquired, "Your family didn't build it?"

"Oh, no. We could never have afforded something like this."

My reply appeared to make him relax slightly. Maybe he'd been thinking I was some rich girl from the city or something. There was a joke. But I could see how that might have made things even more awkward between us; I knew most of my state's Native American residents weren't exactly rolling in cash.

Well, neither was my family, so I added, "I found some paperwork when I was going through the house. The guy who built it was a real estate developer from Phoenix. I doubt he's going to be showing up any time soon."

A nod, although I could see the way Jason was surveying the kitchen, from the gleaming stainless-steel appliances to the custom cupboards and granite countertops. I had no idea what he might be thinking. In that moment, I was only strangely glad that I'd been so careful about keeping the place clean. In the past, I hadn't been what you might call the world's greatest housekeeper, but now I found cleaning the house helped to distract me, and used up some of the empty hours.

His next question surprised me. "You came from Albuquerque. We were pretty cut off in Taos. Did you ever hear anything more about the disease...where it started, mortality rates, anything like that?"

That was the last thing I wanted to talk about, but Jace clearly wanted more information than he'd gotten back home. Not that I had a lot to give him. Even so, I thought it best to stall a little while I figured out how much I should say.

"Water?" I asked, and he blinked, clearly startled by the non sequitur, then replied,

"Yes, thanks."

So I got a glass from the cupboard and filled it up with water from the refrigerator door. When I went to hand it to him, I realized how tall he was, how there were definitely some impressive muscles under the loose-fitting flannel shirt he wore. And even though he had to have been living rough for the past few weeks, I could tell he was clean. In fact, I caught the faintest scent of wood smoke coming from his clothes, and something about the aroma made a little thrill go through me.

I definitely needed to get it together.

Stepping away from him, pretending that I needed to go check on the bread, I said, "Things fell apart pretty quickly in Albuquerque, too. We never got a straight story about where it started or anything like that. Afterward...." I let the words trail off as I flashed back to that dark Walgreens, and the man I had confronted there. "I did meet someone who said he'd worked for emergency management downtown. He said the mortality rate was 99.8 percent."

"Shit." With his brown skin, Jace couldn't exactly go pale, but I still saw the blood appear to drain from his face. Then his dark eyes seemed to go sharp as he focused on what I'd just said. "Wait—you *met* another survivor? Where is he?"

Shit was right. I'd just met Jace. Was I supposed to tell him that I'd murdered a man?

I didn't see much of a way around it. If we were really going to be sharing this house, I wasn't sure I wanted to keep that big a secret from him. He needed to know, so he could decide if it was worth the risk to stay.

"He's dead," I said, my voice flat, harsh. "He tried to take my vehicle away from me, all the supplies I'd put together. He pulled a gun on me. So I shot him."

Silence. Jace stared at me, obviously trying to process what I'd just said. When he spoke, his tone was a lot gentler than I'd expected. "Because he was trying to steal from you, and you would've been dead without that vehicle and those supplies."

The question was, *would* I have been? I could have gone foraging all over again if necessary, could've found one of the abandoned vehicles and hot-wired it, another skill my father had taught me. I wasn't sure what happened to car keys if they were actually on a victim of the Heat, in a pocket or something, when they went to dust. All their clothes and jewelry seemed to disappear, so obviously the heat in their bodies was so extreme that it could destroy everything around them. Or was the explanation that simple? I hadn't actually stopped to puzzle it out, mostly because I knew in the end it didn't really matter. Those people were gone, and so were the belongings they had on them.

"I thought so at the time," I said slowly. As Jason kept looking at me with that concerned expression on his face, I felt something give way inside, the words flowing out, even though I hadn't meant to mention anything else of what had happened. "And he had this *look* on his face, and the night before that, crazy Chris Bowman had broken into my house and *attacked* me, and—"

I couldn't go on, because out of nowhere tears were streaming down my face, and, to my dismay, I'd begun to sob, the horror of it all coming back to me, something dark and terrible that had only been lurking in the murky sediment at the bottom of my mind, just waiting to return and overwhelm me.

Jason crossed the kitchen and pulled me against him, his hand smoothing my hair, his warm voice murmuring my name as I wept into his shirt, the flannel soft against my cheek. He smelled of wood smoke and pine needles, and underneath that, clean male sweat, and I breathed him in, reassured beyond measure at the feel of someone so solid, so real.

And then I realized what I was doing, that I was sobbing in the arms of a man I had just met, and I pushed myself away, shaking my head. "I—I'm sorry," I gasped. "That was just—that came out of nowhere. I'm sorry."

"It's okay," he said. His dark eyes seemed alight with compassion, with understanding. "I can't imagine how rough this must have been for you. And I'm sorry that you...did what you had to do. But I don't think you can blame yourself for that."

I went to the paper towel dispenser and tore off a partial sheet, then blotted my eyes. Good thing I hadn't bothered with makeup since I'd gotten here, except for some gloss to keep my lips from cracking in the dry, cold weather. "Thank you," I said simply. "But I do blame myself. There had to be something else I could have done—"

"I don't know about that," he said. "Sounds like you were kind of up against a wall." Again I was struck by the warmth in his expression...but it wasn't *that* kind of warmth, more that he was sorry I'd had to go through anything so terrible. "But I'm glad you told me the truth."

So was I, oddly enough. I'd just told him the worst thing about me, and he hadn't even blinked. That had to be a good sign.

"I'm glad, too," I told him, wanting to put the whole thing behind me. Somehow I knew Jace wouldn't press the issue any further. "Now, how about some of this bread?"

And like that, Jason Little River came to live at the compound. He took over the larger of the secondary bedrooms, putting his meager belongings in the closet there. I noticed that he hadn't brought any personal items with him, no photographs of family or anything like that, unlike the wedding photo of my parents that now lived on the mantel in the living room, or the shot of all of us at one of Devin's football games, which was now sitting on the dresser in the master bedroom.

When I asked him about his family, his expression grew shuttered. "All gone now," he said, and didn't seem to want to talk about it anymore. Since I understood all too well what it felt like to lose everyone around you, I didn't press the issue. Although I didn't know a whole lot about life on the pueblo, I knew it had to be a fairly close-knit community, a sort of huge extended family very unlike what I'd grown up with. His loss was probably even more painful than mine. If he wanted to open up about it later, after he'd had time to work through it in his own way, then I would be there to listen to him.

He was impressed by the compound, by all the lengths its builder had gone to so it would be self-sustaining. Even so, after one morning of walking around and inspecting everything, just a day or two after he moved in, he told me, "We should really be thinking about getting some livestock. This place isn't big enough for cattle, but maybe some goats?"

"Goats?" I repeated, not bothering to keep the skepticism out of my voice. "You're not suggesting we *eat* a goat, are you?"

His teeth flashed in the morning sun as he grinned at me. It was a bright, brisk day, the sky dappled with clouds, but the sunlight still fiercely bright. Despite the glaring sun, I could feel the bite in the wind, the unmistakable signs that winter was coming...and that it was going to be a lot colder than anything I'd experienced down in Albuquerque.

"The original *barbacoa* was made with goat," he pointed out. I only raised an eyebrow, and he laughed and went on, "I was thinking more in terms of milk and cheese. The cheese you have now isn't going to last forever."

Well, that was true. We had plenty of other staples, but some of the perishables like the cheese and the butter were about on their last legs. "Do you know how to milk a goat?" I asked.

"No, but I've milked cows. The technique can't be all that different."

The way he said it, halfway arch, halfway teasing, just made me shake my head. "Okay, I'll let you do it. Assuming we can even find any goats. They weren't exactly thick on the ground, the last time I checked."

"Maybe not, but there were probably people on the outskirts of town who kept livestock, and I know I saw animal pens up in Nambe as I came down into town."

"Oh?" I asked. It was the first time he'd made any mention of his journey here. I hadn't pressed, because

I knew better than anyone else that there were some things people just didn't want to talk about. Even so, I'd wondered about the long walk from Taos, and what he'd encountered on it.

"Yeah." He wasn't looking at me, was instead staring to the north and east, presumably in the direction from which he'd come. "Part of the reason it took me so long to get here was that I took the High Road down from Taos. I figured it might be safer to stay off the main roads."

"And you walked that whole way?" I asked, staring at him with some incredulity. I'd heard of the High Road, but I'd never been on it. The scenic side trip was one that my family had discussed taking a few times, but those plans had never materialized. My father had always been a Point A to Point B kind of guy and was more intent on the destination than on the road that led to it.

Jace gave me a rueful smile. "Not at first. I had a motorcycle, and I'd ridden it before with my backpack, although I know that's not really recommended. But I thought I could do it if I kept my speed down. Besides, a motorcycle is a lot easier to maneuver around abandoned vehicles."

I couldn't argue with that. But a motorcycle wouldn't have worked for me. I had too much stuff to bring, and besides, there was Dutchie. Well, maybe a sidecar....

Turning away from me, Jason surveyed the horizon again. The wind picked up, pulling strands of heavy dark hair out of the piece of thin leather he had wrapped around his ponytail. His hair hung a few inches below his shoulders, and so far I hadn't seen it in anything but that heavy tail down his back. That hadn't stopped me from wondering what it would look like, sleek and loose over those broad shoulders.

Which was exactly the wrong thing to be thinking. After I'd lost it the day we'd met, and he'd held me and comforted me, we'd maintained a careful distance between us. I hadn't noted even a flicker of interest from him. Maybe I wasn't his type, or maybe it was the far more stark fact that he'd lost not just his family, but his people, his entire way of life. He seemed to be bouncing back fairly well, but it was probably a little self-absorbed of me to think he'd be interested in any sort of romantic entanglements so soon after suffering that kind of shock.

Besides, I wasn't even sure whether *I* was interested in anything like that. Yes, Jace was extremely good-looking, and he had an easygoing way about him that I appreciated, after some of the high-strung guys I'd dated in the past, but our focus should be on survival first and foremost. Those other sorts of complications were pretty far down my list of priorities.

And anyway, break-ups were bad enough when you had a decent chance of never seeing the other person again. I didn't exactly have that luxury at the moment.

Jace didn't seem to have noticed my preoccupation, since he appeared to be absorbed in studying the far-off outlines of the Jemez mountain range. I noticed that he held something in his hand, a leather thong knotted through a hole in a smooth-polished black stone. His thumb moved over it, the motion reminding me of the worry beads sometimes used by Greek men.

Then he said, "But I picked up something in my tire in Placita. I had a patch kit in my backpack, but it wasn't just a nail that had blown the tire, but a sharp rock. I lost two nights there, trying to fix it, scavenging around to see if I could find anything to replace it with, but that was a no-go."

"No one there, either?" I asked, although I already knew what the answer would be.

"No. Not a soul. I did some foraging to replenish my supplies, which was what delayed me even more. Or maybe I just wasn't looking forward to that long, long walk."

It would have been that. Even with the part of the trip he'd shaved off by riding his motorcycle, he still had to have walked a good forty miles or so. Farther, actually, because it was still about fifteen miles from Nambe to the heart of Santa Fe, and then another five miles to this hidden fold of the hills where the compound was located.

"But you did it anyway."

He nodded, then shoved the polished stone he'd been holding back into his pocket. "There was nothing left in Taos. I wandered there for about a day and a half—I was at the pueblo when the illness hit, and our healers couldn't do anything to combat it. No one could. People were being told to stay at home, that the local medical center didn't have the resources to treat that many victims at once. So...I stayed there and watched everyone die around me."

"And waited to find out when it would be your turn," I said quietly.

Finally, he shifted so his gaze fell upon me, rather than that far-off, jagged horizon. Those jet-black eyes, in their fringe of equally black lashes, were startled, but then he nodded in understanding. "Yes. That's exactly what I did. But then after another day passed, and everyone was gone, leaving behind only dust, I realized I wouldn't be lucky enough to join all my people in the afterlife. I was doomed to drift here, in a world I hadn't chosen."

I probably wouldn't have phrased it that way, but he was right—that's exactly what it felt like. Being cast adrift on dark waters, paddling desperately, although you had no idea why you'd been pushed out onto that black ocean in the first place. "So you left then?"

He nodded, and once again his attention moved back to the horizon, to the mountains that blocked his view of the place he had once called home. "Well, I went from the pueblo to my apartment. At least I'd had the motorcycle with me at the pueblo, so the trip didn't take long. The whole way I didn't see anyone, just cars left along the side of the road. Same thing at my apartment—it was a small building, only four units, but all the hotels were equally deserted."

His shoulders lifted under the leather jacket he wore, although I wasn't quite sure of the reason for the shrug. Dismissing his futile attempts to find any survivors? I didn't know him well enough to guess.

"Anyway," he continued. "I could tell that staying in Taos probably wasn't a good idea. It's a small town... was, I mean...and the chances of finding anyone who'd lived through the Heat were pretty low. I packed what I could and left. I did see that one woman as I was heading out of town, but, as I said, she took off the second she saw me. Maybe she thought I was a ghost." He did smile then, but grimly, just the slightest lift at the corners of his mouth.

Or a rapist, I thought, recalling my own experiences. I didn't say anything aloud, though. Whatever he might be, Jason Little River was clearly *not* a rapist. "And the wine?" I asked.

"The La Chiripada tasting room was just down the street from where I lived. Since no one was around, I figured it wouldn't matter if I liberated a couple of bottles. I had a feeling I might need a drink in the near future. Or," he added, with a real smile this time, his expression warming as he looked over at me, "a peace offering."

I tried not to blush, but I wasn't sure how successful I was at it. With any luck, he'd think the flush in my cheeks had come from the brisk wind blowing down from the north, and not the way he'd just looked at me. "Speaking of the wine," I said, my tone probably too casual, "we should have something special to drink it with. Frozen tamales probably aren't festive enough."

"You like rabbit?" Jace asked, a gleam in those black eyes.

"I don't know," I replied uncertainly. I had a feeling I knew what he was going to suggest. "I've never had it."

"Well, time to change that." He glanced over at the house, then back at me. "That is, assuming you have a .22 in that gun safe of yours."

At least he didn't ask me to go with him. In the back of my mind, I'd understood that at some point I'd have to start eating game meats, but I wasn't sure I could handle watching Jace shoot a fluffy little bunny and then expect to roast it or whatever a few hours later.

He did take Dutchie along, saying she might as well start to learn what it meant to be an outdoor dog. I knew he was right; her days as a pampered suburban pooch were long over. Anyway, she was more than happy to go along on the hunting expedition, trotting off at Jace's side without even a backward glance toward the house. I only hoped she wouldn't scare off every rabbit in a five-mile radius.

In the meantime, I had to scour the cookbooks that sat on the shelf mounted to the kitchen wall to see if I could find anything about cooking rabbit. Actually, that didn't take me much time at all, because in addition to the standard *Joy of Cooking* and *Better Homes and Gardens* cookbooks, I found several specialty ones, including a title dedicated to cooking all sorts of game meats, starting with rabbit and quail and moving up from there.

After that, it was a matter of poring over the recipes and deciding which sounded best—and one for which I had actually had all the ingredients on hand. I decided that the rabbit with mustard sauce variation sounded good. Since I'd already harvested some onions and garlic from the greenhouse a few days earlier, all I had to do was rescue the onion from the fridge and the garlic from the little terra-cotta keeper that sat on the counter.

While I did that, I couldn't help worrying that Jace would come back with a couple of rabbit carcasses and expect me to skin and dress them, his work as the he-man hunter done. I didn't know the first thing about doing any of that. Hell, I could barely cut up a whole chicken properly. My mother showed me how to do it once, but I'd protested the whole time that you could buy already cut-up chicken, so what was the point? Wasting a half hour on that sort of exercise just to save a dollar or so on the price of the meat had hardly seemed worth it to me.

That had annoyed her, I could tell; she was probably flashing back to when she and my father first got married, when she was substitute teaching while trying to get a full-time position, and he was still a rookie right out of the Academy. Money had been tight. I understood that intellectually, but twenty-five years later, it seemed a little extreme to be worrying about a few cents a pound for chicken.

But at least she had taught me to cook—not Cordon Bleu or anything, but how to make a roast and how to prepare a variety of potato dishes and lots of veggies, sauces, that sort of thing. I knew I wouldn't have to worry about poisoning Jace if he did somehow manage to bring back a rabbit, even with Dutchie's help.

Until they did return, I wasn't about to get anything started. I assembled the ingredients on the kitchen counter, went down to the cellar to get some potatoes, and then found a tablecloth and some matching napkins on one of the shelves in the laundry room. This would be the first time we'd sat down at the dining room table, as his first few nights here, Jace had eaten with me at the little breakfast set in the kitchen nook. For some reason, that had felt safer to me. There was a certain ritual associated with sitting down to a real meal at a dining room table.

Maybe I was making too much out of his going rabbit-hunting. It wasn't as if we wouldn't be eating a lot of that sort of thing in the future, if it turned out he really was handy with that .22. Then again, making an occasion out of it might make us both feel a little better about our current situation.

That thought seemed to reassure me, so I went ahead and finished setting the table, completing the setup with the long wrought-iron candleholder that had been sitting on the sideboard. It held five pillar candles, and would provide plenty of light.

Candlelit dinners? I asked myself. *Boy, you really are asking for trouble.*

I decided if Jace asked, I'd say it was a good way to save energy.

He returned an hour or so later, Dutchie bounding along beside him, and a very messy bundle of rabbit dangling from a bag in one hand. So he had done the butchering for me, probably guessing that asking me to handle that particular duty would have damaged my delicate sensibilities.

"Thanks," I said, taking the bundle from him. "I found a recipe with mustard sauce. Does that sound okay to you?"

"Sounds great," he replied. He was windblown, but looked far more relaxed and happy than he had when he was telling me about how he had left Taos. Getting out in the fresh air and away from the house seemed to have done him a world of good. "I need to get cleaned up. Can you manage things from here?"

In another world, I might have complained about having to do the typical female thing of cooking, now that he'd bagged his bunnies. Actually, though, I was just grateful that he even had the ability to go out and get us food. He knew how to hunt; I knew how to cook. It seemed a pretty fair division of labor from where I stood.

The bundle of rabbit parts was a little bloodier than something I would have gotten from the supermarket, but I wasn't so squeamish that I couldn't handle it. I rinsed everything off and patted it dry, then sprinkled the pieces with salt and pepper while warming up some olive oil in a pan. As the rabbit was browning, Jace returned to the kitchen, face and hands looking freshly scrubbed, and asked if I needed help peeling the potatoes.

Okay, so much for my worry about thinking he was going to sit on his ass and watch a DVD of *Die Hard* or something while I labored away in the kitchen.

"Yes," I said. "Thanks."

He went to work, being sparing with the water, for which I was grateful. So far it seemed as if the well could manage just about anything we threw at it, including daily showers for the two of us, but it never hurt to be careful. I used to take long, hot showers, the kind that would basically kill all the hot water in the place by the time I was done, but once I got here, I retrained myself so the whole procedure only took five minutes. Not the easiest of tasks at first, but things did get sped up when you didn't have to worry about shaving your legs.

I risked a glance at Jace, thinking I wouldn't mind having to go back to the whole leg-shaving thing if the situation warranted it. But that day seemed far off—if it ever came at all—so in the meantime, I was pretty sure my five-minute showers were safe.

Neither of us spoke, but it was a companionable sort of silence, him peeling the potatoes, me working away at the sauté pan, following the steps of the recipe. He did stop to ask whether I wanted the potatoes sliced or cut up or whatever, but since I was planning on mashing them, he didn't have to do much besides quarter them and put them in a pot of cold water.

"Don't you need milk for mashed potatoes?" he asked.

"There's evaporated milk in the pantry. It won't be quite the same, but I think it'll be okay."

I could tell by the way his brows drew together that he wasn't exactly thrilled by the idea of evaporated milk, but he didn't say anything, only went over to fetch the box and then mix up a batch for me. Well, if it was that big a problem, the next day I'd send him off in search of any stray goats that might be wandering the area, looking for a home. Dutchie would probably be ecstatic at the prospect of that sort of expedition.

The dog had definitely latched on to Jace. Maybe she'd been more bonded with Mr. Munoz, back in Albuquerque. Or maybe Jace was one of those people whom dogs tended to love. I didn't know, and in the end, it didn't matter. Jace was Dutchie's new best friend. It didn't bother me as much as I thought it might have, simply because Dutchie had proved herself to be a decent judge of character. If she liked Jace, it must mean he was okay.

It was dark by the time dinner was ready. Jace and I carried the various platters and bowls to the dining room table, and I brought out some matches I'd found in the kitchen so I could light the pillars in their wrought-iron holder. Without my asking, Jace turned off the overhead fixture, so all we had was the candlelight. It danced off the heavy glass goblets, the dark bottle of cabernet that sat waiting to be drunk. The walls in this room were a warm parchment yellow, and seemed to reflect the glow of the candles and multiply it.

"Wow," Jace murmured. "I hadn't expected to see anything like this ever again." Then he shook his head. "Wait—I don't think I'd ever seen anything like this *before,* either. It looks beautiful, Jessica."

"Thanks," I said, my tone almost shy. Now that I was with him in this intimate space, would he take all this for more than I had intended, as some sort of seduction or something?

Well, there wasn't anything I could do about it now. I pulled out my chair—obscurely glad that he hadn't offered to do it for me—and sat down. A second later, he followed suit, lifting the cloth napkin I'd set out and placing it in his lap. Then he raised the bottle of wine, which he'd already opened back in the kitchen, and poured some of the cabernet into my glass first, and then his.

"I think we should have a toast," he said.

"What should we toast to?" Not being dead seemed the obvious choice, but it seemed crass to voice the thought aloud.

He seemed to think about it for a moment, his glass a few inches off the tabletop. The candlelight gleamed against his raven-dark hair, and again I wondered what it would feel like to run my fingers through it.

"To sanctuary," he said at last.

I was definitely on board with that. Even if nothing ever happened between Jace and me, we had found a quiet haven here, a place to shelter from whatever might be going on outside in the world. "To sanctuary," I echoed, raising my glass as well and clinking it against his.

A brief silence fell as we both swallowed some of the wine. It wasn't as heavy as the Montepulciano I'd drunk a few days earlier. I could taste the fruit in it, and thought it was probably a good choice to go along with the sharpness of the mustard sauce I'd made for the rabbit.

Then we both dug into the main dish, which turned out to be excellent. I wasn't sure why I'd avoided rabbit before this, because I found myself liking the taste.

Good thing, too, I thought, *because you're probably going to be eating a lot of it in the future.*

And the mashed potatoes actually were fine, even with the evaporated milk, and there was fresh bread and butter and roasted carrots. It really was quite the feast, especially considering I'd had to work with what was available in the cellar and the greenhouse. No more popping down to the grocery store to get that one special ingredient.

"This is...amazing," Jace finally said, after making some serious inroads into the food on his plate. "Were you a chef or something?"

"Hardly." I took a sip of wine to cover my embarrassment, cheeks flaming. I really needed to get this blushing thing under control one way or another. "My mother taught me how to cook. That is, she pointed out that it was mostly following directions, at least for the basic stuff. So...that's what I did tonight. Followed directions."

"It's still pretty incredible." Expression thoughtful, he drank some of his own wine. "So what did you do? Before, I mean."

"I was getting my master's at UNM, so I T.A.'d a couple of courses. English—a lot of paper grading, mostly." I broke off a piece of bread but didn't eat it, just sort of rolled it between my finger and thumb. "What about you?"

"I graduated from UNM four years ago, then came back to Taos." He looked at me directly then, as if studying my features, and it was difficult to remain as I was, to not glance away. "We must have been there at the same time, but I guess there wouldn't have been much overlap. You'd have been a freshman when I was a senior."

I could have sworn his expression was somewhat regretful, but I didn't want to read too much into it. That way only lay disappointment.

"Anyway," he went on, "after that I went back to Taos. I conducted tours at the pueblo part of the time, and the rest of the time I worked on getting my business going."

"What kind of business?" I asked, after finally remembering to eat the piece of bread I was holding.

"Website and graphic design. I did some work for the local businesses. Mostly advertising stuff. The tours paid a lot better."

That revelation surprised me. "They did?"

"Oh, yeah." He got himself a piece of bread, then buttered it. When he went on, he wore a rather sardonic smile. "You'd be amazed how much the tourists were willing to part with. On a good day, I could make around three hundred bucks. White guilt is expensive, I guess."

I just stared at him, and he hurried to say,

"No offense. But I think that's part of why they're willing to hand over a twenty—or more—for a half-hour tour of the pueblo." His gaze sharpened on me, and again I had to force myself to look back at him directly. "Anyway, I'd say to look at you, you must have some First Nations blood back in the woodpile yourself. Or am I overreaching?"

So that was it—he was just inspecting my appearance in an attempt to determine my own origins. Fair enough. Would he feel better, knowing I had a Native American heritage of my own? "No, you're not over-reaching," I replied, glad I sounded calm and unruffled. "Family legend has it that my great-great-great-grandmother was full-blood Ute."

"Even better," Jace said, a certain warmth in his eyes doing unexpected things to my midsection. "The

Ute and the Pueblo were on very good terms back in the day."

What in the world was I supposed to say to that? Was Jace hoping that he and I would be, as he put it, "on very good terms"? Not that I thought I would be opposed to such a shift in our relationship, but we'd only known each other for a couple of days. I certainly didn't intend to rush into anything.

"Well, that's good to know," I remarked. "At least I won't have to worry about tribal warfare breaking out in the laundry room or something."

For a second or two, he didn't reply, only stared at me, and I hoped I hadn't offended him. But then he chuckled, reached for the wine bottle, and poured some more into my glass. Still smiling, he said, "No, I don't think we have to worry about any conflict here."

It was all I could do not to shiver. No matter what he said, though, I wouldn't take for granted this current harmony and goodwill lasting indefinitely.

How could it, when we were such strangers to one another?

CHAPTER TWELVE

BUT SOMEHOW, STRANGELY, THAT COOPERATION did continue. We fell into a sort of pattern after a few days—rising early, eating breakfast, which was toast or oatmeal most of the time, taking turns with our showers, getting dressed, then doing whatever needed to be done around the place. Jace was full of plans, abetted by some of the books and manuals he found in the office.

"We really should build a henhouse," he said one morning, about a week after he showed up. "I know people in the area had to have kept chickens. Eggs are a good, steady source of protein."

"So are rabbits," I replied, not bothering to point out that we'd been eating rabbit at least every other day. Wile E. Coyote would have been jealous.

"Now they are," he said. "In the dead of winter, it might be more difficult. But those plans I found for a henhouse look dead easy. We just need to get some supplies."

"What, you're a carpenter and a web designer?" I asked, teasing. Sort of. What I knew about building henhouses was roughly the same as what I knew about brain surgery—that is, nothing. I didn't think I was going to be much help.

He shrugged. "I picked up a few things here and there. It'll be fine."

And so, later that morning, we headed down into Santa Fe in search of a Home Depot, which wasn't as easy as it might seem, considering we couldn't exactly Google its location. But we found a yellow pages inside an abandoned dentist's office, and tracked down the store from there. It was a good ways outside the city center, so I was doubly glad that we'd looked it up instead of driving aimlessly all over the place.

Jace had a list of everything he needed, and we "liberated" one of the trailers you used to be able to rent to haul your building supplies home. Thank God my father had invested in a tow package for the Cherokee, even though we'd never actually had any reason to use it. There just never seemed to be quite enough in the family budget to buy a trailer or an ATV.

It took a while to locate and then load all the necessary supplies—partly because we both kept finding things we thought would be useful and figured we might as well add them to the haul. But after the back of the SUV was packed to the rafters, and the trailer similarly loaded down, we drove off, moving slowly through the streets, since I had to keep zigging and zagging to avoid abandoned cars and trucks. We'd left Dutchie at home, much to her dismay, since we'd known we would need all the available cargo space in the Cherokee.

"It's kind of strange, don't you think?" I asked Jace after we'd cut back up on Cerrillo and were heading to Alameda.

"What's strange?" he replied, his attention still on the list he held. Maybe he was worried that we'd forgotten something.

"That we haven't seen *anybody*. I mean, even with a 99.8% mortality rate, there should still be a couple hundred people wandering around Santa Fe, right? Where are they?"

He did look up at that question, his gaze drifting to the empty sidewalks and dark windows of the businesses on either side of the street. "Lying low?"

"Maybe," I said, but I wasn't sure I believed it. By that point, it had been almost a month since the Heat first began to spread across the country. Anyone who was going to die was long dead. You'd think the survivors would be out foraging in earnest, getting ready for winter. "It's just weird that we haven't seen a single person."

"Do you want to find more people?" His tone was almost sharp as he asked that question, as if he thought I wasn't satisfied with his company, that I needed something more.

"I don't know," I replied. It was only the truth. Part of me wanted to know what had happened to everyone, but after my experiences in Albuquerque, I wasn't sure being around other people was such a good thing. Yes, Jace had turned out to be all right—more than all right, really—but could I count on being that lucky a second time?

"They could be hiding," he said, his tone thoughtful. "Or gone to Albuquerque, thinking that maybe if any center of government still existed, it would be there, in a place where there would be more survivors. There are probably a lot of reasons why we're not seeing anybody."

That explanation sounded logical enough. If it hadn't been for the voice urging me to get out, would I have left my hometown, or would I have stayed there in the hope that people might gather in what had been the state's most populous area?

I wouldn't second-guess myself, not now. I really didn't know. Then again, my run-ins with Chris Bowman and the man outside Walgreens might have been enough to convince me that it was time to get out of Dodge.

"You're right, of course," I said, and he smiled.

"It's okay, Jess. *We're* okay. That's all we have to worry about right now."

Oh, how I wanted to believe him. I just wasn't sure if I did.

The henhouse did go together with surprising speed, and within three days' time, we had a full-on chicken coop with space for six hens to nest, a perch that Jace built from a closet rod, and an enclosed run. He also hung a light overhead so the hens would be encouraged to lay even on gray winter days. It was all perfect, except...no chickens.

So we got in the Cherokee again, this time taking Dutchie with us, and started scouring the rural and semi-rural areas outside Santa Fe for any rogue chickens who needed a home. It actually didn't take as long as I'd thought; about an hour into our search, we found a house with a flock of chickens scratching away happily in the backyard, apparently unaware that the apocalypse had happened and they'd been left on their own. We gathered up six hens and the rooster, who was less than pleased at being plucked out of his yard and put in the back of an SUV. Jace was a little scratched up by the time the procedure was over, but in the end we had everything we needed. All I could say was that I was very glad I'd had the forethought to lay down some plastic trash bags in the bed of the SUV before dumping the chickens back there. If he'd had a proper grave, my father would have been rolling over in it.

It took a few days for the chickens to settle down and start laying, but after that we were able to have eggs pretty much every morning.

"Next, the goats," Jace said at dinner not too long after that.

"Are you still on that kick?" I asked. All right, I had to say that the whole chicken thing was working out pretty well. But the thought of having goats roaming around the property intimidated me more than I wanted to admit. When I was a little kid, maybe five or six, my parents had taken me to a petting zoo. All had gone well until one of the goats decided to eat part of my sweater. I'd screamed bloody murder, and my father had grimly lifted me out of the pen and carried me away. Needless to say, goats weren't exactly my favorite animals.

"Yes, I'm still on that kick. We ate the last of the cheese two days ago." His dark eyes caught mine, and he grinned at me, a wicked grin I'd come to know over the past few weeks...and one that invariably made my knees go a little wobbly. So far I didn't think Jace had noticed what kind of an effect it had on me, but still, I couldn't help getting annoyed with myself for not having better self-control. He clasped his hands together and said in mock-earnest tones, "Jessica, do you want to consign me to a cheese-less future?"

"Oh, for God's sake...." I couldn't help smiling back at him, though, and I spread my hands in a gesture of surrender. "Okay, I give up. So, say we find some goats. How do you plan on getting them back here?"

"Easy," he replied. His grin now had an element of triumph in it. "We'll just find a horse trailer and put them in there."

Easy. Right.

As with the henhouse supplies, we went foraging for the trailer first. There were a number of horse properties in the area, so that wasn't too difficult. The odd thing was, just as I hadn't seen any people on any of our expeditions, so, too, were there no horses in evidence anywhere. They could have bolted, kicked down the fences and gates when it became clear no one was coming to feed them or give them fresh water.

I didn't see any signs of that, though, and the voice's words came back to me: *The animals will be taken care of.* So apparently I didn't need to worry about the horses. I couldn't help wondering, though.

Just as I couldn't help wondering what had happened to the voice. By that point, I hadn't heard him for more than a week. Now that it seemed I was truly settled with Jace, maybe the voice had moved on, deeming me no longer in need of any assistance.

I wasn't sure why, but that thought saddened me a little. I hardly wanted to admit it even to myself, but I missed the voice. If nothing else, he would have given me someone else to talk to...if he'd stuck around. A few times when Jace was out of the house and occupied with some task or another, I'd tried calling out to the voice. It never replied, though, and at last I'd given up, telling myself that if the voice didn't need me, well, I didn't need it, either. Intellectually, I knew I should let it go. But its absence bothered and worried me, despite my best attempts to think about other matters.

Jace and I hit the goat jackpot on our second stop. Not only did we find a nice, largish horse trailer, but the property actually had goats roaming around, keeping the lawn cropped, doing their usual job of eating anything that wasn't nailed down.

So we hooked up the trailer to the Cherokee, then had a little convo in which we decided having four goats to start should work—three does and a buck. If it turned out the does didn't produce enough milk or whatever, we could always come back and collect more of the herd. There seemed to be fifteen or so of them, although it was hard to get an exact count, what with the way they kept milling around.

Choosing was difficult, because I had no idea what to look for in a goat. Thank God Jace wasn't quite as clueless, and he managed to get two of the does with the most developed milk bags up into the trailer without too much trouble. All right, that looked easy enough, so I started to do my best to urge another doe, a pretty animal with a sleek black coat and fawn-colored tipping, in the general direction of the trailer. She just bleated at me and trotted off, so I followed her grimly, wishing Jace would stop messing around with the two he'd already gotten in the trailer so he could help me.

Then, out of nowhere—wham! Something hard hit me square in the butt, and I went flying onto the ground. I blinked, wondering what the hell had happened, and then realized it was the buck, who was standing a few paces away and glaring at me out if his dark amber eyes. It seemed he'd taken exception to my maneuvering that one doe, and had butted me right in the ass.

From the trailer, I heard laughter, and I scowled. Jace came out, grinning at me where I sat on the ground in a pile of dirt and dead weeds.

"Very funny," I snapped. "You come over here and deal with this bastard."

"Sorry, but the way he got you right in the—"

"Point taken." I began to push myself to my feet, only to be stared down by a very angry-looking buck. Fine. I'd wait here until Jace took care of him.

Which he did, somehow managing to circle the beast and then urge him up the ramp into the trailer. How, I wasn't quite sure. Hypnotism? Some magical Native American goat-charming trick?

Whatever it was, it worked. The buck headed right into the trailer as if it were full of a harem of does in heat, and the last doe, the one I'd been trying to manhandle, trotted after him, tail swishing.

Frigging goats.

Jace came over to me and extended a hand. "Need help?"

I scowled at him but took his hand anyway, letting him pull me to my feet. In fact, he yanked me up with such vigor that I lost my balance and pitched right into him, colliding chest to chest. He took me by the arms and steadied me, holding me for a second or two longer than he really needed to.

"You all right?" he asked.

"Uh—" Was I all right? My rear end ached, and I knew my jeans were covered in dirt, but in that moment all I was really conscious of were his hands on my arms, the strength of the fingers wrapped around my biceps. Our faces were only inches apart. Blood tingled all through me, and I knew all I had to do was go up on my toes, bring my mouth to his....

No, that was insane. This was the first time he'd even touched me since he held me when I wept, on the day he had first come to the compound. Other than a few sideways looks and glances I'd probably misinterpreted, he had done absolutely nothing to show he had any interest in me other than as a companion and friend.

Somehow I gathered myself, saying, "I'm fine," and then gently pulled my arms from his grasp. He didn't try to stop me, didn't tighten his grip or attempt to bring me closer.

Well, there was my answer.

I dug the car key out of my pocket and headed to the driver-side door of the Cherokee, while Jace went around the other side. So far I hadn't let him drive the SUV, and he hadn't pushed the matter, somehow sensing that having control over the vehicle was important to me. Besides, he'd taken to driving the Polaris all over the area around the compound, had used it to bring back a buck he'd shot one Saturday afternoon. The freezers were full of venison. Yes, Jace was very handy to have around.

Even so, I didn't say anything to him on the trip back home.

The awkwardness eased itself soon enough, as it had to. We were so busy with getting the goats set up and then foraging for feed, reading up on their care and what we needed to do to ensure the does were properly producing milk, that the moment we shared back in their corral was soon pushed aside, if not forgotten.

Of course, the awkward part was realizing that we needed to breed the goats now so they would have babies in the spring, and therefore more milk. Oh, yeah, discussing breeding options for farm animals with a guy you have a serious amount of unresolved sexual tension with is a whole new species of fun.

To be fair, Jace was very mellow about the whole thing, and didn't make any rude jokes or indulge in any cringe-worthy innuendo. He spelled out the whole thing logically and factually, and then let the goats do the rest. It really wasn't that difficult; a buck is going to do what a buck is going to do, after all. I was just glad that I managed to avoid seeing them actually do the deed.

One thing we didn't have to worry about was the goats escaping the compound. They might come through and eat the ornamental plants in the garden area directly off the back of the house, but there was no way even the most ambitious goat could jump a seven-foot-high solid adobe wall.

Jace did have to teach me to milk the damn things, which at first scared me to no end, since I was sure I was going to end up with a hoof in my face the second I put one of my unpracticed hands on the animal's teat.

"You can just do it, you know," I told him, hovering nervously in the background as he sat down to give me a demonstration.

"Oh, no," he replied. "Equal division of labor on this farm."

I made a face but didn't argue. It was true; I might have done most of the cooking, but he did the hunting, and even cleaned out the chicken coop when my one foray into doing so proved I didn't have the world's strongest stomach. In return, I happily did his laundry. At least that way I was able to learn that he favored dark-toned boxer-briefs over tighty-whiteys.

"It's not that hard," he went on, his voice almost too coaxing. "Just watch."

He placed his thumb and forefinger near the top of the doe's teat, squeezing it, and then exerted pressure with his remaining fingers on the lower part of the teat. A thin stream of white liquid emerged and went into the glass jar he'd set beneath it. "See?"

"Oh, yeah. Easy peasy."

"Actually, it isn't. You have to exert a good deal of force. But that's okay. She wants to be milked." He did it again, and I watched his long fingers squeezing against her flesh. For a second, I had a brief flash of those fingers cupping my breast, squeezing, and I had to force the thought out of my mind. No way was I going to let myself get turned on by watching Jace milk a goat. He glanced up at me. "You want to give it a try?"

I really didn't. To stall for time, I responded with a question of my own. "Is there anything you can't do?"

He appeared to consider, then said, "I don't know how to play the violin. Now come over here and start learning how to milk this goat."

Heaving a sigh didn't really seem appropriate, given the situation, so I waited while he got out of the way and then sat down on the old packing crate we were using as a milking stool. I did take a breath, though, before placing my fingers more or less in the same position Jace had put his.

"Good," he said, watching my hands, not my face. "Now squeeze with those two fingers while using the rest to push the milk out of the teat."

Oh, boy. I squeezed, tentatively at first, and the goat, who we'd named Aster because of the little star-shaped mark on her haunch, shot me a look of pure irritation over her shoulder. But at least she hadn't kicked me.

"Harder than that," Jace instructed me, but his voice sounded more coaxing than annoyed.

I definitely didn't want him annoyed with me. This time I squeezed harder, exerting so much pressure that I was certain Aster was going to step on my foot in protest. Instead, milk squirted into the bottle, and she seemed to relax slightly, letting me do what I needed to do.

After letting out a little exhalation of relief, I went back to milking her. More and more milk kept squirting out, but within five minutes, the fingers of my right hand were aching like you wouldn't believe. I tried switching to the other hand, but couldn't get the angle right. After another minute, I sat back, shaking my head. "I can't do any more."

"It's okay," Jace said. His hand dropped to my shoulder and gave it a squeeze. "It's going to take some time to develop those muscles. I can finish up."

That was probably my signal to relinquish the packing crate to him so he could sit down, but I found I didn't want to move. Not with his warm hand on my shoulder, the pressure of it somehow delicious, even through the flannel shirt and heavy canvas anorak I wore.

He seemed to realize that as well, because he moved his arm, breaking the contact. At the same time, attempting to cover up the awkwardness of the moment, I got to my feet.

"Thanks, Jace. I'll just get back to the house, then."

Grinning, he asked, "How's the butter project coming?"

"Good. I'm just about to break out the mixer and have at it."

Making butter had turned out to be a bigger task than I'd expected, but after some trial and error, I'd gotten enough buttermilk ready to go so I could move on to the next step. At least we had power in the house, and the kitchen had come equipped with a fancy stand mixer. Much better than having to stand around with a butter churn the way they did it in the bad old days.

We'd made the decision to use a good deal of the milk for making butter and cheese, since neither Jace nor I was what you would call a big milk drinker. Both of those projects weren't exactly what you'd call user-friendly, but it was sort of amazing how much extra time you had on your hands when you weren't spending half the day chatting with your friends on Facebook or whatever.

I still hadn't decided whether that was a good thing or not.

A week after that, I stood at the window in the living room, looking out over the drive, past the wall to the landscape beyond. Heavy clouds blocked the sky, and I wondered how much we would get out of the solar panels today. We had a backup generator, but we hadn't needed it yet. I was glad of that—the procedure to switch over from the solar collector to the electric generator didn't sound all that simple. But the oven ran on propane, so I'd still be able to use that, even if we decided to dial back on our power consumption for the day. All the heat came from the various fireplaces and the wood-fired stove in the sitting room, so the interior temperature of the house wouldn't be affected, one way or another.

Anyway, it wasn't the possible loss of power that had me staring out at the brooding vista. What with one thing or another, I hadn't been paying that much attention to what day it was, although I'd dutifully marked off each one on the calendar in the office, just so I wouldn't completely lose track of time. But today, when I'd picked up the Sharpie to draw that thick black line, I'd paused and frowned at the date I was crossing out.

October 31st.

"Something wrong?" Jace asked, coming into the living room. He looked a bit surprised, and I supposed I couldn't blame him. We didn't spend much time in there, beautiful as the room was. Usually we were either in the kitchen or the family room, or, more rarely, the office.

"No," I said, then paused. "It's Halloween."

"And?" His expression told me he wasn't particularly impressed by that piece of information. "Did you want to go trick-or-treating or something?"

"Ha," I replied. My trick-or-treating days were long behind me, although Elena and Tori and I had still gone out on Halloween, mostly as an excuse to get dressed up and go to bars. I'm not going to lie—the year before, we all did variations on the "sexy" something, me as a witch, since it suited my long near-black hair, Tori as an angel, and Elena...well, I still wasn't entirely clear what her costume was supposed to be, except that it was black and red and sparkly, and showed way more leg than I would ever have dared. Needless to say, we didn't have to buy any of our own drinks that night.

"It's not the trick-or-treating," I said slowly. "It's more...I don't know. Like the date is telling me it's been more than a month since...well, since."

The light of humor in his dark eyes abruptly disappeared. "You're right. I guess I hadn't really thought
about it, what with everything we've been doing." He
closed the distance between us, coming to stand next
to me in front of the window. So close, and yet...and
yet, he might have been a million miles away. I knew I
didn't have the courage to reach out and take his hand
in mine, to feel the reassurance of his touch. Then he
shifted so he was halfway facing toward me, his gaze
fixed on my profile. "I have an idea."

"You do?" I didn't dare move, didn't want him to
see any of the yearning currently pulsing within me.
I wished it could be different, but I just wasn't brave
enough.

"Tomorrow's the Day of the Dead. *Díos de los
Muertos.*"

"And?"

He smiled, but it was a grave, quiet smile. "I think
there are a lot of dead who need to be honored."

CHAPTER THIRTEEN

We'd been meaning to go back into town anyway, but had been putting it off for one reason or another. Well, today we had a mission.

I drove, of course, since I still felt hinky about letting Jace get behind the wheel of my father's Cherokee. This time we went to a place we'd avoided, the Albertson's grocery store near the center of town. So far, we'd either had everything we needed on hand, or we hunted or foraged for it. Although there were items we could have used from the store, neither of us thought it a very good idea to go in there, not with all that food spoiling inside.

Neither did we know for sure what it would be like now, after having the power cut off for more than a month, but it was the best place we could think of to get some of those saints' candles for our Day of the Dead observance. Maybe Santa Fe had a Hispanic grocery store somewhere, but I remembered the Albertson's because that's where the girls and I stocked up on booze when we came to stay at Elena's parents' timeshare.

I pulled into the parking lot of the Albertson's, then reached down and pulled the bandanna I had wrapped around my neck up and over my mouth. Jace did the same. We looked like we were there to hold up the place, but it seemed the best solution, since we didn't have access to any surgical masks.

"Ready?" he asked.

Probably not, but it was too late to back out now. Besides the candles, there were a number of nonperishable goods we wanted to grab—paper towels, toilet paper, rice, flour, sugar, spices. Of course Jace didn't know the store at all, but I had a hazy idea of where some things were located, based on my previous visits here. I'd just have to hope it would be enough to get us in and out as quickly as possible.

"Ready," I said, my voice muffled by the bandanna tied over my mouth.

We got out of the Cherokee and headed toward the entrance to the store. Shopping carts had been abandoned in haphazard order in front of the building, and we each grabbed one. We also both held big crank-operated flashlights, part of the emergency supplies at the compound, since my experience inside the Walgreens in Albuquerque had taught me that those little pen-sized ones really didn't cut it when you were trying to carry out a salvage operation.

The glass in the door had been broken out and lay scattered all over the place, so it was a good thing that Jace and I both wore heavy hiking boots. Shards of glass crunched underfoot as we pushed our way inside, flashlights bobbing this way and that.

It was fairly cold that day; the outside temperature reading in the Cherokee had put it at around forty-six degrees. Maybe that was a good thing, as it kept the smell from being too overwhelming, even with my nose covered. Oh, it was definitely there, something sickly sweet and yet acrid at the same time, but not so overpowering that I couldn't ignore the odor. It did seem to catch at the back of my throat, and I found myself breathing shallowly, pushing the cart grimly ahead while Jace cut off to the right to canvass that side of the store.

Some people might have said that was foolish, to separate like that, but since neither of us had seen another living soul in weeks, we decided it was a risk we were willing to take. This way we could be in and out more quickly.

As I moved along, panning my flashlight over the shelves, I could again see evidence of looting, of items that had been taken. Breakfast cereals seemed to be popular, for some reason. The vitamin aisle had also been almost cleaned out, although I found some bottles of multis that had been left behind. The same with the paper goods—a lot had been taken, but not all. I grabbed what I could, stacking big packages of toilet paper and paper towels in my shopping cart.

Then I came around the corner and found the real reason why we'd come there: the Hispanic food section. I was sort of surprised to see that all the saint candles seemed undisturbed. Maybe people had been more interested in seeing to their physical needs than their spiritual ones, or possibly it was just that they hadn't thought to use the candles for lighting after the power failed. Whatever. It didn't matter now. What mattered was that I was able to scoop up a dozen of the things, packing them in and around the toilet paper and the boxes of Kleenex and all the other items I'd picked up.

"Got 'em!" I called out.

Jace's voice came back to me from the other side of the store. "Great! Go on out to the Jeep—I'm almost done."

I wasn't sad to hear that at all. This grocery store wasn't quite as creepy as the Walgreens had been, since the flashlight I held was far more effective than the one I'd had then. Besides, I knew Jace would come running the second I gave the alarm, should anything strange happen. All the same, I was glad to get out of there, out of the lingering stench and the mournful realization that nobody would be coming by to restock those shelves or pick up the items that had been knocked to the floor.

As I was beginning to load my haul into the cargo area of the Cherokee, Jace came out as well, his cart full to the brim with those big economy-size bags of rice, boxes of salt, pepper grinders, container after container of spices—you name it, he seemed to have nabbed it from the bakery aisle, including some much-needed tins of olive oil. We had some, but not nearly enough. This would definitely help to extend our supplies for a good many more months.

"Looks like you plan to keep me chained to the stove for a good while longer," I joked.

He slanted me one of those dark-lashed looks I loved so much. "Oh, I might give you time off for good behavior."

"That a fact?"

"Absolutely."

A hint of a smile had been playing around the corners of his mouth, but as I watched, it faded. When I followed his gaze, I thought I understood why. I'd excavated my cart to the point where all that was left were the saints candles. He reached in and picked one up, turning it over in his hands. From her blue robe, I guessed the saint depicted on it was the Virgin Mary, but I didn't know for sure. My family wasn't Catholic.

Elena would have known, but she was long gone.

"I suppose we're done here," Jace said. It wasn't a question.

"Yes," I told him. "Let's go."

Although we hadn't discussed our plan in any detail, somehow we were both drawn to the monument at the center of the plaza. It seemed that here, in the heart of the city, was the best place to pay our respects.

Dead leaves had scattered over the walkways, but otherwise the place looked as if it hadn't been touched since the last time I was here, when the voice had summoned the wind to sweep up the mess the looters had left behind. True, many of the stores had their windows broken in, but unlike at the Albertson's, there was no glass scattered on the ground.

I had to wonder how much of that detail Jace took in as we walked from the Jeep to the center of the plaza. Some, it seemed, if the tight lines of his mouth and the puzzled furrow in his brow were any indication. But he didn't ask any questions, only continued to the monument and the low wall that surrounded it.

The day had remained dark, the clouds threatening, although it hadn't rained. It smelled like it might, though, heavy and damp. If it did, then these candles wouldn't last very long. But at least we would have made the effort.

Still not speaking, we each took our burden of candles and placed them at regular intervals along the low wall surrounding the monument. Jace produced a box of strike-anywhere matches from the inner pocket of his jacket, then took one out and used the rough concrete of the wall to get it started. It flared up, and he cupped it in his hand, moving from candle to candle and lighting them one by one. They flickered in the chilly wind but didn't go out.

We'd waited to go out on this expedition until late afternoon, and now it was almost dusk. It was the first time I'd ventured out into the city at anywhere close to dark, and I realized how very black it would soon become, especially with the cloud cover blocking out any possible moonlight or starlight. But we had our flashlights, and, for the moment at least, the candles themselves were giving off far more illumination than I had expected they would.

Jace glanced over at me, and I nodded. This had been his idea, after all, and so I thought he should be the one to make the speeches.

For a long moment, he didn't speak, but only stood there in front of the candle with the Virgin Mary on it, the blue of her robe seeming to glow from within. Then he said, "We honor all those who walk in the paths of their ancestors. Those of us who are left here behind have so many questions, questions we know will never be answered. But our thoughts are with you, and we hope you have all found peace in the next world."

The next words he uttered, I couldn't understand, and I realized he must be speaking the language of the Pueblo. The sound of it was slow and sad, but strong and rich as well, and I found something inside me unclenching for the first time since I'd left Albuquerque. True, I had written something of the time before, in the little sketches I'd jotted down during my first days at the compound. After that, though, I had walled away my grief, thinking that the only way to survive and go on was not to think of everyone who was gone, of everyone I had lost. Now, hearing Jace speak, I knew that had been the wrong approach. I needed to celebrate who they were and what they had done, not pretend they had never existed. That was doing them no service, giving them no honor.

Jace fell silent, and I could see the way he looked over at me, clearly expecting me to say something. How I was supposed to follow that, I had no idea. But no, that was foolish. This wasn't a competition.

"I miss you all," I said simply, then turned and began to walk away from the monument. I didn't bother to turn on my flashlight, even though the sun had gone down by then. The illumination from the candles was enough to light my path.

From behind me, I heard the sound of Jace's footsteps, hurrying a little so he could catch up with me.

And then I felt his hand slip into mine, his fingers warm and strong, even though it was cold enough that we really should have been wearing gloves. My own fingers felt as if they'd been dipped in ice water.

Neither of us said anything. It was enough then to walk hand in hand back to the Jeep, to take comfort in the feel of human flesh pressed against mine, reassuring in the dark and the cold. When it was time to pull the car key out of my pocket, I hesitated for a fraction of a second. I didn't want to let go of him, to relinquish my grip on his fingers.

He seemed to detect my reluctance, because he stood there next to me for a moment, his grip tensing. But then he let go and said, "Let's get home."

I couldn't argue with that. The night wind was drilling through the anorak I wore as if it were made of gauze rather than sturdy canvas, and right then the thought of being surrounded in the warmth of our house seemed even more attractive than usual.

So I nodded and unlocked the Cherokee, and we both climbed in. After I'd pulled away from where we were parked and was negotiating the narrow, car-choked streets—a task far more difficult after dark than it was during the day—I felt Jace's hand cover mine where it rested on the gearshift.

"You okay?" he asked.

I couldn't take my eyes off the road, but I nodded. "I think so. That was—" The exact word seemed to elude me. Moving? Sad? Satisfying? All those, and more. "It helped," I finally said, hoping he would understand what I meant.

It appeared he did, because his fingers tightened around mine. All he said, though, was, "Good." And then he let go, seeming to realize that I needed to focus on driving. Although I'd gone back and forth along this route several times, it had always been during the day, and of course there were no streetlights to guide me along my way.

I flicked on the high-beams and slowed down. Good thing, too, because when I finally got to it, I almost missed the turn-off to Upper Canyon Road. Muttering a curse, I angled the Cherokee onto the street at almost the last minute. In the passenger seat, Jace shifted, but he remained silent, as if he knew any comments on my driving were the last thing I needed right then.

We bumped along, and then there was gravel under our wheels as we left the paved road and began to head up the winding dirt track that led to the compound. I slowed so I could shift into four-wheel drive, and when I looked up, I let out a little screech. Three pairs of eyes seemed to glow red as they stared straight into the Jeep's headlights.

"Coyotes," Jace murmured. "It's okay—just drive forward slowly. They'll get out of the way."

Which they did, as I began to inch toward them. Somehow, though, their movements seemed almost leisurely, as if they weren't too worried about me running them over. Almost at the last minute they got out of the way, but they only moved to the side of the road, where they stood and stared as we passed them by.

Something about their posture, about the way they were watching the Jeep, made the hairs stand up on the back of my neck. It wasn't the cold; I'd turned on the heater as soon as we got inside the SUV. No, their unblinking surveillance just felt...wrong. Unnatural. I'll admit I wasn't the world's foremost authority on coyotes, but in general, wild animals tended to scatter when confronted by something as large and intimidating as a Jeep Grand Cherokee.

I shot a sideways glance at Jace. He wasn't looking at me, though, and instead was staring out the passenger window. I didn't know how much he could even see, since the high-beams were illuminating the road ahead of us, not either side.

"That was weird," I said, once we were past the coyotes and they'd melted away into the darkness.

"A little," he agreed. Then I saw his shoulders lift. "Maybe they're getting bold now that they don't have to worry about getting run over every time they come out of hiding."

That sounded plausible. But still a note of wrongness seemed to echo inside me, and I couldn't help thinking there had to be more to it than that. Then again, the world had ended in a way no one could have ever predicted. Things had been wrong for weeks now.

Well, mainly. I risked a sideways glance at Jace and saw that he was looking out the window again, his fine profile faintly illuminated by the glow from the dashboard lights.

Looking at him, I knew there was one thing right in my life.

Although I cast worried glances from side to side as we approached the compound and I pushed the remote to open the gate, I saw nothing in the darkness, no gleaming red or yellow eyes of various wildlife just waiting to pounce. We came onto the property without incident, although I activated the controls for the gate as soon as our rear bumper had cleared it. The motion-activated lights above the garage door turned on as we approached.

Off in the distance, I did see a shimmer of eyes glowing in the darkness, and I jumped.

"It's okay," Jace said softly. "It's just the goats."

I didn't quite relax, but I did let out my breath. "Oh, right."

Was that a chuckle? When I glanced over at him, his expression was sober enough, but that didn't necessarily mean anything. Fine, if he wanted to laugh at me for jumping at shadows—or glowing eyeballs, in this case—I'd let him. I didn't see anything wrong with staying on my guard.

But the unpacking of the Cherokee passed without incident, although it took longer than I'd expected to unload all that stuff and get it safely stowed. Dutchie kept wandering between us, trying to track all the new and interesting smells we were bringing in the house, until at last I bribed her with a chewy treat so she'd get out from underfoot.

By then it was moving on toward seven o'clock, and far past time for dinner. When I had all afternoon to figure out what to make and plenty of time to prepare it, I really didn't mind cooking. Right now, though, I thought I might have sold my soul for pizza delivery. Or Chinese takeout.

Jace must have noticed my lack of enthusiasm for the task at hand, because he said, "It's not that bad. Look what I brought back." And I saw that he held a package of fettucini in one hand and a jar of vodka cream sauce in the other. "Add some of that rabbit sausage you made a few days ago, and we're set."

I could have kissed him. Actually, I realized I would have loved to have an excuse to go over and kiss him, but I wasn't sure dry pasta and pre-made sauce were a good enough reason. I had to settle for smiling and saying, "That sounds perfect. Can you feed Dutchie while I get this going?"

He nodded, setting the pasta and the jar of sauce down on the countertop. The dog, seeing that he was heading toward the pantry, got up from her rug and went bounding over to him, tail wagging wildly. At least she wasn't the type to turn up her nose at kibble. She still got as excited about it as though we were feeding her T-bone steak or something.

While they were occupied, I filled a big stock pot with water and set it on the stove, then found a smaller pan and dumped the sauce into it, setting it on low heat on the back burner. The sausages were being stored in an airtight container in the fridge, so I got them out and started them cooking, too. Actually, I was sort of surprised that they'd turned out as well as they had. Let's just say that making sausages hadn't exactly been in my cooking repertoire before this, but they really weren't that difficult, once you figured out how it all worked.

They were just starting to sizzle away when Jace came over to the stove and paused to sniff the air. "Those smell good."

"You said the same thing two days ago when we had them for the first time."

One eyebrow went up. "So? Two days shouldn't make them taste any less good."

Maybe not. I wasn't going to argue the point, especially with him standing that close to me, barely a foot away. He'd taken off his jacket, and I could see the way the knit henley shirt he wore molded to the muscles in his arms and chest, the smooth golden-brown skin where he'd left one button undone.

Shit. I shouldn't be staring. Was I staring?

I had a feeling I was staring.

Blood rose to my cheeks, and I turned back to the skillet, making something of a show of turning the sausages over. I also took a pot holder and lifted the lid on the pot of pasta water to check on it, but it wasn't boiling yet.

As I was setting the pot holder down on the counter, I felt a hand settle on my waist, turn me around. Jace was even closer now, dark eyes fixed on my face. The touch of his fingers through the long-sleeved T-shirt I wore seemed to burn like fire.

I swallowed, thinking I needed to say something. But words had fled, leaving me alone with him, with the need I now saw in those dark eyes. I recognized it at once, because I'd felt the same thing myself.

And then...oh, God...he was bending toward me, his mouth suddenly on mine, his lips strong, urgent. I tasted him, felt him taste me, and then I was pressed against him, feeling the shocking solidity of his body, the power of the muscles in the arms that were now going around me, bringing me even closer, as if he needed every inch of me to be touching every inch of him.

Why now? some part of me asked, but the rest of my mind and body and soul, all those parts that had been aching for him for days...for weeks...they didn't care so much. It was enough that here, in this moment, Jace was kissing me, and I was kissing him back, letting him know I'd wanted this, too, more than he could ever know. Every nerve and cell in my body seemed to be responding, pulsing with heat. Had it ever felt like this before? I didn't know, because Jace kissing me seemed to have wiped away my memories of every other kiss I'd ever experienced.

A hissing sound interrupted us, though, and Jace let go of me abruptly. "The water's boiling," he said.

That's not the only thing boiling, I thought, but I didn't answer, only lunged for the pot holder so I could lift the lid on the stock pot and then turn down the heat to a more reasonable level. Those mundane tasks helped me gather myself a bit, although I could still feel the blood thrumming and throbbing in my veins. That wasn't the only thing throbbing, either. I wouldn't say I was the kind of person who got turned on easily—as my asshole ex-boyfriend had complained on more than one occasion—but right then I was so aroused that Jace probably could have laid me out flat on the kitchen counter and taken me there with absolutely no complaints.

He'd backed away slightly, though, seemed content to watch as I dumped some fettucini into the boiling water and then turned the sausages over once again. It was only after I gave the vodka sauce a quick stir that he said, "You didn't...mind that, did you?"

"Mind it?" I asked. We now stood facing one another, my back to the stove. He looked calm enough, but I thought I could detect a certain hard, bright glint in his eyes that I'd never seen before. Arousal? I couldn't tell.

I realized I didn't know him well enough to guess. Yes, we'd been living under the same roof for almost three weeks now, but we'd always been careful around one another, making sure we didn't cross any lines, didn't blunder through any barriers.

Well, those barriers were pretty well knocked down now.

"I didn't—I didn't want you to think I was forcing you or anything."

Now he appeared almost worried, the gleam gone from his eyes, leaving them sober and dark, so dark I couldn't really tell where the pupils ended and the irises began.

Forcing me? That was a joke. I'd wanted that kiss, but had worried that my growing feelings for him weren't reciprocated.

"I mean, after what happened to you in Albuquerque—"

Time to disabuse him of that notion. I set the spoon down on the little stone rest we used to keep our cooking utensils off the counter, then went over and took his hands in mine, right before I went on my tiptoes and kissed him on the lips. A fast kiss, not like the breath-stealing, knee-knocking one we'd shared a few moments earlier, but still enough that he should understand that I liked kissing him very much indeed.

"This isn't Albuquerque," I told him. "And you're nothing like...either of them." To be fair, I didn't even know for sure that the man who'd wanted to steal the Cherokee had the same designs on me that Chris Bowman did, but I'd gotten the impression his intentions weren't exactly benign. "And I've wanted...this...for a long time. I just wasn't sure it was what *you* wanted."

The tense set of his shoulders seemed to relax slightly, and he even grinned. "Oh, I wanted it, too. But I didn't want to push you. I could tell you'd been through a lot."

"We both have," I said simply. No need to go into it any more than that. He'd lost everything, and I'd lost everything. Through some miracle, though, we'd both come to this place, come to the one spot in the world where we'd be safe to grow into knowing one another, caring for one another.

And again I couldn't help wondering if this was somehow the doing of my guardian angel, the voice. Had he given Jace the same prompting he'd given me?

Eyes flickering as he seemed to study my face, Jace asked, "What is it?"

Did I dare mention the voice? We'd just opened up so much to each other; the last thing I wanted was for him to think I was crazy, or at least slightly unbalanced by everything I'd experienced since the Heat stole everything I loved. But I didn't want to keep it a secret from him, either.

"Did you...." I began, then stopped. He was still holding my hands, fingers strong and somehow comforting. I never wanted him to let go, although I knew he'd have to at some point, just to let me get back to making dinner. But that could wait another minute or two. His gaze was still resting on my face, expectant, wondering what I was trying to ask. And there was simply no good way to ask.

"Did you ever hear anything?" I blurted. "Afterward, I mean. Like a voice guiding you, telling you where you should go. Telling you should come here."

A long, long pause. At least he hadn't let go of my hands, but I could see him weighing the question in his mind, trying to see if I was serious. "No, nothing like that," he said at last. "Like I said, I came to Santa Fe because no one seemed to be left in Taos, and I had a friend here. The world's longest shot, I know." He hesitated, then asked, his tone soft, "Did you hear something like that?"

I wanted to deny it. But that would also seem like a denial of all the assistance the voice...guardian angel...whatever...had given me. "Yes," I said. "It's how I found this house. I would never have gotten out of Albuquerque alive if not for the voice."

"'The voice,'" he repeated. Nothing in the calm, even set of his features told me what he was thinking, and so I could only stand there in agony, wondering when he was going to let go and back away from me. Away from the crazy woman.

Somehow I managed to stand there, waiting.

"You've been blessed, I think," Jace said at last. "Some guiding spirit looked down on you and knew you were worthy, that you needed to survive."

Relief washed over me. So he didn't think I was crazy. Then again, although I'd never much believed in such things, I guessed that his people thought differently. The dividing line between our world and the world of the spirits was definitely thinner for them.

"You really think that?" I asked, my voice barely above a whisper. Up until that moment, I hadn't realized how important it was that he believed me.

"Oh, yes," he replied, pulling me closer to him, his lips finding mine. "So let's make sure our survival matters."

CHAPTER FOURTEEN

Dinner was...well, dinner was wonderful. It might have only been left-over sausage and sauce out of a jar, leavened a little by some zucchini from the greenhouse that I steamed to go along with the pasta, but I might as well have been eating at a five-star restaurant for as exhilarated as I felt. Jace had kissed me. Jace wanted me, had only been holding back because he didn't want to pressure me or frighten me off.

Some people might have said it was inevitable, that if you put two healthy, attractive people of the same sexual orientation in the same place, sharing the same home, eventually they'd end up together. Propinquity, or whatever they called it.

I didn't believe that for a second, though. There were plenty of guys I'd known over the years who, if they'd shown up on my doorstep the way Jace had, I could've lived in platonic harmony with and never had the slightest inclination for anything more than a quick hug on a birthday or something.

Jace, on the other hand...well, I'd been thinking how hot he was from the first moment I laid eyes on him, even as I was confronting him at the gate to the compound, shotgun in hand. That sudden, unexpected flare of admiration had shifted into attraction as the days had gone on, and now was...what?

Far more than simple attraction, even if I was too scared to put a label on it right then.

He'd opened a bottle of wine, some more of the Black Mesa Montepulciano, which, as it turned out, was also a New Mexico wine. I'd been so rattled when I arrived at the compound that I hadn't even read the label that closely. It did go well with the simple meal I'd prepared. More than that, it gave the evening a sense of celebration, that this was just the beginning of something far more.

Was I ready for that? Yes, I'd been dutifully taking my pill every night, knew I'd be protected in that way, if nothing else. Maybe I should've been worrying whether Jace had packed some condoms as part of his "surviving the apocalypse" kit, but for some reason, I didn't think that was necessary. He certainly didn't give off the man-whore vibe. It should be fine.

"Dollar for your thoughts," Jace said, and I startled, knowing I could never tell him I'd been pondering contraceptive options. By then we were winding down, only a few bites left on our plates.

"A whole dollar?" I teased, glad that we were eating by candlelight. With any luck, he wouldn't have noticed the way the hot blood rose to my cheeks.

"Well, a penny's probably worth more than a dollar now, since at least you could melt a penny down and get the copper out of it." He set down his fork and leaned forward slightly, a smile touching those full lips, the ones that had felt so delicious when pressed against mine. "But your choice."

"I—I wasn't thinking about anything in particular," I said.

An eyebrow went up.

"Seriously." I lifted my glass of wine and took a quick swallow.

The other eyebrow went up.

Oh, boy. I could stall and I could hedge, but it was pretty obvious that Jace would see through any of those machinations. "Okay, fine," I told him, setting my wine glass back down and taking a breath. "If you have to know, I was thinking about whether you'd packed any condoms when you bailed out of Taos."

He let out a breath, both eyebrows still raised. "You don't beat around the bush, do you?"

"Well, you *asked*."

For a second or two, he didn't say anything, only looked at me. I tried not to blink or glance away, but damn, that was hard. My cheeks felt like they were on fire.

At last he said, "No, I didn't. Sorry...I guess I was thinking more about the world ending or something than whether I was going to get laid in the near future."

I winced, and he shook his head as if exasperated with himself.

"Jessica, I'm sorry. That's not what I meant." His hands flattened on the tabletop, as if by exerting pressure against the cool copper surface, he could take back what he'd just said. "That is, if we—if we were together, I think you know it would be a lot more than just getting laid."

My heart seemed to start beating again. "It would?"

"You know it would," he said, his tone quiet, but no less intense for all that.

I smiled at him. "It's fine. I'm on the pill."

After that...well, I'm still not sure who moved first, but almost in a single motion, we were on our feet, pushing our chairs away from the table, Jace reaching out to take me by the hand. He pulled me into him, kissing me, his mouth sweet with wine. I felt as if I could never get enough of tasting him.

But he broke the kiss after a few seconds, leading me down the hallway to my bedroom. He'd never been in here before, of course, although I left it unlocked most of the time, except for the occasions when I was getting dressed. Since Dutchie liked to wander between our rooms at night, I didn't have the heart to shut the door. Because of that, though, I always kept it tidy. I knew I didn't have to worry about Jace tripping over a discarded bra or something when we entered.

It was cold, though, away from the fireplace in the family room, which did a pretty good job of heating the dining room as well, since they were right next to each other. Jace let go of my hand—with some reluctance, it seemed—and asked, "Okay if I get a fire going?"

"You already have," I said, smiling, but I nodded. "We could use one. It's probably going to get below freezing tonight."

He went to the fireplace and began expertly stacking some logs within it. We were burning a lot already, but I wasn't too worried. The house had an enormous log room built on the north side, with wood stacked almost to the rafters on every wall. Jace had taken one look at the stockpile and said we could have fires in every room through July if necessary.

So I allowed myself to enjoy the warmth that began to spread through the room after he got the fire going, and not fret over whether we were going to run out of wood halfway through the winter. And I'd be lying if I said I didn't also enjoy watching the way Jace's jeans hugged his backside as he bent over, coaxing the fire to life.

Afterward, he turned around, then came over to me where I sat on the foot of the bed. "Better?"

"Yes," I replied. "Although it'll probably still be smart to get under those covers quickly."

"I can help with that." His fingers tugged my shirt loose from the waistband of my jeans, then undid my belt buckle. At the same time, I was working at his belt as well before undoing the buttons on his faded Levi's. I hooked my thumbs through the belt loops of his pants, easing them down. I could tell he was already aroused, the bulge in the dark gray boxer-briefs he wore evidence that stopping to get the fire going hadn't put him too much off his stride, so to speak.

He stepped out of the jeans but didn't let that distract him from pulling my T-shirt up and over my head. After dropping it on top of his jeans, he reached down and undid the front clasp of my bra, releasing a long, drawn-out breath as his hands closed over my bare breasts.

I gasped, closing my eyes as he caressed me, fingers sliding over my skin. Then he was tugging at my jeans, getting them out of the way, and I stepped out of them, letting him lead me over to the bed. With one hand, he yanked back the covers, and I collapsed onto the mattress, bringing him with me, bare skin to bare skin, our mouths finding one another in the fire-lit darkness. The sheets were icy cold, but I hardly noticed.

Because oh, God, he was reaching between my legs, stroking me as his mouth closed on my nipple. My heart was pounding, my breath coming in great, heaving gasps. I had done all these things before, but never with Jace. And it had never felt like this with anyone else.

My own hand moved lower, touching him, wrapping around him, feeling the heat and the strength of his arousal. He moaned as I touched him, the sound seeming to reverberate through every inch of my body. Or maybe it was just the approaching wave of the orgasm that I could feel bearing down on me, building up until I couldn't do anything except allow Jace to touch me, to flick his tongue against the bud of my breast, and then it tore through me like a swollen river breaking down a dam, my voice calling his name, my body heaving against his.

Yes, it had been a while, but it was more than that. It was Jace, all of it—the way he'd made me come, the way I felt as if I had been some strange half-alive being before this, hiding in the darkness until he brought me into the light.

Then he was shifting, moving, and I could feel him pushing against me, against my entrance. I'd never wanted anything more than I wanted him inside me, filling me. "Please, Jace," I breathed.

That was all he needed. In that instant, he was there, in me, moving deeper and deeper as I rocked my hips against his, drawing him into me, our bodies locked together, finding the rhythm, the perfect push and pull of man and woman, Jace and me. I clung to him, one hand moving up to clutch his neck, feeling the leather cord that held his hair back. One tug, and it was loose, his raven hair spilling over his shoulders, brushing against my cheek, and that was it, the last push I needed. Crying out, calling his name, gasping, my body convulsing against his, and then I could feel him let loose, heard him groan, his hips driving him into me, my legs wrapped around him, until finally he stilled, went quiet, his mouth by my ear, my name a soft breath in the silent room.

"Jessica...."

We lay there for uncounted moments, flesh to flesh, drinking in each other's warmth. Finally, he shifted, pulling away from me, but only so he could lie on his side, his chest touching my arm, as if he didn't want any real distance to come between us. I understood the feeling all too well. In a moment, I'd have to force myself out of bed and go to the bathroom, get myself cleaned up, but right then I only wanted to be next to him, to breathe him in, to reassure myself that he truly was real, that this actually had happened.

He reached out and pushed a strand of hair away from my face. Such a tender gesture, so different from the wild abandon of a few minutes earlier. Because the room was so dimly lit, I couldn't precisely decipher his expression. But I definitely wasn't expecting what came next.

"I love you, Jessica."

Out of nowhere. Or not nowhere, not really. I could have seen those words in the way he looked at me when he thought I wouldn't notice, in how careful he was to listen to my suggestions...in the very reticence that had kept him from making a move until he was certain it wouldn't be rebuffed.

And because he'd been brave enough to say it first, I didn't hesitate. Not now. I'd been denying this to myself, coming up with reasons why it couldn't be true, but there was no point in denying it any longer.

"I love you, Jace." It was true. I knew it, accepted it, let my heart and mind and soul become open to the idea. I loved Jason Little River. The sound of his voice. The crinkle at the corner of his eyes when he laughed. The long, strong fingers of his hands. The way he asked for my opinion on things and never made me feel foolish for not knowing as much as he did about raising animals or gardening or...well, most things. I'd led a sheltered life, while I got the impression he hadn't. His hands were beautiful, but they had the calluses and scars of someone who hadn't spent his entire life behind a desk. I supposed that was from the time he spent at the pueblo, even though his own start-up business had involved computers.

All these details and contradictions, all the elements that made Jace uniquely Jace...they were what made me realize I loved him. And, by some miracle, he loved me in return.

He pulled me against him, and I burrowed my face into his chest, breathing in the warm, delicious scent of his skin, hearing his heart beat, strong and sure. I couldn't remember a time when I'd been this happy.

Happy. Was I allowed to be happy, when most of the world was gone?

I didn't know. I tried to tell myself that my parents would have wanted me to be happy, that they wouldn't have wanted me to wallow in sorrow for the rest of my days, just because they were gone. But even in the warm afterglow of our lovemaking, of hearing Jace say that he loved me, I couldn't help feeling a twinge of guilt.

He pushed a lock of hair away from my face, trailed his fingers across my cheek and down to my mouth. I pressed my lips very softly against his forefinger, and he smiled. But then his expression sobered, and he gave me a very direct look.

"Don't do this to yourself," he said.

"Do what?" But I was pretty sure what he meant.

"You can't beat yourself up just because you've found some happiness in your life. The Dying wasn't your fault. All you can do is live your life to the best of your ability, make your survival mean something."

The Dying. It was the first time I'd heard him use that phrase, but it was apt enough. Because that was what had irrevocably changed the world... all that death.

"I know," I whispered. "It's just sometimes...it comes rushing over me like a wave, you know? I put it aside, and I'm fine, because I'm here with you, and I know we're safe, but...."

His arms went around me, keeping me close to him, close to the security of that strongly beating heart and the soothing warmth of his flesh. "I know." The words came in a murmur, gentle. "You're stronger than you know, Jessica. It's human to feel doubt and worry. But...don't let it get between us. Please?"

There was a note of concern in his voice that I hadn't heard before, and I shifted so I could look up into his eyes. "Oh, no," I told him then. "I'll never let anything come between us."

We slept in each other's arms that night, and awoke to a chilly morning where the roof of the garage was white with frost. The fire had guttered down to coals, and Jace wrapped one of the blankets around himself as he got up to set new logs in the hearth and get a fresh blaze going. Dutchie watched all this with approval; it looked as if she hadn't moved since she curled up in front of the fireplace the night before. I got the distinct impression that she was happy with our new sleeping arrangements, since it meant she wouldn't have to split her time between Jace's and my room anymore.

Even with the fire going, I was loath to get out of bed. But I wasn't a city girl any longer; I needed to get moving, shower, check on the goats, start breakfast. All these things were speeded up by Jace and me sharing the shower in the master bath, which was roomy enough that we fit quite nicely. Okay, we didn't save quite as much time as I'd thought, because we got lost in lathering up each other's bodies, running soapy hands over bare skin, until I was pressed up against the wall and he was inside me again, one of my legs wrapped around him, holding him in place while he thrust into me. We had to clean up all over again afterward, but it was worth it.

At last, though, we got out of the shower—mostly because the hot water heater began to run out of steam—and got dressed, then dried our hair. A pang went through me as he fished another one of those leather cords out of his pocket and began winding it around his hair.

"Don't," I said, and he turned toward me with a quizzical look.

"Don't what?"

"Don't tie it up. I like it down."

A slow smile spread over his lips then, and he shrugged and shoved the cord back into the pocket of his jeans. "Okay. But if it starts getting in my face when I'm out in the wind—"

"Then okay, you can tie it back again." I went to him and gave him a quick kiss on the cheek. "I'm not totally unreasonable, you know."

"Oh, I know." He gave my own ponytail the side-eye, and I couldn't help laughing.

"Yeah, do as I say and all that."

We went out to check on the goats before breakfast, our breath puffing up into the icy air. They seemed all right, but Jace looked at the frost on the ground and shook his head.

"We need to get them some kind of protection from the cold. It's only going to get worse after this, and when we have our first snowfall...." He didn't bother to finish the sentence, but I knew what he meant. Our little herd needed someplace to go.

"So what are you thinking?" I asked, looking around the walled-in landscape. From within the chicken coop, I could hear the hens clucking away happily. It was obvious they hadn't suffered too much from the cold.

"It doesn't need to be fancy, but some kind of shed, someplace where they can go inside if they need to. The henhouse went together pretty quickly, so I'm sure I can do something like that for the goats, too."

I saw another foray to Home Depot in our near future. We'd stocked up on food just the day before, but if we were going to Santa Fe anyway, I was going to put in a request to raid an outdoor gear store or something similar. My outerwear definitely wasn't up to snuff, and I had a feeling that adding some thermal underwear to my repertoire wouldn't be a bad idea, either.

So I asked about that, and Jace nodded. "I could use a few things, too. So we'll do that first, and then we'll go the hardware store. I need to check the library here, though—I'm pretty sure I saw a book with plans for different kinds of outbuildings, and that'll help me figure out how much to bring back."

With that settled, he headed back into the house to start making notes, and I popped into the henhouse to scoop up some fresh eggs for breakfast, then hurried to the kitchen. At least in there it was relatively warm and cheery. My fingers gradually thawed out as I made scrambled eggs and toast, and a pot of fresh coffee. I reflected then that Jace was right—I couldn't let survivor's guilt get in the way of enjoying the life I had now. I had him, and we had this beautiful place to live, with plenty of food and no one bothering us. In this post-Dying world, that was about as close to heaven as I would probably get.

After breakfast, we patted Dutchie and went out to the garage. I'd been thinking this over while Jace took care of this dishes, and I realized it was time for me to show how much I really did trust him.

"Wait," I said as he began to head to the passenger side of the Jeep. He glanced back toward me, and I opened my hand to reveal the key fob lying on my palm. "You want to drive?"

His dark eyes lit up, but he didn't move. "Are you sure?"

I nodded, and he came back to me, taking the key from my hand as he leaned down to kiss me. Mmm, coffee and the faintest trace of butter, rich and friendly, welcoming, just like the man who was kissing me.

"Thank you," he said, then went to climb in the driver-side door.

It felt strange to go around to the passenger side, to get in and then watch Jace back the Cherokee out of the garage and maneuver it down the steeply sloping drive to the gate. I had a new perspective on things this way, could concentrate on my surroundings rather than merely on the road.

Not that there was a lot to look at up here. The junipers didn't change much with the seasons, and the grass had already been sere and yellow even before the frost hit. But the sky was a deep, deep blue, overlaid with faint traceries of high clouds, and in the Sangre de Cristo mountains above town, I could see the patches of bright yellow aspens now looking faded as they lost more and more of their leaves, settling in for winter.

We came down onto Upper Canyon road and wended our way into town. "Any ideas on outdoor supply places?" Jace asked.

"Not really," I admitted. "When I came here with my friends, we were more interested in partying than hiking. And of course you can't Yelp something after the apocalypse."

His mouth seemed to twitch, but when he turned slightly to look at me, his expression was grim enough. "Is that what you think this is? The apocalypse?"

"Well, close enough as makes no difference." We'd slowed to maybe twenty miles an hour at the most, partly because Jace was weaving in and out of the abandoned cars on the streets, but also because I had a feeling he didn't have any idea where he was supposed to go. "I mean, most of the world is dead, and the life we had back then is gone. No, I suppose there weren't any four horsemen and blood-red moons and flaming swords and all that, but...."

He didn't reply, but I could almost feel him turning over the idea in his head. My knowledge of Native American mythology was scanty at best, and so I didn't know if his people had their own vision of the end of the world. The terminology I'd used was purely Revelations sort of stuff, but that was my only frame of reference. At least, those were the kinds of things you'd always hear quoted in movies dealing with the end times.

"I have an idea," he said, in a very different tone. "Let's stop and go into that hotel. They had to have phone books and local directories at the concierge desk, right?"

He had a point. I couldn't remember the last time I'd used a phone book, since I either used Yelp or Google Maps to find things with my cell phone, but maybe not everyone was as firmly rooted in the digital age as I had been before the world collapsed. Checking at the hotel sounded like a good idea.

So he pulled up onto the sidewalk in front of the La Fonda Hotel, in a spot where once bellhops had probably assisted people with their luggage but was now free of cars. And actually, as I got out of the Jeep and looked around quickly, it somehow seemed as if the street wasn't quite as choked with vehicles as I remembered it.

"What's the matter?" Jace asked, seeming to notice the way I was scanning the street. "Do you see something?" His hand went to his belt, and for the first time I realized he was wearing his long knife in its sheath. I hadn't even thought to bring one of the guns with me. Maybe Jace made me feel a little *too* safe. I was getting sloppy.

"No," I replied, quickly so he wouldn't get too nervous. "That is...I could have sworn there were more cars here the last time I drove through. It's as if some of them are just...gone."

His eyebrows went up, and I could see him look past me to the street the hotel faced. What good that would do, I wasn't sure, because I didn't think he'd even come this way when he passed through town. There were obvious gaps in the lines of cars parked at the sidewalk, but that didn't have to mean anything, except that no one had been parked there in the first place.

"You're sure?" he asked, and now I thought I detected a note of patience in his voice, as if he was trying to humor me.

"No, I'm not sure, because I wasn't memorizing everything I saw when I drove through here. It just feels...off."

"Well, all the more reason for us to see if we can find a phone book and a map, and then get out of here."

I decided I couldn't argue with that logic, and followed him into the lobby of the hotel.

Luckily for us, the concierge's desk did have an area phone book, as well as a detailed map of downtown and a larger one for the greater Santa Fe area. I took a quick glance around, remembering how Tori and Elena and I had gone up to the rooftop bar for drinks. Back then the place had been packed. Now the tiled floors echoed under our footsteps, and I had to work hard not to look at the flurries of gray ash that stray drafts must have blown against the floorboards and into the corners.

It felt good to be out in the sun again, despite the brisk wind, although we got into the Jeep quickly enough. I paged through the phone book and discovered that there was an REI probably less than five minutes from our current location. Jace seemed cheered by that, and we headed there in silence, although I kept looking at the streets as they passed by, trying to determine if they felt less impacted by abandoned vehicles than I'd previously thought. It was hard to say for sure, as I'd never gone down this particular road. It did seem less crowded than it should be, although I was basing that observation on pure gut feeling and not much more.

The store was located almost on the railroad tracks, just off Market Street. While there were a few vehicles parked nearby, the place still felt far more deserted than some of the other shops I'd visited. Again, people probably weren't thinking of outdoor supplies as they were succumbing one by one to the Heat.

Jace and I got out of the Jeep and headed to the store entrance. The glass wasn't smashed, but the doors seemed to have gotten stuck halfway open. Convenient, since we wouldn't have to worry about breaking in.

When we entered the store, though, I still got the feeling that it had been carefully ransacked, although it wasn't a mess. No, it was more that the stock seemed far leaner than it should have been. The glass case with the GPS devices had been emptied of its contents, and it looked as if a bunch of the mountain bikes were gone, too.

But at least the low-dollar stuff like the thermal underwear and the gloves hadn't been totally depleted. I got a shopping cart and started adding anything in my size, while Jace went to the men's section and basically did the same thing. He dumped in all his items, then went back for a thigh-length down-filled jacket. Before he put it in the cart, he looked at the price tag and shook his head.

"What?" I asked.

"That coat cost more than I paid for my motorcycle."

Ouch. Well, retail prices were definitely a thing of the past, so it wasn't as if we had to worry about whether we could afford any of this stuff. "Yes," I said, "but a motorcycle won't keep you warm at night."

A corner of his mouth quirked, even as a warm gleam came and went in his eyes. "Oh, I've got something way better than a jacket for keeping me warm at night."

I could feel heat as well, running through my core, but I knew we needed to stay focused on the task at hand. "Anything else?"

"That about does it for me. I like my boots, so I'm not going to bother replacing them. You?"

"Same." Maybe there were some fancy outdoor shoes that would have suited me better, but my hiking boots were sturdy and comfortable. They'd cost me a good chunk back in the day as well, come to think of it. Money well spent, as far as I was concerned, considering everything they'd gotten me through during the past few weeks.

So we pushed our haul out to the Cherokee and stowed everything in the back. "Who do you think took that other stuff?" I asked Jace, just as he was closing the hatch to the cargo area.

He shrugged. "Other survivors, I suppose."

"Don't you think it's weird that we still haven't seen anyone?" Something felt strange. I couldn't put my finger on it, since I really didn't have any frame of reference for what things were supposed to feel like after the apocalypse. Still, you'd think that any survivors in Santa Fe would have seen Jace and me coming and going, would have realized we didn't pose any kind of threat. At least, I didn't think we looked terribly intimidating.

"I don't know. Maybe." He turned the key over in his hand, fiddling with it. "I'll bet if you crunched the numbers, you'd realize the odds of us running across any of the few hundred survivors in the area on any given day really aren't that great. We'd have to keep coming down here day after day, looking for them. Are you ready to do that?"

Part of me was. Oh, I didn't really need anyone other than Jace, and we'd done just fine—more than fine—on our own, but still....

I wanted to know.

However, I could tell from the expression Jace currently wore that he didn't share this particular thirst for knowledge, and I decided I'd better not push it. After all, before I'd met him, my run-ins with survivors of the Dying hadn't exactly been all that pleasant.

"No," I said, and gave him what I hoped was a convincing smile. "I've got better things to do with my time."

CHAPTER FIFTEEN

Strangely, although at first glance the Home Depot looked exactly the same as the last time we'd left it after we'd gotten the supplies for the chicken coop, when we went to fetch a trailer to haul the lumber home, only one was still sitting there. The other three were gone.

That did take Jace aback; he stood there for a moment, hand on his chin, staring at the spaces where the trailers had been parked. Finally he said, "What the hell?"

"So you'll admit they're gone."

"Of course they're gone. It's kind of obvious, don't you think?" Then he shook his head. "Sorry, Jess. Didn't mean to snap at you. But this is just weird."

That was a good word for it. I could see survivors making off with GPS devices and hiking boots and multi-packs of toilet paper. But equipment trailers?

"Well, at least they left us one," I offered.

That didn't seem to mollify him much. He stood there, hands shoved in his pockets, clearly discomfited by this evidence that there were survivors, and that they seemed to be organized enough to make off with most of the store's trailers. I saw the troubled glance he sent toward the entrance at the lumberyard end of the building, and guessed he was worried that the stock inside would be similarly picked over.

We were here now, though, so we might as well go in and see what we could find, once we had the trailer hooked up to the Cherokee. That didn't take long, though, and afterward we headed toward the building, both of us grimly silent.

Several big orange flatbed carts sat near the entrance, so Jace took one and wheeled it in, glass crunching underfoot as he did so. It seemed clear enough, even from a quick glance around, that someone had been in here since our last visit. The battery displays were almost all emptied out, and a lot of tools seemed to be missing, too. But at least the lumberyard didn't look as if it had been raided, so Jace was able to get the supplies he needed. Tools we already had back at the compound, up to and including a belt sander and a jigsaw, so the looters were welcome to take anything that still remained here.

"I wonder what they're doing with all of it," I ventured as he began shifting the lumber from the cart and into the trailer.

"Who knows?" he replied. "They're probably people like us—you know, with a place where they're holed up and safe but still need assorted odds and ends. Actually, I have a feeling they would need more, since our compound was so well stocked when you found it. And you're probably used to seeing stores getting restocked on a regular basis. Things can start to look pretty picked over when no one's coming in with new products all the time."

Well, that made sense. It was true that I didn't have much experience yet of a world where stores weren't magically restocked when supplies ran low. Even so, something didn't feel right to me. Batteries and hammers I could understand. But the trailers? I supposed if they had enough stuff to haul away, it made some sense. But that would have to be a *lot* of stuff.

Jace finished tying down the lumber, then threw the nails and fasteners and other small items he'd collected into the cargo area of the Jeep. From the way the corners of his mouth were turned down, I could tell he wasn't thrilled at the prospect of having to compete with other survivors for supplies we might need to get through the winter.

But no, that wouldn't happen. We were stocked on food, and now we had milk and eggs and cheese and butter, so really, once we got the goats sheltered, we wouldn't have much need to come back down to Santa Fe proper unless we were just dying to. And I didn't see that happening anytime soon.

Thinking about our goats made me recall the herd we'd taken them from. They were just as much out in the cold, although I thought I remembered seeing a few ramshackle outbuildings on the property where they were grazing. Still, it couldn't hurt to check on them. It wasn't that out of our way.

When I mentioned my concerns to Jace, he nodded. "That's probably a good idea. They would have more shelter there than our own goats, but we might as well look. If they're in trouble, we can unload this stuff, get the horse trailer, and then bring them back to the compound. It might take a couple of trips, though."

I said I wouldn't mind that at all, so we got into the Cherokee and drove off, angling away from our normal route so we could get to the edge of town and the small ranch where we'd first found the goats. But when we got there, the animals were all gone. I would have said they'd wandered off on their own, but I could see tire tracks in the dirt, tracks that were fatter and wider than those of my Jeep. Some big off-road truck, if I had to guess.

Jace seemed to be of the same opinion, because he squatted down to take a closer look, one finger digging into the rutted earth. "Probably a half-ton pickup, judging by the tread and how deep it is." He stood, following the tracks along the narrow dirt road that led to the pasture gate. We'd come in that same way, but it looked like the truck had turned and headed west afterward, rather than to the east, the direction of town and our own hidden compound.

"Where do you think they were going?" I asked.

"I have no idea. I don't think there's much out that way, unless they were headed to the highway. And if that's the case, their home base could be anywhere."

"So you don't think they're local?"

For a second or two, Jace didn't answer me. He just stood there, gazing off to the west, straight brows pulled together in a frown. The wind blew his loose hair, turning it into a shining raven cloud around his head, but for some reason, I didn't find myself quite as lost in admiration as I might otherwise have been. Instead, a shiver of apprehension went down my spine. Whatever thoughts might be occupying his mind, they didn't look as if they were pleasant ones.

"I don't know if they're from around here," he said at last. "Maybe, maybe not. Maybe one of the survivors knew this ranch existed, then noticed some of the goats were missing and came back to get the rest before they disappeared, too. And maybe they're holed up some-place remote, just like we are." He turned and began heading back to the Jeep, walking quickly. I practically had to jog to keep up with him.

I almost asked what the rush was, but he seemed to know what I was thinking. Jaw tense, he told me,

"I think it's better that we get back. We've been gone long enough."

Nothing else, but the implication was enough to make me hurry into the passenger seat, to hold on as he drove faster than he really should have on the way home, the trailer rattling and bumping behind us. It was a beautiful, brisk fall day, but I couldn't enjoy the scenery. I just wanted to get home and make sure everything was all right.

If anything had happened to Dutchie....

But when we pulled up and opened the gate, everything looked fine. The goats were still wandering around, eating dried grass, and I could hear the hens clucking away in the chicken coop. Jace maneuvered the Jeep around so he could back the trailer up to the edge of the yard. That way, he wouldn't have to carry the lumber as far. He left it, though, to come with me to the house.

"Let me go in first," he said, and I did as he asked, allowing him to walk in front of me.

All that did was subject him to the first of Dutchie's onslaught. She came bounding up to us, panting, tail wagging, nose busily sniffing the bags we carried. Since all they held was the clothing we'd pilfered from REI, she lost interest soon enough, instead hanging out by the pantry, clearly angling for a chewy treat.

"I think it's safe," I told Jace, going to get the dog her treat. Maybe she hadn't exactly earned it, but I was so happy to see her and the rest of the property safe that I didn't much care.

"Probably. I'll go drop this stuff in the bedroom, though. That way I can check the rest of the house."

I didn't bother to stop him. If it made him feel better, he was welcome to search every inch of the property.

After I gave Dutchie her treat, I paused and surveyed the kitchen. Nothing appeared out of place, unless you wanted to count some water slopped on the floor around the dog's bowl. The world's neatest drinker she was not. Otherwise, though, it was tidy enough, the dishes stacked in the wooden drainer on the counter, everything I'd used to make breakfast either put back in the refrigerator or the pantry.

Jace entered the kitchen then, relief plain on his face. "Everything looks fine."

"Were you really worried it wouldn't?"

"I don't know. I suppose—" He stopped there, clearly trying to decide what he really wanted to say. "I suppose seeing all that stuff taken rattled me. I'm not sure why. Maybe because the last time we were in town, I didn't see any evidence of other survivors. Now, though...." His shoulders lifted; I noticed that he'd taken off the leather jacket he'd worn on our expedition. "I know it's stupid. They have just as much right to help themselves to supplies as we do. But the way they came in and took all the rest of the goats? It feels... greedy, I guess. We only took what we needed."

I could see what he was thinking, but at the same time, I wasn't sure I wanted to ascribe any negative intentions to the people who'd collected the rest of the herd. "Maybe...or maybe they saw them and were worried about them, the same way we were, and took them all because they had more room for them. There could be all sorts of reasons."

"You're probably right." The square set of his shoulders seemed to relax a little, and he came over to me and took me in his arms, holding me tightly against him. Something of the cool juniper-scented wind outdoors seemed to have clung to his hair, and I breathed it in, marveling at how the feel of him could drive all worries right out of my head. Whoever had absconded with the goats, it really didn't matter in the grand scheme of things. We had enough to keep our own little homestead going, and would have more goats in the spring, once the does gave birth. Really, in a couple of seasons we'd be swimming in animals and wondering what the heck we were supposed to do with all of them.

"I'll make some sandwiches," I offered, after I glanced at the clock and realized it was nearly one-thirty, past the time when we'd usually eat lunch.

Jace nodded, but I could tell from the way his mouth was set that he was still turning the problem over in his head. Well, if he wanted to brood over it, I couldn't stop him.

I just knew it would be fine. It had to be.

The days seemed to blur after that, running together until I realized that we were less than a week away from Thanksgiving. Jace had spent long hours building the shed for the goats, doing his best to make sure they didn't have to be exposed to the elements any longer than absolutely necessary. And they did seem grateful for the shelter we provided, going in there without any urging from us.

As a child, I'd read all those "Little House" books about Laura Ingalls Wilder and her family moving from place to place, homesteading, farming, and although I thought I'd absorbed most of the details, it wasn't until I was doing roughly the same thing myself that I understood how time-consuming having to do everything yourself actually was. And yes, I realized that Jace and I were living in a modern, up-to-date house with a lot of conveniences that Ms. Wilder could never have conceived of. Even so, there was still housework and laundry and cooking and so much more, like making cheese and sausage and butter, collecting eggs, making sure the goats had fresh water and were milked twice a day, tending the plants in the greenhouse and determining what was ready to be eaten and what still needed a few days. By the time we were done with dinner and the clean-up afterward, Jace and I were practically asleep on our feet. Every once in a great while, we'd sit down and watch a movie from the collection in the family room, but that happened maybe every ten days or so, if that. And no, we never watched any of the real estate developer's porn. Jace had looked at the row of Blue-Rays and chuckled, shooting me an inquiring look.

"No way in hell," I'd told him, and he'd let it go. I wasn't about to confess that I actually had tried to watch one of them in the first week I'd been here, lonely and scared and thinking maybe giving myself an orgasm would help to relax me. But about five minutes of looking at the actors with their unnaturally waxed bodies and the women with their fake breasts and equally fake moans made me less inclined toward sex than I'd ever been in my life, and I took the disc out of the player and put it away, knowing I could never watch one of those movies again.

And now, I had no need to.

By some unspoken agreement, Jace and I had begun making love in the morning, while the world was still dark and the day hadn't wrung every last drop of energy from us. Sometimes one of us would wake up in the middle of the night and reach out for the other, and we'd cling together in a sort of frenzy before passing out again, but it wasn't a common occurrence.

Even so, it was a good life. The weariness I felt every day when I lay down to sleep...it was a good kind of tired, the kind you got when you'd spent your day doing something that felt useful, worthwhile. I could tell that Jace viewed our existence the same way, that he didn't have any regrets about the life we were living. In a post-industrial world, this seemed to be the new normal.

Behind all that, though, I still had this nagging sensation at the back of my mind, as if I was missing something vitally important, that if I could only put the pieces together in the right order, I'd figure out what had been bothering me all this time. It was sort of like looking at one of those "magic eye" pictures and attempting to puzzle out what exactly the hidden image was. I was never very good at that, either. No matter how hard I tried, I could only see a blur of color that didn't mean anything.

In the meantime, Thanksgiving came, and we feasted on pheasant, which I found I enjoyed far more than turkey. Maybe that was simply because, although my mother knew her way around a turkey, my Aunt

Susan really didn't, and so on alternating Thanksgivings I'd had to eat dried-out bird smothered in cranberry sauce to give it a decent flavor.

No such worries with the pheasant Jace brought home, which was moist and delicious, especially paired with a sauce I made from currants he'd found during one of his hunting expeditions. And combined with wild rice and sautéed green beans from the greenhouse—well, it was probably the best Thanksgiving meal I'd ever consumed, even if I couldn't help looking at all the empty seats around that huge dining room table and thinking it would have been wonderful to have friends and family there to share the meal with us.

But that world was long gone, and if I were destined to spend the rest of my life around only one person, I couldn't think of anyone better than Jace to share it with. During that meal, he'd gone quiet a time or two, and I had a feeling he was thinking the same thing, that Thanksgiving was supposed to be about sharing, about being with loved ones, and now ours were all gone.

Those somber moments were fleeting, though, and I could tell he wasn't about to let the memories of what once was ruin what we had now. He joked about Dutchie wanting to eat that pheasant whole before it even hit the back of the ATV, and praised my cooking, raising a glass to honor my efforts. It did feel good. Before all this, I would never have said I was particularly domestic, but I'd risen to the occasion with more success than I could have imagined.

Also, I'd surprised him by putting on the black dress I'd brought from Albuquerque, and my jeweled sandals, and those amazing tanzanite earrings that had so mysteriously shown up in my pocket after my first visit to the plaza in Santa Fe. Actual makeup, my hair styled as best I could, since I hadn't brought any curling irons or hot rollers with me, thinking I'd never need them again. Jace had taken one look at me and asked, "You expect me to be patient all through dinner with you looking like that?"

I'd given him a sphinx-like smile and continued teetering my way back and forth from the kitchen, bringing food to the table. Funny how just a month or so in hiking boots had apparently killed all my ability to walk in heels.

And after dinner, Jace surprised me by taking me in his arms, actually lifting me away from the dining room table and carrying me to the bedroom, where he proceeded to show me exactly how much he appreciated me, mouth moving with teasing slowness across my skin, his fingers stroking me, finding exactly the right spot to wring moans of ecstasy from a place so deep that before I'd been with him, I hadn't even known it existed. Then we were together once more, bodies locked, moving in a rhythm that had become second nature to us by now.

That was really how it felt...natural, as if my body had been made to fit with his, and the reason it had never worked with anyone else was simply that they hadn't been the *one*. We fell asleep in one another's arms, a perfect end to a perfect day.

A week after that, we had our first snowfall. At first, I didn't even know what was happening, only caught an odd flicker of movement out of the corner of my eye while I was clearing up the breakfast dishes. The skies had been heavy and gray when we woke up that morning, and Jace said it smelled like snow. I'd laughed at him over that remark, although really, he would know more about it than I would, since he'd grown up in Taos. When I was in high school, Albuquerque had been hit by a freak snowstorm that basically shut the city down, but that was my only real experience with snow, save for a light flurry here and there that didn't stick around long enough to cause any trouble.

This, though—it drifted downward, light and delicate, the flakes settling on the goats' shed and the chicken coop and the evergreens in the backyard, giving everything a soft sugar frosting. I stood at the window, a dish still in my hands, and stared at the miracle of it, how beautiful it was.

I was so transfixed that I didn't even realize Jace had come up behind me, not until his arms wrapped around my waist and his breath came warm against my neck as he said, "Looks like winter is really here now."

"And we're all safe and snug inside," I responded, setting the dish in the drain before I could drop it. The sensation of having him there, pressed up against me, was enough to send all sorts of tingles up and down my spine.

"That we are. I'll go out and check on the goats in a bit, just to make sure there aren't any leaks in the shed or anything, but I think we'll ride this out just fine." He shifted, as if glancing up at the ceiling, then added, "But we may not have lights for much longer. With cloud cover this thick, the solar's not going to do us much good."

"Then we'll spend our day by candlelight," I replied. "I'll turn off anything extraneous—maybe that way, there'll be enough of a trickle to keep the refrigerator going."

"Not a bad plan. You may want to go scrounge some extra candles from the basement."

"I'll do that as soon as I'm finished with these dishes."

His lips brushed against my cheek as he gave me a soft kiss, an acknowledgment of my words. Then he let go of me, heading toward the laundry room and the mudroom beyond that, where he could get into his jacket and gloves and brave the snow to check on the livestock.

There really weren't that many dishes to do, so I was done in the next few minutes. After that, I went from room to room, making sure we hadn't left any lights on. In general, we were pretty careful about that sort of thing, but I did realize that I needed to put the computer in sleep mode so it wouldn't draw any more power than was strictly necessary. If something happened to set off one of the periphery alarms, it would turn back on right away, but in the meantime it could hibernate.

After that I got a flashlight from the drawer in the kitchen where we kept them, and headed down into the basement. It had its own lights, of course, but if we really were in for a snowy day, I didn't want to turn them on and waste more power. The flashlight would do well enough, even if it was a little creepy to be wandering around down there with only a narrow beam to show me what I was doing.

I'd come down here once before to fetch the candles, but that had been weeks ago, before Jace had even shown up at the compound. The basement actually was very organized, with rows of metal shelving and the items on them arranged according to use. Even so, I couldn't exactly recall where I'd found the candles that last time. On the left, about five rows down?

Figuring it was worth a try, I shone the flashlight's beam in that general direction, but saw only bins of what looked like bundles of wire and cable, possibly intended for repairs to the home's electrical system, should the occasion warrant. Undeterred, I moved to the next row, only to have my foot bump into a cardboard box sitting on the ground next to one of the shelving units rather than placed directly on it. That was strange, simply because everything else I'd encountered in the basement so far had shown an almost fanatical adherence to order on the part of the person who had put it there.

I frowned and moved the flashlight's beam over the box. It had clearly come from some kind of a manufacturer; there was even a shipping label still affixed to it. Crouching down, I read the name and address.

Cory Berman
28-A Skyline Trail
Santa Fe, NM 87501

Cory Berman. So was that the name of the developer from Phoenix who'd built the property, or the caretaker who'd kept watch over it? Maybe it didn't really matter. They were both gone, after all.

What did matter, as I read the lettering stamped on the box itself, was what had been sent to him.

Yaesu FT-857D Amateur Radio Transceiver

Holy crap.

A ham radio?

A way to make contact with other survivors.

Heart pounding, I shone the flashlight around and saw another package, a much longer one, that seemed to contain the antenna to go with the radio. Damn.

I didn't know the first thing about setting up a ham radio, or its antenna, but maybe Jace would. Or at least could puzzle out the instructions. We'd have to wait for the snowstorm to blow over before we could go up on the roof to mount the antenna, but in the meantime we could read up on how to use the radio itself.

This could change everything.

I was halfway to the cellar stairs before I remembered I'd come down here in the first place to pick up some spare candles. After going up and down a few more rows of shelving, I found them—pack after pack of shrink-wrapped pillars and votives and tapers, the sort of thing you'd buy in bulk for a wedding or some other large event. I grabbed a flat of pillar candles and headed back to the stairway, then hurried up to the main level of the house.

Jace was nowhere in evidence as I set the package of candles down on the breakfast table in the nook. When I peered out the window, though, I could see him hauling something from the garage to the shed. A sack of the pellets we used to supplement the goats' diet, it looked like. That made sense—they probably weren't going to head out to forage until the snow stopped.

About ten minutes later, I heard him come in, then waited as he stopped in the mudroom to get rid of his coat and scrape the snow from his boots. In the meantime, I'd gone around the house and lit a number of candles, as it was clear from the lowering skies outside that we probably wouldn't see any sun today. Actually, it was so dark that it almost felt as if dusk was coming early, which of course was ridiculous. At this time of year, the days were short, but they weren't *that* short.

"What's up?" he asked, almost as soon as he entered the kitchen. I supposed he could tell I was fairly dancing with impatience.

"Guess what I found in the basement?"

One brow lifted slightly. "You know, that question generally doesn't have a good answer."

"I'm serious."

"So am I." But I could tell by the twitch at the corner of his full lips that he wasn't...not really.

"A ham radio," I announced. Jace appeared nonplussed by that revelation, so I went on, "It's still in its original packing...I think it was delivered here but never used. And there's an antenna, too."

"And?" he asked.

I felt a stir of impatience. "What do you mean, 'and'? With that radio, we can try to reach out to any other survivors, find out where they are, how they're doing."

"Maybe they don't want to be found. It seems as if they've done a pretty good job of hiding so far."

"So have we," I pointed out. "But it doesn't mean we don't want people to find us. Or...do we?"

Without replying, he went to one of the cupboards and got out a glass, then filled it with water. He drank some, his gaze not fixed on me, but on the increasingly snowy landscape outside the window. "I don't know," he said at last. "You wouldn't think there'd be much of a struggle for resources, not with so few of us left, but after hearing what happened to you in Albuquerque, I'm not sure I'm willing to trust anyone right now. What if there's a bigger, more organized group out there, one that decides what we have here is better than where they're living? We have weapons, but there are only two of us. Would you be willing to risk that?"

When he put it that way.... Involuntarily, my mind flashed back to the man in the Walgreens, to the greed in his watery brown eyes, and I shivered.

"No," I admitted, hoping Jace hadn't noticed my shudder. "Of course I don't want to do anything that would put us in harm's way. But maybe if we set it up and just listened, didn't transmit?" That seemed like a good compromise to me, but Jace's grim expression didn't change. After a perceptible pause, he said,

"Maybe. But we'll have to wait for better weather. No way am I climbing up on the roof in a snowstorm, just so I can install an antenna."

"Of course not."

"And it may need hardware we don't have, so then we'd have to go back into town."

A prospect I didn't particularly relish, and it seemed clear enough to me that Jace wasn't looking forward to it, either.

"Well, we can figure out the logistics later," I said. "It's nothing that has to happen right now."

He nodded, and I let the matter go, instead went on to ask him what sounded good for dinner that night. Something in the tense set of his shoulders appeared to relax. It didn't take a genius to figure out he was glad that I didn't intend to press him on the issue.

Exactly why, I didn't know. Was he really that worried about the consequences of contacting other survivors?

Or did he have some other reason why he wanted us to stay isolated here?

CHAPTER SIXTEEN

ACTUALLY, DESPITE HIS OBVIOUS RELUCTANCE TO do so, Jace did get to work on the antenna situation a few days later, after the weather had cleared. We bumped along the icy, muddy roads to go back to the hardware store, since, as he'd guessed, we didn't have all the little bits and pieces necessary for the installation.

Although a good deal of the snow had melted by then, there was still enough of it around to make driving treacherous, and I was more than happy to have Jace behind the wheel. He had experience driving in snow and ice, and I sure didn't. And as I stared out at the streets while we drove along, it suddenly hit me, the thing that had been niggling at the back of my mind for so long.

"None of the cars are missing," I said, and Jace took his eyes off the road for just long enough to shoot me a quizzical glance before returning his attention to the icy pavement.

"What?"

I glanced back out the window, wanting to confirm the notion that had finally taken coherent shape in my brain. "You know how I said that it seemed like there weren't as many vehicles around as I remembered, that some seemed to have gone missing, but I couldn't quite figure it out?"

A nod.

"Well, the *cars* are all here. And sure, there are still SUVs and trucks all over the place. But...." I let the words trail off as I focused on the patterns I now saw on the streets around us.

"But what?"

"I bet if we stopped and made a survey, we'd see that the SUVs and trucks left behind are the ones without much utility. Two-wheel drive, small engines...you know, passenger cars with SUV bodies. The ones that can pull their own weight, like this Jeep—I have a feeling we won't find as many of those around."

By then we were almost at the Home Depot, so Jace didn't say anything until after he'd pulled into the parking lot and stopped. "You mean someone's been coming here and systematically taking the trucks and the four-wheel-drive SUVs?"

"Well, I doubt I could prove it, but...yeah, something like that."

He shook his head and pulled the key from the ignition, then slipped it into his pocket. "In a way it makes sense, I suppose. Whoever and wherever the other survivors are, they're going to have to do a lot more for themselves. So having vehicles that can tow things and haul things and get around on unplowed roads would be vital." His brows had been pulled together as he pondered the conundrum, but then he seemed to relax, and although the air was sharp and cold, a flicker of warmth went through me as he gave me an admiring glance. "That was some pretty good detective work, Jess. I don't think I would have even noticed."

"Well, it's just a theory," I said deprecatingly, trying to convince myself as much as him.

"Better than anything I could come up with." Then he hesitated, looking past me down the street that fronted the store. Of course it was completely deserted, but I could tell he was worried. "Maybe you should stay here. You know—keep an eye on the car."

I really didn't want to do that, but if it turned out I was right about the way the abandoned vehicles were being cherry-picked, then it made sense for me to stand watch. At least this time I'd remembered to bring a sidearm. It was hanging in a holster against my hip, a reminder that we could never relax all the way when we came into town. Jace had one as well, the big S&W, which was better suited to his height anyway.

"No problem," I said. All right, so I didn't sound terribly enthusiastic, but neither had I argued with him.

He leaned down and kissed me on the cheek, his lips warm against my wind-chilled skin. "I'll be less than five minutes. I just need some brackets and wire. It'll be fast."

I nodded, and he reached into his pocket and pulled out the car key.

"Just in case."

In case of what? I wanted to ask. I didn't, though, only took the key from him and slid it into my coat pocket.

After that, he turned away from me and headed into the store, walking quickly despite the patches of ice that lingered on the asphalt. I supposed I could have gotten back inside the Cherokee where it would be warmer, but I didn't. Instead, I leaned against the driver-side door, my eyes scanning in all directions for... what? A batch of marauders out of a Mad Max movie, bearing down on me, intent on stealing my SUV?

No sign of anything like that—no movement at all, except a crow that came flapping down the street and then perched on one of the tall lights in the parking lot. It shook out its wings and settled down, fixing me with a baleful yellow gaze.

Crap on my car, and I'll use you for target practice, I thought, but the bird didn't move, only sat on the lamppost, surveying the parking lot. In happier days, it might have had some pickings there—the uneaten fries from some kid's Happy Meal, a spilled Coke. Now, however, the lot was bare of anything except the abandoned vehicles that still remained there, waiting for owners who would never return, and some patches of unmelted snow.

But even though I didn't see anyone else, and I knew I was perfectly safe, I couldn't help the wave of relief that washed over me when I saw Jace coming back out of the store, carrying several bags' worth of supplies.

"It looks like they—whoever they are—came back. More stuff is gone." Jace handed me the bags, and I got the car key out of my pocket and gave it to him.

"Stuff you needed?" I asked anxiously.

"No, everything we came here to get is pretty eso-teric. But now the batteries are totally cleared out, and the solar garden lights, and—well, just a lot of different things."

The batteries would have worried me, except that we had flats of the things back in our basement, both regular and rechargeable. And solar garden lights? Our property was outfitted with those, too. It seemed who-ever was looting the Home Depot, they were coming from a place of a lot more need than either Jace or I.

But we'd have to figure that out later. Or never. The weather seemed to be holding, and I had to hope it would stay that way for a few days, long enough so Jace could get the antenna installed. Maybe after that we could start to get some answers.

Right then, though, it was a lot more important that we get home. We had no evidence to show that anyone knew of our hideaway, but leaving it unattended always made me feel nervous. Dutchie would bark up a storm, but I doubted her doing so would be enough to scare off anyone who was determined to break in and take what they could.

Either no one had yet discovered the compound, or any survivors in the area had decided it was easier pickings in town, because once again we returned to find everything as we had left it. We gave Dutchie her usual greeting of some scratching behind the ears and a treat, and then Jace went to survey the area outside the office.

"We're in luck," he said, after prodding at the mud and driving a piece of rebar down into the ground. "It's not frozen."

"And that's relevant because...?" I was standing a few feet from him, close enough to see what he was doing but not so close that I would be in the way.

"Because I have to install a ground rod in addition to running co-ax from the antenna to the unit in the office." At my blank look, he sort of grinned and shook his head. "It's a little more complicated than sticking a TV aerial on your roof."

"Can you do it?" As soon as the words left my mouth, I realized that I probably should have asked that question before we went to all the trouble of getting supplies.

"I think so. I've read over the instructions a few times. Good thing I learned to solder in my shop class in high school."

And here I'd thought all we'd have to do was install the antenna on the roof, run some wire, and *voilà,* we'd be chatting it up with survivors around the globe. I should have known nothing would be that easy.

But he got to it in earnest after that, producing a ladder from the garage and climbing up to the roof, then letting me hand the antenna up to him from a point midway on the same ladder. I had to loiter there for some time, waiting so I could catch the bundle of coaxial cable as he tossed it to me once one end had been attached to the antenna. After he was done on the roof, Jace came down and fastened the wire to the exterior wall of the house with a series of brackets.

"I can handle it from here," he told me. "You'd better go inside—your lips are starting to turn blue."

"They are not," I protested, although truthfully, it was fairly cold outside, probably only a few degrees above freezing.

"I can see them. You can't." He grinned at me. "Really, I've got this. Isn't it around time for you to be starting dinner anyway?"

"Chained to the stove, just like I thought," I remarked, but I leavened the tartness of my words by giving him a quick kiss on the cheek. "Don't stay out so long that *your* lips start to turn blue."

"I won't."

I had to be satisfied with that, so I went in the house and started rummaging around in the kitchen. Outside, the daylight slanted its way toward dusk, and before it got full dark, I heard Jace come inside, although he seemed to go straight to the office rather than stopping in the kitchen to check on the ETA for dinner. Since I was making quickie rabbit stew that didn't really need babysitting, as it was now in the "let it sit in the pot until you're ready to eat it" stage, I headed back to the office, where I found Jace under the table we'd designated as the ham radio workstation.

"Everything okay?" I asked.

"Yeah," came his voice, somewhat muffled, since he was facing the wall. "Just need to make this last connection."

Since I really didn't have anything better to do, I leaned against the doorframe and waited as he wrenched on something. A few minutes and a couple of muffled curses later, he was pushing himself out from beneath the table and getting to his feet.

"I think that should be it."

"So let's fire it up and see if we can find anything."

He set down the screwdriver he was holding and crossed his arms. "We don't have to rush into this, you know."

"After you just spent all afternoon working on it?" I said, both perplexed and irritated by his reluctance to use the radio. "If you didn't think it was a good idea, then why waste so much time and effort on it?"

"I'm not saying that," he replied, digging in his pocket for another of those interminable leather cords so he could pull his hair out of his face. I wondered why he hadn't done that earlier, but maybe having his hair down on his neck had helped to keep him warm while he was up working on the roof.

"Then what are you saying?" I crossed my arms and tried hard not to scowl. "I guess I just can't figure out why you're so reluctant to even *attempt* to find other survivors, especially since we wouldn't be talking to them, just scanning to see if there is even anyone else out there."

A long pause. I could tell from the way his mouth tightened and he didn't quite look at me that he wasn't particularly eager to explain himself. Maybe not, but I wasn't about to let this go.

Finally, he jammed his hands into his jeans pockets and said, "All right, what if we listen in and find some survivors, then decide they sound all right and that we should reach out to them? What if they turn out to not be all right?"

"'Not all right' as in...what?" I asked, wondering what he was driving at. I tried to think of the worst-case scenario and added, "Like, cannibals or something?"

A grim smile touched his lips. "No, I don't think cannibalism is going to be an issue, not with all the wild game to be had around here. More like...." The words died away, and he hesitated again. "More like, what if they turn out to be a bunch of good old boys who aren't exactly thrilled to find an Indian shacked up with a white girl?"

I stared at him. "That's...." I'd been about to say, *That's ridiculous,* but then I realized maybe it wasn't. It should have been, but...I'd seen enough ugly incidents involving my friend Elena to know prejudice wasn't exactly a thing of the past, even for someone who was beautiful and talented and came from a family with money. The worst incident had been at a frat party in college, when some drunk asshole told her, "Hey, *chiquita,* you're pretty hot. Why don't you come over here and suck my *chalupa?*" Luckily, Tori was standing right there and responded by dumping her cup of cheap keg beer over the guy's head, but I'd never forgotten that scene. I knew Elena hadn't, either, even though she'd blown it off at the time, telling us the guy was too wasted to know what he was saying. That wasn't true, though...he'd known *exactly* what he was saying. And so had she, despite trying to act as if it was no big deal.

So as much as I wanted to brush off Jace's concerns as being completely unfounded, I knew they weren't. Just because the calendar said it was the twenty-first century, it didn't mean that everyone had gotten the memo.

And while intellectually I could understand where he was coming from, I knew I'd never be able to feel that doubt, those misgivings, the way he did, because I'd come from a completely different world. I was a white girl. Sure, I had a Ute great-great-grandmother—if the family legend was even true—but that didn't mean I could relate to his experiences as someone who'd grown up on the pueblo, who'd come at life in twenty-first-century America from a completely different angle than I had.

"So you see what I mean," he said quietly.

"Yes." His expression brightened a little at that, and I went on, "But...can't we just try it to see if it works? No one will know we're doing that if we don't transmit anything, right?"

At least he didn't try to equivocate. "No, no one will know that we're listening in. If there's even anything to listen to. But we'll give it a shot."

Jace went to the ham radio receiver and switched it on. When he'd set it up, he'd told me that it was designed to be portable, that if we could locate a different antenna setup, we could even take it along with us in the Jeep if we wanted. Why we'd want to do that,

I didn't particularly know, but it could possibly come in handy one day.

"Well, here goes," he said, pressing the power button.

A soft hiss began to emerge from the small speakers set up to either side of the receiver. Jace began scanning along the bands, going slowly enough that he could stop if he came across something interesting. All I heard was that hiss, sometimes louder, sometimes softer, but even I knew it was all merely dead air.

And then...what sounded like a faint, tinny voice, a single syllable. "Lo—"

It cut off with a screech and was replaced by more static. "Damn it," Jace said, scanning back to the band where the sound had come from. But there was no voice this time, only an angry, crackling hiss.

"What happened to it?" I asked, coming closer, as if somehow I thought my presence would help the tuner lock back on to the signal.

"I don't know." He sounded irritated, and I didn't blame him. All that work, for something that might or might not have been an actual person?

"Keep scanning," I suggested, and he expelled a breath and continued his slow sweep across the bands. Just more hissing, more static.

My stomach clenched, and I told myself to calm down. Just because we weren't picking up anything now didn't mean there was no one out there. The other survivors might not have the skill to operate ham radio equipment, or hadn't managed to set theirs up yet. It wasn't as if Jace and I were alone on the planet—the missing supplies and those mysteriously vanished trucks and SUVs told me other people were out there somewhere, and, from the look of it, they seemed to be fairly well-organized. Sooner or later, we'd have to cross paths. Although now, after what Jace had confided in me about his misgivings on that score, I wasn't sure meeting up with other people would be as beneficial as I'd previously hoped.

"I'm not getting anything," Jace said at last, then shut off the receiver before turning back toward me. "Maybe I screwed up something in the installation, but it's dark out now, so I won't be able to check until tomorrow morning."

"It's fine," I told him, even though I didn't know if it really was. "I think you did have it working. I just think...no one's transmitting."

"Still, I'll investigate more tomorrow." He glanced away from me, sniffed the air. "Smells like dinner's ready."

"Almost," I said, knowing that he'd changed the topic on purpose. Still, what did it matter? We weren't getting anything out of that ham radio tonight.

So we went to the kitchen, which was warm and smelled of good and savory things—proven by Dutchie, who was loitering much closer to the stove than she should be. I shooed her away, and then dished up our food while Jace got her some kibble. Just another normal night...or as normal as things could ever be now.

That syllable was still rattling around in my head, though. Lo.... "Lo" what? The transmission had cut off so quickly that I didn't even know whether it truly had been part of an actual broadcast of some sort, or merely a weird distortion that sounded like part of a word but was in fact only a nonsense note generated by a rogue sound wave or something.

I didn't speak of my concerns to Jace, though. The subject of the ham radio was a sore one already, and he *had* tried. I'd let it go for now, and maybe someday I'd learn if there truly had been someone broadcasting out there...or whether I was only imagining things.

We checked the radio every day after that, but got nothing but static and hiss. It was frustrating—for me, anyway—but as there didn't seem to be much we could do about the communications blackout, we put it aside so we could focus on more important things, like surviving the winter.

Well, it wasn't that bad, but I still could tell I hadn't become acclimated to the cold. Santa Fe probably averaged around ten to fifteen degrees colder than Albuquerque most of the time, but when that difference is between fifty-five degrees and forty, believe me, you can *feel* it. We had the wood stove in the sitting room going all the time, and the fireplaces in the living room and family room as well, but you could still sense the drop in temperature when you went out of the range of any of them. Jace got in the habit of going to our bedroom immediately after dinner and starting a fire so it would be comfortable enough to get undressed by the time we went in there.

Of course it could have been much worse, and the conditions were certainly endurable, but all the same, I found myself missing the central forced heat at my parents' house or even the wall unit in my studio apartment over the garage. That thing had heated up fast.

But those appliances were long gone, along with a million other comforts and conveniences I hadn't even appreciated until I didn't have them anymore, and so I told myself not to worry about them, that I was damn lucky to be where I was now.

Especially since I could be here with Jace.

We talked about the coming spring, about what we might be able to plant outside the greenhouse to supplement the crops we grew there. Because of the goats, we'd have to build a separate enclosure for another garden, since otherwise it would get eaten before we had a chance to harvest anything, but Jace thought he could manage it, especially if the stores of lumber down at the Home Depot didn't get pilfered by whatever survivors were still lurking around the area.

And occasionally, after I was done hurriedly washing my face and brushing my teeth, because the heat from the fireplace in the main part of the bedroom didn't quite reach into the bathroom, I'd pull out my packet of pills and hesitate before taking one. We hadn't discussed that kind of future, but it seemed clear to me that Jace didn't intend to go anywhere, that he was planning on a future with me in it. Was it crazy to consider starting a family? After all, someone needed to begin repopulating the earth.

But after that wild moment of hesitation, I always popped the pill in my mouth and swallowed it resolutely. Having a baby was a crazy idea. With no doctors, no medical facilities...no epidurals?

No, thanks.

The funny thing was, I'd never been all that invested in the idea of having a family. Elena was the one who wanted to get married and have lots of kids (and a nanny, of course) and do all that domestic stuff, and Tori wanted to be a social worker and focus on other people's kids, not her own. As for me, well, most of the time my main concern had been finding someone to have a few dates with and then break up with before things got serious. I'd tried serious once, and all that had gotten me was taking multiple exams for a bewildering variety of social diseases, thanks to my cheating ex.

With Jace, though...it was different. So different that some days I could barely wrap my head around it. I thought it would probably be wonderful to have a child with him, because I had a feeling he'd be a great father. He certainly possessed the patience and the quiet good humor. I knew I could count on him to be steady under pressure...a lot steadier than I, when you got right down to it.

Also, he was so gorgeous that it seemed a real shame to let all that amazing DNA go to waste.

More important than all that, however, was that I loved him. I wanted to bring something into the world that came from our shared love, that showed our commitment to one another.

I knew better than to bring up the subject, though. One day, the time would be right to discuss a future beyond the next planting season, but I didn't think we were there. Not quite yet, anyway.

The cold days slid past. It snowed here and there, but never enough to completely bury us, just enough to make the world pretty to look at and a pain to get around in. Christmas would be here in less than a week, and I had no idea what to do about that. I wanted to give Jace something, but I couldn't exactly nip out to the mall and buy him a sweater. Yes, we could go into town together and split up while we picked out presents for one another, but that didn't sound very safe.

When I mentioned Christmas to him, that I wished I could get him something, he'd pulled me against him and given me a strong, lingering kiss, the kind that made me want to drag him back to the bedroom and tear all his clothes off, although we'd have to pause long enough to get a fire started before I could safely do that. And he'd said,

"You're the only present I need."

How was I supposed to respond to that statement? By kissing him back, of course, and telling myself that presents didn't matter, that being here together was what mattered.

The next day he went out with the ATV, saying he was going hunting, and since he went on these expeditions a few times a week, I didn't think all that much of it.

But then he returned carrying a beautiful pine tree, a little bit taller than he was, and I realized he had given me my present, the one thing I'd really wanted all along.

"How did you know I wanted a Christmas tree?" I asked, watching as he settled it in a corner of the living room. It had a stand made of two pieces of wood attached to the bottom of the trunk, so he must have stopped at the garage first to hammer those on before coming to the house.

"I guessed. I saw the look in your eyes when you were talking about Christmas, and...." His shoulders lifted, and he reached out to make a minute adjustment so the tree sat more squarely in the corner. "I thought you should have some sort of holiday, even if it can't be like what you were used to."

"It's perfect," I said sincerely. And it was, especially because I knew Jace wasn't Christian, and might not have even had a tree while he was growing up. But he'd still realized how important following these traditions was to me.

"Glad you like it." He stepped back a few feet from the tree, looking at it with narrowed eyes, as if making sure it stood as straight as it possibly could. "I didn't have anything to use as a bowl, so I'm not sure how we'll keep it fresh."

"I'll get some paper towels and dampen them, then wrap them around the bottom of the trunk. It should work okay." I gazed at the tree, wondering what to do to decorate it. Go to town and raid the nearest Michael's? No, that wouldn't work, even if I could convince Jace to take me on such a frivolous expedition. The Heat had struck in late September, and even a store as gung-ho for Christmas as Michael's wouldn't have had any decorations out then. Should we raid random houses along Upper Canyon Road and see if they had any boxes of Christmas decorations hidden in their garages?

That sounded even worse.

Then I remembered the jars of popping corn in the pantry. Perfect. Old-fashioned, but it suited the way we were living now. "We can make popcorn strings, and I'll use one of the spare Mexican blankets in the linen closet to wrap around the base. It'll look great."

Jace nodded. "Sounds good. I'll try not to eat all the popcorn before you get it on the string."

"Better not," I warned him, and went to kiss him on the cheek before heading off to the kitchen. I had no idea how much popcorn to make to cover a seven-foot tree, but I got the feeling I was about to find out.

A good deal, as it turned out, and although Jace didn't eat all of it, or even anything close, I did catch him popping quite a few kernels into his mouth as he worked at making his own strings to decorate the tree. It was so lovely being there with him in the living room, a fire blazing away in the hearth, candles burning on the tables and on the mantelpiece of twisted juniper, that I couldn't even get angry about the way a good portion of the popcorn in his bowl was going into his mouth rather than onto the thread he held. Then again, maybe that had something to do with the half bottle of wine we'd brought out here with us after we were done eating dinner.

Either way, I was feeling more than a little mellow as we hung the popcorn strings on the tree, then topped it with a five-pointed star that Jace had fashioned out of aluminum foil and tied on with some extra thread.

"I want to make a wish," I said.

"Is that a tradition?" he asked. "To make a wish when you put the star on the tree?"

"I don't know if it was for everyone. But we always did it in my family." A flicker of sadness went over me then as I thought of all those family Christmases when I was younger, the wrapping paper strewn everywhere, hot cocoa for Devin and me and coffee for my parents. Regret, too, that they'd never get to meet Jace. I had a feeling they would have liked him.

"All right," he said. "What's your wish?"

So many I could have made—that the world would somehow heal itself, that the Dying had never happened. Those things were out of my hands, though, so I wished for the one thing I truly wanted that was reasonable. "I wish that it will always be like this—the two of us here, together."

A glow touched his dark eyes, a glow that had nothing to do with the flicker of the fireplace or the gleam of the candles all around us. "I think I can make that wish come true."

He moved close, pulling me into his arms, and then he was kissing me, mouth warm, lips insistent against mine. Just like the first time we'd kissed, I could taste the wine on his tongue, and heat flamed through me, awakening a deep throbbing in my core. I knew this was one night when we wouldn't fall asleep exhausted without touching one another.

No, we were hurrying down the hallway to the bedroom, laughing at the chilly air, Jace fumbling with the logs so he could get the fire going.

"You should have come in here right after dinner like you were supposed to," I teased him.

"I would have, except someone insisted I come with her to make popcorn strings."

"Oh, right. Well, I hope that won't take you *too* long." I pulled the sweater I wore over my head, followed by the long-sleeved T-shirt I had on underneath. It was cold enough that I broke out in goose bumps, but I wouldn't let that stop me. While Jace was busy with the lighter, his back to me, I took off my boots, then stepped out of my jeans. All that remained were my socks and my bra and panties, and I made short work of those.

When he turned around, his mouth dropped slightly. "Damn, Jessica." He took in a breath, then added, his voice husky, "You are so beautiful."

Heat went over me, despite how cold it was in the room. "Th-thanks," I said, my teeth chattering slightly. "Now come over here so I can tell you the same thing."

He was across the room in a flash, my fingers working the buttons of his flannel shirt while he undid his belt buckle and then the buttons of his Levi's. Oh, how I loved the smooth, heavy muscles of his chest, his flat stomach. If anything, he'd gotten bigger and harder during his months here, probably from all the manual labor.

Speaking of bigger and harder....

I sank to my knees, stroking him, and then brought him into my mouth, tasting salt and a faint, faint musk. He moaned and tipped his head back, his fingers tightening on my shoulders. "Man, Jessica," he breathed. "I'll have to remember to bring you Christmas trees more often."

Chuckling, I continued to move my hand up and down his shaft, my tongue swiping over him. After that, he didn't seem capable of speech, only continued to hold on to me, until he pulled himself from my mouth and raised me to my feet, then pushed me down on the bed, his hands warm on my ass.

We didn't have sex in this position very often, but I loved it when we did. He pushed into me, hands shifting slightly so they were wrapped around my hips as he rocked against me, in me, and I gasped, my own palms flat on the bed as I took him in, took all of him, pushing deeper, stronger, until I felt the throbbing warmth growing within me and knew I was close...so close.

As was Jace, because I felt him clench, then cry out, and as he released, I did so as well, my body clamping down on him, pulsing, squeezing. I gasped. "Oh, God, Jace...."

That was about all I could manage before I collapsed on the bed. He slid down next to me, his chest heaving, and then pulled me against him. How perfect the warmth of his skin, the way our bodies fit together. We held each other in silence like that for a few moments, and then he said,

"Happy?"

I didn't even have to stop to think. "I've never been this happy."

He kissed me then, not fiercely as he had before, but with a touch of his lips to my skin as soft as a snowflake settling there. "That's all I've ever wanted. To make you happy."

Because I could already feel myself slipping into sleep, I didn't really stop to puzzle that out, how he could've always wanted such a thing when we'd only known each other for less than two months. Instead, I cradled my head against his chest, and let myself drift into darkness.

CHAPTER SEVENTEEN

Voices in the darkness woke me. I blinked and sat up, holding myself still for a second or two, since the room wanted to spin around me. For some reason, I felt positively thick-headed, like the one time in college I'd tried an over-the-counter sleep aid because I was stressed from exams and the breakup with Colin, and I was having a hard time falling asleep. That didn't make sense, though, since I hadn't had anything more than a glass of wine with dinner, and another one while we were in the living room, making popcorn strings.

Instinctively, I reached to my right, where Jace should have been sleeping. But the bed was empty, although I knew we couldn't have been asleep for too long, as the fire was still burning brightly. Dutchie was passed out in front of it, nose and tail almost touching, her heavy breaths not quite a snore.

Once again I heard that strange murmur, and I sat very still, ears straining to make out individual words. But the voices were far enough off that I couldn't catch anything, although one of them sounded like it could be Jace. Had he gotten up and tested the radio, and this time actually made contact with someone? I would have thought he'd come and wake me up for something that momentous, but maybe he'd thought it best to let me sleep.

I blinked, fighting off the last of that strange drowsiness, pushed back the covers, retrieved my panties from where they were lying on the floor, and then went to the closet to get my flannel sleep shirt and thick robe. Yes, lying naked next to each other was very romantic, but by the time 4 a.m. rolled around, it was also damn cold. Luckily, Jace didn't seem to mind the sleep shirt, which was covered in penguins. One time he even told me he thought it was cute. He could have been lying, but I think it was more that he wanted me to know he thought I was sexy no matter what I might be wearing to bed.

As I tied the robe around me, I went to the doorway, then paused. The voices should have been coming from my right, down the hall in the direction of the office. But they weren't—instead, they seemed to originate in the living room.

That didn't make any sense. Even if the unthink-able had happened and another survivor had shown up on our doorstep, I should have heard something, no matter how deeply asleep I was. If nothing else, Dutchie would have barked her head off. But she was passed out on the floor of the bedroom, so conked she looked like someone had drugged her.

Frowning, I slipped out into the corridor, the tile floor icy against my bare feet. It wasn't quite pitch dark, since, in our rush to get to the bedroom, Jace and I had left the pillar candles burning on the coffee table and on the mantel. Because of that, as I approached I could make out clearly enough who was in the living room.

Only...my brain couldn't quite grasp what it was seeing. Two men. At least, they looked like men, but... they couldn't be. Not hovering in midair, approxi-mately a foot and a half above the floor, as if they had no need of solid ground.

One of them was Jace. Or rather, he resembled Jace, except somehow older and harder, his jaw and eyes stern. His hair seemed longer than its current inch or so below shoulder length, almost as long as mine, and floated around him, appearing to wave in an unseen wind, a wind that stirred the branches of the Christmas tree and made all the flames in the pillar candles on the mantel and coffee table dance and sway. Just as when he'd fallen asleep, his chest and arms were bare, but now thick cuffs of silvery-blue metal surrounded his wrists, and he wore full-legged pants made of a shimmering dark blue fabric, possibly silk.

The other man...or whatever he was...stood in profile to me, so I couldn't get all that good a look at him. And actually, I wasn't sure I wanted to. There was something cruel in his hawkish profile, in the set of his jaw and mouth. His hair was pulled back into a severe ponytail and banded with reddish metal—copper, maybe, or even rose gold. More reddish metal gleamed at his wrists, and his pants, similar in construction to the ones Jace wore, were a dark burnt-umber sort of shade.

Stranger than his presence, and even stranger than the way he floated above the floor, however, was the way odd little flames seemed to dance around his feet and swirl in the air directly above his head, as if he were somehow made of fire, and had only taken on physical form so he could have this conversation.

I flattened myself against the wall, glad of my bare feet, which had made no sound as I approached, and the relative darkness of the hallway where I hid. Jace...that oddly altered Jace...and the stranger would have had to look directly at me to see me at all, and it seemed clear enough that they were occupied with one another, not sparing a glance for the supposedly sleeping house around them.

"...wasted enough time here already," the stranger was saying. His voice was deeper than Jace's, harsh, and something about it made chills go up and down my spine. "It is time to come join the rest of us."

"Surely a few days more won't matter," Jace replied. "After Christmas has passed—"

The stranger made a sound of disgust. "Christmas? What foolishness is this? That day means nothing to us, and you have coddled the woman long enough. Tell her the truth, or as much of it as you deem necessary, but we will not wait much longer."

"What is the rush?" Jace crossed his arms and stared directly into the other man's eyes, something I didn't think I'd have had the courage to do. "What does it matter if we wait out the winter here, and then come to you in the spring?"

For the briefest second, the stranger hesitated, his hands tightening into fists at his sides, even as the flames dancing around his feet and above his head flared brighter, shifting from warm orange to an acid yellow. From annoyance...or something else? "Because it may not be safe to do so. We are disturbed by some of the developments among the Immune. They've gathered in a place not far from here, and although we do not know how they are managing it, they are blocking us from scrying them, or indeed from coming within miles of their compound so we might finish them off."

"The Immune"? I thought. *Other survivors? And what the hell does he mean by "finish them off"?*

"That is troubling," Jace said, and it seemed the unseen wind that swirled around him gained in force, wildly blowing at his hair and causing the flames of several of the candles to almost snuff themselves. "No one has been able to get close?"

"No. There is one road in and one road out, both heavily guarded. Several of the Chosen volunteered to investigate, since they would be able to get far closer to the Immune than we would, but we have had no contact with any of them since, and it is feared they have been lost."

It was hard for me to tell for certain, but it almost seemed as if Jace winced when he received that particular piece of information, as if it was more painful to him than the rest of what he had just heard. "That is a grievous loss."

The stranger shrugged. Clearly, he was not overly concerned about the loss of these "Chosen," whoever they might be. "They volunteered for the mission. Their partners will find replacements, if they wish."

From the set of his shoulders, it appeared that Jace wasn't quite so blithe about the fate of the Chosen who had disappeared. "How long has it been? Perhaps you are not giving them enough time."

"Two weeks, as such things are counted here. Time enough." The stranger straightened, his eyes on a level with Jace's. "I am telling you this because your safety here is not guaranteed. Better for you to be with the rest of us." Then he paused, and my heart seemed to stop in my chest as he glanced over in my direction. "Your paramour is awake. It seems she was not quite as deeply asleep as you thought. You will have some explaining to do, I think."

That appeared to be his parting shot, because after he made that remark, the flames which had been licking at his feet seemed to grow and swell, rising until they engulfed him. Then they went out, and Jace was alone in the living room.

His eyes met mine, and I saw him draw in a breath, then lower himself to the floor. As he did so, his appearance shifted back to the Jace I knew...or thought I knew. At the same time, the lamp in the corner of the room flared to life, although neither of us had touched a light switch.

"Jessica," he said, his arms reaching out to me as he began to move in my direction.

"Don't," I retorted, still hugging the wall. "Stay back."

He stopped at once, but I could see the pleading in his dark eyes. "Jessica, I can explain—"

"Oh, you'd better explain." The cool plaster of the wall against my back gave me a little courage. At least this way, he'd have to face me, couldn't sneak up on me from behind. "Who—*what* are you?"

His shoulders seemed to droop then. He looked so pitiful that, under normal circumstances, I would have gone to him at once and put my arms around him, attempted to comfort him. But there would be no comfort here. Not after what I had just seen.

"Please, come and sit down," he said. "We must have this conversation, but we don't need to have it like this."

I shook my head. "I don't think that's such a good idea."

"Jessica." This time he sounded different, his voice deeper, the way it had been when he was speaking with that—whoever he was. At the same time, he backed off, going to sit down on the couch. "Look. Here I am. You can sit in that chair. I promise I won't move unless you say it's all right."

For a second or two, I didn't do anything, only watched him through narrowed eyes. He was sitting there quietly, his hands planted on his knees. He certainly didn't look as if he intended to launch at me, but how could I trust him when it was clear he was definitely not who he had pretended to be?

Then again, I did want answers, and if he might be more inclined to give them if I sat down as he'd asked, then that seemed to be what I should do. Not taking my eyes off him, I crossed over to the chair and sank into it. Actually, that did feel a bit better, although the spurious sensation of relief could have had something to do with the rug under my bare, icy feet and the warmth of the fire as it reached out to heat the room.

I pulled in a breath. "So...this you I'm looking at right now. Is it the real you, or the other one?"

In answer, his features seemed to shift and harden, becoming those of the man I'd seen floating above the floor a few minutes earlier. Still handsome...in a way, more handsome, because those features had somehow become more chiseled, more refined, even though he was recognizable as the Jace I'd thought I had known. "This is my true aspect," he said.

Right then, I wasn't sure which was upsetting me more—knowing that Jace wasn't real, was some sort of disguise worn by this...being—or the casual way he flipped from one appearance to the other. I tightened my fingers on my knees, feeling the soft nap of the robe I wore and realizing that now it was giving me absolutely no comfort. "And your true name?"

"Jasreel."

So he was still Jace, in a way...although I doubted I'd ever feel comfortable enough to call him that again. The thought made incongruous tears sting my eyes, and I swallowed. Could I mourn the loss of something I'd never truly had?

Maybe, at some point. Right then, I had to man up and get some answers.

"So what are you?" I asked, my voice deliberately hard. "Some kind of demon...angel...what?"

"Neither." He reached up to touch the smooth stone he wore around his neck, and I wondered then if it was some sort of talisman, rather than the simple souvenir I'd thought it must be. "I am a djinn."

I blinked at him. "What, you mean like *I Dream of Jeannie,* and the big blue guy in the lamp from *Aladdin?*"

His mouth tightened. "Not like that at all, even though your people have simplified the idea of the djinn to something as foolish as a being who can grant wishes."

"So you don't grant wishes?"

"When called by a powerful enough magician, perhaps. But we do not enjoy the process and will do whatever we can do free ourselves from such bonds."

Okay. First djinn...and now magicians? My head was spinning. "All right, so you're a djinn. I can't really deny that, not when I saw you floating two feet above the floor and watched your friend vanish in a puff of smoke."

Jace's...*Jasreel's*...brows drew together. "He is not my friend, not in any way you would understand."

I decided to let it go for now. That other djinn had seemed like a nasty customer anyway. There was a far more important question I wanted to ask. "All right, then...*why?*"

A long, long silence. He stared at me, dark eyes sorrowful. "You should know...beloved."

Every single vein in my body seemed to be filled with ice. I tried to draw in a breath, but it got caught somewhere in my throat, choking me. I stared at him, then finally forced the words out. "That was you? The voice was *you?*"

"Yes," he said simply. "I had chosen you, and so I would do whatever was necessary to keep you safe."

In my mind's eye, I saw Chris Bowman's limp body being thrown across the yard as if it had been made of rags, saw a bullet stop an inch away from my face, then bounce harmlessly off some invisible shield. Yes, this Jasreel had been there all along, watching over me, then leading me here. But for what purpose? I found it hard to believe that some sort of supernatural, supremely powerful being would go to all that trouble just for a little booty.

"That word," I said. "*Chosen*. I heard your visitor mention it, too. What does it mean, really?"

Jasreel stared at me with those sad, sad eyes. How could I be terrified of him, and angry with him...and yet still want to reach out to comfort him? No, that was crazy. Bad enough that only a few hours earlier we'd—

My brain shut down that line of thought with an almost audible *click*. I could not let myself think about that, or I really would go mad.

"It will be difficult to hear," he said quietly.

"And it'll be even more difficult for me not to know the truth," I replied. "So tell me."

His fingers clenched on his knees. For the first time, I noticed that although his face and body had shifted to those of what he called his true self, he wasn't wearing those silk pantaloon things, but a pair of flannel pajama bottoms he routinely wore to bed when he was pretending to be "Jace." The contrast was jarring.

Then he said, "This world was ours once, uncounted ages ago. When God made man, He—"

"Wait, what?" I broke in. "God? Like, *the* God?"

"Yes, *the* God." This was accompanied by a flicker of a smile, but Jasreel's expression sobered quickly enough afterward. "When God made man, the djinn were cast out, and this world given over to mankind. We are not flesh precisely as you understand it, although we can make ourselves corporeal as it suits us. We spent long ages in exile, only coming to this world when summoned, or during brief stolen moments. During that time, the world changed a good deal, and mankind along with it. We watched from our exile, saw how you were destroying this gift you were given. And so, among certain quarters, the decision was made to take back that which had been stolen from us."

That did not sound good at all. I pulled my robe more tightly around me, although I didn't think that was going to do much to combat the chill which seemed to be creeping through every limb.

"Many years were given over to the task, but at last the means of mankind's destruction was perfected—an illness so grave that it would take almost the entire population of the earth with it."

"You—*you* did that?" I demanded, sour bile churning in my stomach at the thought that this—*thing*—had been behind the death and destruction of everyone and everything I had cared about. I got to my feet, not even thinking, just knowing I had to get away from him, had to run—

But he'd risen as well, his hand clamping on my arm like iron, preventing me from fleeing. "No, *I* did not do that. There were those of us who protested, who said we could not support such a vile act. We were outnumbered, though, overruled."

His fingers felt as if they were burning into my flesh. "Let go of me," I gritted from between clenched teeth.

To my surprise, he did release me, raising his hands as if in surrender. "Jessica, I am sorry. The only compromise we were allowed was that those of us who did not support such extreme measures would be able to choose from among the Immune, to find someone who would be under our protection, who would not be subject to the final purge."

"'Final purge'?" I echoed, my stomach clenching once again. Just when I'd thought it couldn't get any worse. "What are you talking about?"

He pulled in a breath, although I noticed he kept his gaze fixed on my face and didn't try to look away.

"Those who created the virus knew that no illness would have a perfect mortality rate. There are now perhaps two million people left alive, scattered across the face of the planet. And so the next task is to eradicate the Immune, leaving behind only the Chosen."

It was so awful that I truly couldn't begin to comprehend the scope of what he was telling me. Two million out of seven billion seemed like a paltry number, but obviously the djinn in charge wouldn't be satisfied with even that many human beings left alive.

My legs gave way, and I slumped back down into my chair. "How many?" I asked. "How many Chosen?"

"A thousand."

One thousand people, out of two million. All those who'd thought they had survived the worst, who even now were struggling to pick up the pieces of a world that had utterly fallen apart...they would have all that stolen from them.

"What will happen to the Immune?" I asked. I wasn't sure where those words had come from. It wasn't as if I'd consciously decided to ask that question.

Jasreel sat down as well, expression troubled. In a way, I was surprised I could read his face so easily, since he wasn't even human. But he looked human enough at the moment, and he'd certainly done a good job of fooling me these past few months.

"They will be hunted down," he said at last. "As one of the dissenters, I am not privy to exactly how and why, and truly, I don't wish to know. I cannot stop it."

"You're really that powerless? How many dissenters are there?"

"As many as there are Chosen. One thousand. The djinn do not number anywhere near what mankind once did, but there are still some twenty thousand of my people, far too many for any of us dissenters to even contemplate confronting them." He sent me an imploring look then, as if pleading for me to understand. "Jessica, we did everything we could to stop this thing from happening. It was beyond our power. All we could do was save that chosen one thousand of you."

My protests died on my lips then. Yes, he had lied about who and what he was, but this Jasreel had been by my side for the better part of two months now, and I saw nothing in his face in that moment but regret and sorrow. Whatever horrors his people had perpetrated, he'd wanted nothing to do with them.

Which left only one question. "Then...why me? Why did you choose me? I'm no one."

He was off the couch and on his knees in one fluid movement. So close, and yet I noticed he didn't try to reach out and touch me. He wouldn't, I realized then, unless I told him it was all right.

Whether or not that would happen...even I didn't know for sure.

His voice was pitched low, but no less intense for all that. "Beloved, you are not *no one*. I recognized your beauty and your strength, and I knew you were the choice of my heart, even out of several million survivors."

What was I supposed to say in response to such a declaration? I stared at him, at a face that was like Jace's, but wasn't, at the broad shoulders, the arms thick with muscle. He looked human, and yet I knew he was anything but a mortal man.

"Please," I whispered. "Please don't call me that. I don't—I don't know what to think."

A stillness settled on his features in that moment, as if he'd finally realized that I wasn't simply going to say, *Oh, it's all right, I still love you, too, all is forgiven.* He glanced away from me, over at the fire, and then back. "I realize this is all difficult for you."

"'Difficult'?" I repeated. "I think we passed difficult about ten minutes ago." I pulled in a breath, then pushed the chair back so I could stand up without bumping into him. "I just—I need some time to process this, okay?"

He didn't get up, but remained there on his knees, still staring up at me with that blank expression on his face. A muscle twitched in his cheek as he said, "You can have as much time as you need."

"Good." I sidled away from the chair, moving toward the hallway. "And—don't come to the bedroom. Go back to your old room. That is, if djinn even need to sleep."

With that parting shot, I made my escape, all but running to get away from him. Even so, I couldn't help taking a quick backward glance as I left the living room. He was still kneeling on the floor, but now his head was bowed, his elbows on the coffee table, as if he needed that support to keep himself from collapsing completely.

At that sight, my throat tightened, and the hall-way around me blurred, tears welling to my eyes and spilling down my cheeks. I stumbled into the master suite and then fell on the bed—the bed where Jace had made love to me so many times—sobs tearing themselves out of my chest. I didn't even know exactly what I was crying about. The loss of what I thought I'd had with Jace? The realization that the Dying had come about not because of some horrible accident of nature, but from directed, malevolent intention? Or knowing that the Dying wasn't even over, and that the survivors, the Immune, would soon be attacked by the djinn, and there wasn't a damn thing I could do about it?

All of those, and so much more.

Dutchie jumped up on the bed and licked my face, and I gave a strangled laugh, then pulled her close, burying my face in her soft fur. No, ordinarily she wasn't allowed on the bed, but in that moment, she knew I needed her.

I clung to her the way a shipwreck survivor might cling to a life preserver, and finally let sleep take me to a place where I could try to forget all the horrors I had just been told.

CHAPTER EIGHTEEN

I STALLED AS LONG AS I COULD. I TOOK A SHOWER, dried my hair, even put on some lip gloss and mascara, things I hadn't bothered with lately, not after I'd swiped some heavy-duty lip balm from REI on our one foraging run there. But all the preparation in the world could only take so much time, and eventually I had to emerge from the master suite, although I noticed that Dutchie had nudged the door open earlier and slipped away.

Or maybe Jasreel had let her out.

Despite my delaying tactics, I knew I wasn't ready to face him. A cowardly part of me was praying that he'd packed up and left, had gone to "join the others," as the strange, cruel-looking djinn had told him to do. Where that supernatural meet-up was supposed to take place, I didn't know. I didn't want to know.

The smell of coffee told me Jasreel was still here, though. I stopped at the entrance to the kitchen and saw him standing at the counter, staring out at the bleak landscape beyond the false lushness of the garden. The goats were already grazing, which meant he must have gone and milked them, taken care of their water, then let them out. Since the snow from the last storm had all melted by then, save for a few drifts directly under the eaves of the house, nothing was stopping them from cropping at the short, yellowed grass.

"You made coffee," I said, my tone flat.

"I thought you could use some."

I noticed he was wearing Jace's clothes—flannel shirt, faded Levi's, worn boots—and yet they couldn't really be Jace's clothes. This Jasreel was just enough bigger, more muscled, that dressing him would require a whole new wardrobe. No, these had to be counterfeits, copies, garments designed to look like what I was used to seeing him wear and therefore intended to put me at ease, when in fact they were doing the exact opposite. His hair was pulled back into a ponytail, and although his expression was serene enough this morning, his eyes looked shadowed. So could djinn suffer from sleepless nights, or was this his attempt at evoking some kind of pity in me?

Normally, I would have said thank you. This morning, though, I went to the cupboard in silence, got out a mug, and poured myself a cup. Getting some goat's milk and a smidgen of sugar to leaven it used up some more time, a few minutes where I didn't have to say anything. I could feel Jasreel's eyes on me, watching every movement I made, and I didn't like it at all.

At last I turned around and made myself face him, although it was one of the harder things I'd done. Now, in the morning light, I could see more of those differences, see how his brows were just slightly more arched, his jaw just a little more square. There were faint laugh lines around the dark, dark eyes, although they were the same, nearly black, and still circled by the kind of lashes most women would kill for.

"Why are you still here?" I asked abruptly, my fingers circled around the coffee mug I held, desperately trying to claim some of its warmth. My hands felt as icy as the world outside the kitchen.

The question seemed to surprise him. His eyebrows lifted, and he said, "You didn't tell me to leave."

All right, I hadn't, in so many words. I'd said he could go back to his old bedroom, which in his mind seemed to have been an open-ended invitation to stay. Last night, I hadn't exactly been thinking all that clearly.

His voice lowered. "Do you want me to leave?"

Did I? Rationally, I knew I should have ordered him out of the house the night before, but in that moment, all I'd been able to think about was him not following me to the bedroom.

"I—I don't know," I said at last, then added, as I saw hope flare in his eyes, "that is, I still have some questions I want to ask."

Mouth thinning to a compressed line, he nodded. "You can ask me anything."

Maybe, I thought, *but that doesn't mean I'm going to get an answer I like.* I sipped some coffee, letting the heat of it course down my throat and begin to thaw that lump of ice at my core. Who knew I could feel so cold, when before Jace had made me so warm?

"Jason Little River," I said, bringing up something I'd been pondering while in the shower. "Is he just someone you made up, or is he a real person?"

"He was a real person," Jasreel said. From the use of "was" and the way Jasreel's mouth tightened as he said it, I had to assume that the Mr. Little River was no longer with us. "Everything I told you about me was true...about him, that is. He grew up in Taos, went to the university in Albuquerque, split his time between the pueblo and building his own business in town. He was also physically similar to me, and that made it much easier to hold the illusion of his appearance for extended periods." A pause while Jasreel drank some of his own coffee, which I noticed was pure black. "Jace" had always taken milk, like me. "Jason Little River died two days after the Heat came to Taos. After he was gone, I took his appearance, and his motorcycle, and began the journey here to Santa Fe."

That part didn't make any sense. I decided for sanity's sake that I'd leave aside the part where Jasreel clearly knew where and when the real Jason was going to die. "His motorcycle? What the hell for? Couldn't you have just...I don't know...materialized on my doorstep?"

Jasreel didn't smile. Still in that same quiet, intense voice, he said, "I could have, but that journey was important for me as well. I needed some time to become Jason, to grow accustomed to being him. Showing up weary and footsore here made me more... believable."

Something about that comment just made me angry, like he'd known I would fall for his act but decided to hedge his bets, just in case. "All right, you suckered me. So why lie in the first place? Why not tell me the truth?"

He set down his mug. I could see the anguish in his eyes, but all he did was ask quietly, "And would you have believed me? If I had to come to you as myself, told you that my race had destroyed mankind but also that you would live because I wished it, what would you have done?"

What would I have done? In that moment, I honestly couldn't say for certain. When I'd found this place, guided here by the voice, I was thinking more or less five minutes ahead, only wanting to survive another night. I was tired, heartsore, drained. Could

I have found it within myself to believe what he told me? Maybe, if he'd given me a little demonstration of that "floating above the ground" trick.

Whether I would have allowed him into my heart and my bed was an entirely different matter.

"I don't know!" I flung at him. "All I do know is that you came here, and you *lied* to me, made me think you were someone else...made me *love* you...and now I have to reconcile that with the truth, with the way you used me—"

Horrible, choking sobs rose in my throat after that, and I had to stop, to drop my mug on the counter and turn away from him so I wouldn't have to look into that face, the face that used to be Jace's and wasn't anymore, tears rising up to blind me all over again. A mercy, because then I couldn't see him clearly.

But I could feel him, warm fingers lacing through mine and pulling me against him, his voice rough with sorrow as he said, "Beloved, it was never my intention to hurt you. I thought perhaps it might be easier—"

"Don't call me that!" I gasped, pushing at him, trying to free myself. He resisted for a scant second, and then released me, backing away and holding up his hands as if to show he had no intention of attempting to touch me again. Angrily, I wiped at my tears with the back of one hand.

"Very well...Jessica." He pulled in a breath, and I noticed how his chest rose and fell, as if he were struggling to gain control of himself. Could djinn experience an accelerated heartbeat, or difficulty breathing? One wouldn't think so, if they truly weren't completely tied to this plane of existence, or a physical body. But Jasreel was giving a good enough imitation of it now. Then again, he'd already proved that he was pretty good at pretending he was something he was not.

Looking a little less wild-eyed, he went on, "Jessica, I came to you as Jason Little River because I thought it would be easier for you. I thought we could grow to be comfortable with one another first, and then, when the time was right, I would tell you who I was really was, the truth behind the Dying. It was never my intention to hurt you. How could it be, when I swore an oath as I chose you that your life would be more precious than all the riches in the world to me?"

He took a step in my direction, and I retreated several feet toward the kitchen entrance. That stopped him, and he raised his hands again, almost as if he were as much telling himself to halt as he was showing that he didn't intend to pursue me or reach out for me. As I stood there, halfway toward the dining room, I realized that poor Dutchie, like most dogs who hate hearing their people fight, had retreated under the little round table in the nook and was staring at us with worried mismatched eyes.

For some reason, seeing her reaction to our quarrel made me calm down a bit. Dutchie loved me, but I remembered that she loved Jace—Jasreel—too. And if she loved Jasreel, surely that meant he couldn't be evil, or anything close to it. I'd seen the way she'd reacted to Chris Bowman, so I knew she wasn't one of those dogs who indiscriminately liked everyone. Whatever lies Jasreel might have told me in order to ease his way into my life, I knew then that he'd told them out of a misguided attempt to protect me, to avoid frightening me.

I was angry with him, and I was scared, almost as scared as the night my father died, but in that moment, I knew I didn't hate him. Some part of my soul wouldn't allow me to hate him.

He'd brought me a Christmas tree. That could have been another manipulation, but I didn't think so. He'd done that because he knew I wanted it, wanted some part of my life to feel normal, even when hardly anything in it was normal anymore.

Maybe something in my expression shifted. I couldn't say for sure, but it must have been enough to give Jasreel some hope, because he said, "Do you still wish for me to go?"

I didn't...but I also didn't know how I could begin to process all this with him around all the time. "I don't know," I replied. "A minute ago, I would have said yes. But—"

"But?"

It was time to take a deep breath of my own. "I suppose I want some more answers. What was that—the other djinn saying about the Immune?"

If he was disconcerted by my change of subject, Jasreel didn't show it. He could have simply been relieved that I was willing to go on talking, even if the topic of conversation had moved away from the two of us and where our relationship currently stood, and on to something more neutral.

"His name is Zahrias. He is the leader of our group in this—sector, I suppose, is the best word for it. The region is not quite analogous to your state of New Mexico, but close enough."

"So this Zahrias came here to, what, warn you?"

"More or less." Jasreel shifted, and I could tell he'd been about to step closer to me, but had pulled back at the last second. "In general, we djinn are able to look in on human affairs with very little interference. If we suddenly can't do so with the group at Los Alamos—"

"Lo," I said, and he stopped and shot me an inquiring look.

"What?"

"That was the transmission, wasn't it?" Another spark that could be fanned to anger. Now I thought I understood what I'd heard so briefly on the ham radio. Voice tight, I said, "The people—the Immune—were transmitting from Los Alamos. And you...cut it off."

"Yes," Jasreel replied, sounding resigned. "And yes, I disrupted the signal. Only because I wanted more time alone with you. Until Zahrias came to see me, I didn't know the group there was any kind of a threat. I only knew they must be Immune, and so their time on this earth was limited."

I decided to put that anger aside to be dealt with later. "So they're a threat just because you can't spy on them?"

"It's more than that, Jessica. The Immune simply should not have the capability to keep us from looking in on their doings. And now that some of the Chosen have disappeared, the ones who volunteered to go where we could not—well, you can see how that would be very troubling."

From his perspective, I supposed it was. For myself, I was more intrigued than anything else. What were they doing at Los Alamos that would allow them to evade djinn surveillance? I didn't know much about the town, except that it was still a place for research and had quite a few government contractor–type businesses. We drove up there once when I was in high school, more to go someplace off the beaten path than for any other reason, and it really did feel like I'd just walked onto the set of that TV show Eureka, the one about a town populated by mad scientists.

But I figured the probability of discovering the truth about what the Immune in Los Alamos were doing was roughly the same as waking up to discover this had all been a terrible dream, so I moved on to my next question. "And the djinn? The ones from this sector, I mean. Zahrias made it sound as if they were all holed up somewhere."

Jasreel gave me an incongruous grin, as if that mental image amused him. "Djinn do not precisely 'hole up,' but they are using Taos as their base of operations."

"Really?" I asked, surprised. A touristy little town didn't seem like quite the right spot for a bunch of supernatural villains to be hanging out. "Why Taos?"

"Since its population was small to begin with, it did not have many survivors, and the one or two who were left were...." He let the sentence trail off, but I got the gist.

"Disposed of?" I volunteered.

A grim nod. "Yes. Also, because it was a travel destination, it has accommodations for a number of people, restaurants with good stores of food, and so on."

"They have power in Taos?"

"In a manner of speaking."

I wondered exactly what he meant by that, but I decided the day-to-day logistics of keeping Taos going under djinn occupation weren't my top concern at the moment. "And because the Immune in Los Alamos are up to something you can't figure out, Zahrias wanted you to leave here and go to Taos."

"Exactly. You and I have been safe on this property, hidden from the world. It's exactly why I chose this place as our sanctuary, our haven. But if what Zahrias says is true, then it might be best if we left and took refuge with the other djinn and the Chosen in Taos."

Crossing my arms, I said, "That's assuming I would go with you."

Now the expression he wore was one of resignation. "I will not force you. I can say that it would be safer. But that is your decision to make."

Oh, thanks for putting it back on me, I thought. But hauling me off to Taos without so much as a by-your-leave would have made me far, far angrier. Jasreel was treating me as a peer now, giving me equal say in what we should do next. I could tell that Zahrias' news about the Immune in Los Alamos had Jasreel worried. For myself, I didn't think I had that much to worry about. After all, they were human beings. I was one of them.

Or...was I? Maybe they would look on me as some kind of co-conspirator, a betrayer of my kind. Of course, I hadn't known Jasreel was djinn, but I had no idea whether that kind of excuse would wash with them or not.

"Let me think about it," I said. "I have to go gather the eggs." That had always been my chore, just as watering the goats and lugging their pellets from the garage to the feeding trough he'd built next to their lean-to was Jace's—Jasreel's—job.

He seemed to recognize that I needed some time alone, because he didn't protest, only said, "Of course," and went to get his neglected cup of coffee. I realized then that I'd only had a few sips out of mine. Oh, well. I didn't want to have to go past him to retrieve my mug, so I wrote it off as a loss and went to put on my coat and gloves.

The djinn didn't try to follow me.

The cold air was bracing, but it didn't do a lot to clear my mind or settle the thoughts that kept racing through it. I gathered eggs mechanically, placing them in the basket with practiced care, the familiar stink of the henhouse around me. Glancing down, I realized it would need to be shoveled again soon. If I asked Jasreel to do it, would he? He'd handled the distasteful chore ever since my one disastrous attempt to handle it, but that was back when he was still trying to convince me he wasn't anyone except a guy from the pueblo, someone who was used to taking on a good deal of manual labor.

Maybe he can just wave his hands and have all this bird poop and dirty straw magically disappear, I thought. *That would be convenient.*

Problem was, I didn't know if his powers—whatever they were, exactly—worked that way.

But even as I pondered such trivialities, my thoughts kept dancing around the real question, the one I didn't know if I could ever answer.

Can I forgive him?

Because it wouldn't be simply forgiving the lies he'd told me. To a certain extent, I could understand why he'd done that. If he'd been watching me for some time, studying me before he made me his Chosen, then he would have known I wasn't the type of person who watched the skies for UFOs or believed in ghosts or any of that other "woo-woo stuff," as my friend Tori used to put it. A djinn? I probably would have burst out laughing—if I hadn't unloaded my shotgun into him first, just to be safe. True, if I'd done that and he'd survived unscathed, then maybe I would have started to believe in his supernatural origins.

No, forgiveness would have to go far, far beyond that. He'd protested that he couldn't stop the Dying, couldn't have kept his people from unleashing their terrible virus on the world. Maybe not; I'd seen this Zahrias, the de facto leader of my little part of the world, and if he was any indicator of the type of people the djinn had running things, then I could understand how pleas for mercy would have fallen on extremely deaf ears. Even so, many would say Jasreel still was guilty by association. It was the djinn who had done this terrible thing, and he was a djinn.

All right, most people would probably think that way. But I wasn't a lot of people. I was me. I had to make this decision for myself, based on what my heart and my gut and my mind told me.

And what they were telling me was that Jasreel loved me. He couldn't save everyone, but he could save me. And he had. He'd saved me, and he'd shown, day in and day out, that he cared for me. In little things, like always making sure he helped clear the table, even though the dishes were my bailiwick, and properly sorting his dirty clothes into the correct bins in the laundry room so I wouldn't have to do it. Bigger things, like that Christmas tree and the aforementioned mucking-out of the henhouse.

The biggest of all...watching over me, keeping me safe, all along knowing that we weren't precisely equals, that he was a being of vastly more power and experience. And yet he had never talked down to me, never discounted my suggestions, always took me seriously. If that wasn't love and respect, what was?

Well, it sounded as if I'd answered my own question.

Feeling lighter by roughly a hundred pounds, I headed back to the house and let myself in the back door, through the mudroom. I scraped off my boots, set down the basket of eggs before I took off my jacket, and then went into the kitchen. Jasreel wasn't there, but I noticed that he'd cleaned out his coffee mug and put it on the dish drain. That wasn't just sucking up, either; he always cleaned up after himself.

"Jasreel?" I called out, the syllables of his proper name feeling strange on my tongue.

"In the living room," he replied.

I wondered what he was doing there. Figuring I'd find out soon enough, I headed in that direction. He was standing in front of the fireplace, which we had going pretty much twenty-four/seven these days. In his right hand he held a log, so it appeared he'd gone in to stoke up the blaze. Dutchie was lying next to him, patting at his leg with one paw. Obviously, someone thought it was time for a belly rub.

Smothering a smile, I said, "So...."

"So?" He set the log on the fire and turned toward me, disrupting the dog's pant-pawing. She gave me a disgusted look and rolled away from Jasreel, toward the hearth.

"So...I'll go to Taos with you. If you think it's for the best."

An expression of such joy spread over his face that, for an instant, all my doubts and worries deserted me. Surely no one who could look like that would ever mean me any kind of harm. He came to me and cupped my cheeks in his hands, turning my face up toward him.

"You're sure?"

Was I? His fingers were warm on my face, reassuring, strong but gentle. No one had ever touched me like that. No one except Jace...Jasreel.

I nodded.

He bent and kissed me then, and it was the first time I had kissed this version of him, the first time I had felt the contours of this particular mouth, the taste of this tongue. Not so very different from "Jace," but different enough that I had to remind myself that it was still him, still the man who had kissed me before, who had made love to me on those cold winter mornings and stood laughing in a field after a billy goat knocked me on my rear end.

But then I felt his body go rigid, and he took a step away from me, one hand going to his throat.

"What is it?" I asked, reaching out to hold on to his fingers. They felt like ice.

His hands had always been warm. Always, no matter how cold it might be outside, as if the weather didn't affect him the same way it affected me.

"Can't...breathe...."

I put my hand on his chest, felt his heart beating wildly within, felt him laboring to pull in a breath. Which he did, a short, shallow gasp. Better than nothing, but it didn't explain what was happening to him.

Dutchie got to her feet, nose pointed toward the doorway. A low, penetrating growl emerged from her throat, and her ears flattened against her head.

What the—

I didn't have time to complete the thought, because in the next second, the front door was flung open, and a group of seven men wearing parkas and heavy boots burst into the living room. Six of them carried guns, and the seventh some sort of strange device, no more than a little black box, really, with lights that seemed to flicker deep within it, as if buried under a layer of dark translucent plastic.

The scream that had been building in my throat died when one of the men with the guns stepped forward and said, "It's all right, Ms. Monroe. We're only here for him." He pointed at Jasreel, who had taken a step backward, toward the hearth. Sweat was beginning to drip down his temples.

"Who—what—" I swallowed, knowing I had to keep it together, at least until I found out what the hell was going on. I began again. "Who are you, and what do you want?"

He nodded at the men who flanked him, most of whom were large, burly types, the kind of guys who once upon a time probably could have been found drinking beer at some back-road dive bar. They went to Jasreel and surrounded him, then began dragging him back toward the man in charge and the other one, the one holding that strange box. He, unlike his compatriots, was slender, of average height, and wore wire-rimmed glasses. Despite the commotion around him, he didn't look up from the box he held, kept his fingertips moving over the surface, as if controlling it via touchpad.

The leader, who held himself like a military man and had the short-cropped hair to match, said, "Ms. Monroe, we're survivors from Los Alamos. We're collecting as many of these scum as we can"—a jerk of his chin in Jasreel's direction— "and are putting them on trial for crimes against humanity. Seems the least we can do, in the name of those who are no longer around to seek justice."

My mouth was so dry it physically hurt to swallow. But somehow I forced myself to do just that, even as I sent an agonized glance toward Jasreel. He had gone pale under his olive-toned skin, his breath coming in short, labored pants. What the hell were they doing to him?

"He's not guilty," I managed to get out. "He hasn't done anything wrong."

"Beg to differ, miss." The leader of the Los Alamos gang gave a faint nod, and the four men holding him began to drag Jasreel out the front door.

"No!" I began to move after them, but another of the group, one of the two men flanking the guy with the black box, took me by the arm.

"I wouldn't," he said in a murmur. "Right now you have the benefit of the doubt, but...." He let the words die away, but I got his meaning. It was Jasreel these men were after, not me. The last thing I should be doing was provoking them.

I gave the fair-haired man, who seemed to be about my age or a little more, the faintest of nods, then held my position, just a few feet away from the guy in charge. "What proof do you have that he's guilty of anything?"

"His nature is proof enough." He gave another of those chin-jerks at the man with the black box and the two men with him. For the first time, the one wearing glasses looked up from his device, whatever it was, then gave a faint nod, right before they went out the front door. The blond one gave me a warning glance before he turned and took up the rear, as if to tell me that I needed to stay put and keep my mouth shut.

Fat chance of that. Instead, I followed them. As soon as I was outside, the chilly air seemed to bite at me, piercing the thermal shirt I wore, but I ignored the momentary discomfort. Parked a little ways down the drive were two Hummers, one bright yellow, the other red. Clearly, these were some of the vehicles "liberated" from Santa Fe and the surrounding area.

I could see Jasreel being bundled into the yellow Hummer and cursed mentally. What was I supposed to do? There were seven of them—all right, the guy with the box seemed peculiarly uninterested in his surroundings and kept fiddling with the device, whatever it was, so maybe he wasn't much of a threat—but the rest of them were all big enough to take me individually, let alone as a group. And all my weapons were currently locked up in the gun safe.

The leader of the group paused and glanced down at me, seeming to really assess my appearance for the first time. He didn't leer, but I could see the look in his eyes take on a certain glint. "You should come with us," he said casually. "We're trying to in-gather as many of the Immune as we can. You'd be safe with us in Los Alamos. We can protect you."

For a second, I actually considered it. Not because I wanted to go with this bastard and his crew, but because that way I'd be closer to Jasreel. I'd still have to figure out some way to free him, but I thought attempting a rescue would be a lot easier if I were nearby.

No, beloved.

The words were barely more than a gasp in my mind. I couldn't speak aloud, not with the leader of the band of thugs standing close by, so in desperation I tried to respond the same way. Amazingly, it seemed to work.

But I want to stay with you!

You will be...better able to help me if you stay away from them, and free.

How?

You will need assistance...and you will not be able to get it if you come with me to Los Alamos now. I do not think they intend to kill me right away.

And that's supposed to be reassuring?

Yes, beloved.

I had to ask. *How are we doing this?*

The bond between us. They have trapped me here on this plane, cut off my powers, but I can still speak to you thus. At least—

But then the thought-speech abruptly broke off, and I realized it must have been because they'd finally hauled Jasreel into the Hummer and shut the door behind him. So our mental connection was limited—by space, and by physical barriers.

Luckily, the entire exchange had taken place in less time than the blink of an eye.

"Thanks for the offer," I told the leader, my tone as casual as I could make it, as if I hadn't just held a desperate mental dialogue with their captive. "But I've got goats and chickens to tend. I think I'll stay right here."

His eyes narrowed. "You sure? It's not safe for a woman alone."

And I'd be so much safer in Los Alamos. Right. Evenly, I replied, "I'll take my chances."

A long hesitation, and I worried that he might try to force me into the other Hummer. But then he shrugged and said, "Door's always open. Come find us there when you're ready."

I nodded, and he seemed to take that as the conclusion of our conversation, because he signaled the three men still waiting outside to get in the red Hummer. Immediately afterward, he crossed to the vehicle and climbed in the passenger seat. A slap on the door, and both vehicles moved off, heading down the drive and out through the gate, which I noticed was standing wide open. They must have shorted out the mechanism or something, although that should have triggered the alarm system. Then again, I didn't know what the black box the weedy-looking man had been holding could do. Maybe it could simultaneously short out the alarm and somehow trap Jasreel here in this world, with no hope of escape. Or maybe one of the men in the Hummers had just stepped out and clipped a couple of wires.

In a minute or two, I'd have to go inspect the gate and see if what they'd done was anything I could fix. In a minute or two, I'd have to take Dutchie back into the house and lock up, and pray that no unfriendly eyes had seen me in my current vulnerable state.

Right then, though, I could only stand there in the driveway and feel the icy tears roll down my cheeks, stinging in the bitter wind that was blowing down from the north. Jasreel was gone.

I turned so I faced west, in the direction the vehicles had disappeared. And although I knew he couldn't hear me, I still sent the words out to him, letting them ride on the wind.

I will find you...beloved.

~~✕~~

The story continues in *Taken*,
Book 2 of The Djinn Wars.